*He couldn't help but travel back,
using her body as a time machine . . .*

He studied her face. The moon had made its way through the haze and was falling on her through the skylight. He was relieved to see that she did look older. This was no visit from the Twilight Zone after all. There were tiny wrinkles around her eyes, smile lines at the sides of her mouth . . .

He felt as if it might be possible to ignore all these details and just close his eyes and go back to a time when they'd both been impossibly young, when they'd wanted each other so much they'd thought they were in love. But what if he did? The morning would still come, her game would be over, and she'd be on her way . . .

He opened his eyes and was thirty-five, with a set of keys digging into his back, lying on the hard dirt floor of a run-down greenhouse, powdered with the summer grime of a Los Angeles August, hugging a woman he hadn't seen or heard from in twelve years . . .

ALWAYS SIX O'CLOCK

*A novel of romance, mystery, and suspense
from the Emmy Award–winning screenwriter of* Cheers

ALWAYS SIX O'CLOCK

Phoef Sutton

B

BERKLEY BOOKS, NEW YORK

ALWAYS SIX O'CLOCK

A Berkley Book / published by arrangement with the author

PRINTING HISTORY
G. P. Putnam's Sons edition / May 1998
Berkley edition / February 1999

The Penguin Putnam Inc. World Wide Web site address is http://www.penguinputnam.com

ISBN: 0-425-16763-1

BERKLEY®
Berkley Books are published by The Berkley Publishing Group, a member of Penguin Putnam Inc., 375 Hudson Street, New York, New York 10014.
BERKLEY and the "B" logo are trademarks belonging to Berkley Publishing Corporation.

PRINTED IN THE UNITED STATES OF AMERICA

10 9 8 7 6 5 4 3 2 1

Acknowledgments

Many thanks to:

—my parents and my brothers and our house full of books.

—my teachers Roger Hall, Les Charles, David Lloyd, Bill Steinkellner, and Cheri Steinkellner for setting me on the path.

—my friends Elliot Webb, Steve Warren, Emily Corey, Randy Hale, and Jeff Peterson for keeping me going.

—Dr. Robert Cowan of Pasadena, whose lucid explanations of the nature of memory helped me write but didn't help me remember to return the books he loaned me.

—my indefatigable agent Molly Friedrich and her team, Paul Cirone and especially Frances Jalet-Miller.

—my editor, Stacy Creamer, for her guidance and support.

—most of all to Dawn and Skylar and Celia and the memories they have given me.

For Dawn

"Well, I'd hardly finished the first verse," said the Hatter, "when the Queen bawled out 'He's murdering the time! Off with his head!' "

"How dreadfully savage!" exclaimed Alice.

"And ever since that," the Hatter went on in a mournful tone, "he won't do a thing I ask! It's always six o'clock now."

Water

She didn't know where the water had come from. It pulled at her and pushed her away. It dragged her down with its cold heaviness and forced its way into her mouth and all the time she fought it, she kept trying to figure out where it had come from and how it could be all around her under the night sky.

She had school tomorrow. She should be home. She should never be here, watching the stars bend and wrinkle beyond the freezing weight of this saltwater. She pulled herself up to the air and tried to swim, but her arms ached as if she'd been swimming for hours. Perhaps she had. Perhaps she'd always been in this dark water. She thought about her little brother and her parents and how sad they were going to be. But her arms were tired and she wanted so much to rest.

She stopped and floated for a second. Then the water got hold of her clothes and pulled them down. She watched the stars grow dimmer and more distorted through the water.

Then they came into focus again and she felt cold air on

her face and a hard grip on her wrist. Something hard slammed into her side, knocking air and water out of her, but all she could see were the stars, which seemed impossibly bright now. She was too weak to answer when a voice asked if she was hurt. Too weak to care when she felt hands searching her body. Too weak to answer the next question, even if she'd been awake to hear it.

"If you're not hurt, where did the blood come from?"

1

Carl pulled into his driveway and the moon-cast shadow of the huge eucalyptus tree washed over the hood of his car and dappled the back of his hand that gripped the steering wheel.

He shut off the engine. In the silence, the music from the car stereo boomed too loudly. Easing his head back against the leather headrest, he turned to look at his house.

Carl was the only person he knew who lived in the house he'd grown up in. He hadn't meant to. When he was seventeen he'd moved out of this cozy Spanish Revival house in Glendale (Glendull, all the young people called it) and over the hill to a grimy room under a storefront on Hollywood Boulevard. No amount of pleading on the part of his parents, no amount of suffering of his own due to poverty or heartbreak or the exciting starvation of youth, could get him to move back in. In the end, it took financial security to do that.

Money had come into his life with the speed of a sudden head cold. One week he'd been scraping together enough money to Xerox programs for a production of his one-act plays in a converted toilet theater on Santa Monica Boulevard, the next he was making two thousand dollars a week as a staff writer on a network TV show. Within two years he was a producer with a salary approaching three hundred thousand a year. Meanwhile, his parents' income had declined while the cost of living had gone up, so the only money they had left was tied up in their house. They didn't want to leave it, and they turned to him for help. The house he'd considered a sterile prison when he was a teenager looked like a worthwhile investment now that he'd hit thirty, so he bought it from them and let them live there for free.

Three years later, just as he was recovering from the breakup of his near-marriage, his mother died, so he moved into the house to keep his dad company. Now that Dad was gone too, there was no reason at all to stay there. He felt like an alien in the neighborhood, which was filled with houses occupied either by elderly white couples or extended Armenian families of twelve.

So sell the house and buy a condo at the beach, he thought, as he sat immobile in the driver's seat, Joan Armatrading blaring out of the CD player. It was two-thirty in the morning. After a day like this, he should be rushing in to fall on the bed. Eight hours spent locked in a room with his partner, Kit, and four other professional manic depressives, rewriting an ill-conceived episode of a CBS half-hour comedy. That's three hours of writing and three hours of bitching about the actors and the network and how shitty all the other shows on television are and how the city is going to hell. And two hours of deciding what to order for dinner.

But he wasn't in bed. He was watching the blue-gray shadow of the tree move on the hood and thinking about all the times that eucalyptus shadow had washed over all the hoods of all the cars he'd known as they'd pulled into this driveway. The Chevrolet station wagon—he was sitting on his mother's lap dribbling ice cream onto her slacks. His father's Dart—he was seventeen, driving home from a date with Jesse and smelling her scent on his fingers. His Maverick—he was driving in from his Hollywood rathole, deliberately too late for Thanksgiving dinner. His BMW—he'd just rushed home after he got the call about his mother's stroke. Too late again, but not deliberately.

He started the engine and eased the Jeep forward to pull up next to the kitchen door, leaving the eucalyptus shadow back on the driveway where he couldn't see it. He looked up at the dark house and it was so empty it made him catch his breath. He could already hear his footsteps echoing on the wood floors. He laughed to himself, entertaining the notion of reclining his seat and spending the night in his car. But somebody had to feed the animals.

He climbed out of the car into the cool, dusty summer night. To hell with the real estate market, he really would put this house up for sale tomorrow. Some people have trouble keeping in touch with their pasts, he thought—I'm going to dump mine on the market at a cut rate.

He set a dish of dried cat food and an overripe avocado on the patio, slipped back through the double doors, settled into a wicker chair he'd pulled up for the purpose, and waited.

His cat jumped clumsily into his lap. It climbed up his chest and breathed in his face, breath ripe with Science Diet for Older Cats. He pushed its head down, gently but firmly, hoping it would curl up in his lap and go to sleep. Instead it climbed up onto his shoulder and started sucking on his hair.

Roxanne was an aged Persian cat. With old age, the flat

face of the breed had turned convex; its teeth were exposed in a permanent werewolf's snarl, and its snuggles of affection were accompanied by a viscous drooling. It was one of the most disgusting animals Carl had ever seen, but he kept scratching behind its ears. He even ignored the hair sucking, a lifelong habit he attributed to a premature separation from its mother's breast and, therefore, never had the heart to resent. He ignored the wet spot growing on his shoulder and peered out through the French doors at the bowl on the patio.

The raccoon showed up about five minutes later, scooping the dried cat food into its mouth by the handful. Roxanne jumped off Carl's lap and hissed at the intruder behind the protection of the patio door. Satisfied that it had done all it could to protect its domain, it went off to the laundry room to vomit.

The raccoon paid no attention, moved on to the avocado, and began to peel it deftly. All the while Carl kept perfectly still, amazed at the size of the creature; it was as big as a small dog. Its haunches were huge and beautifully formed. He marveled at the ringed black tail and the black mask— like something out of a nature documentary right here in his own backyard.

For no reason that he could figure, it started suddenly and glanced up at him. Its black marble eyes met his, and he tried to smile in a way that a raccoon might find friendly. It kept its eyes fixed on his as it ate the avocado.

He'd first started to suspect its presence about a week ago. He'd left a bowl of cat food out by the door overnight by mistake and the next morning had found tiny handlike prints around the empty bowl. Since then he'd left out more food and found it gone every morning. Four nights ago he'd come in, late as usual, and switched on the light in time to see something that looked like a small bear waddling off into the dark.

So he'd spent the last few nights like this, sitting for a time in a chair in front of his patio window, hoping to catch a glimpse of the beast. Now it was here, staring at him, apparently unimpressed. Carl couldn't imagine how an animal of that size could live in an urban area. He knew that coyotes and even deer lived up in the hills, but he felt sure this fellow hadn't traveled that far. Somehow it had managed to eke out a living in suburbia. That was a miracle for any creature.

The animal dropped the bare avocado pit and trundled off into the darkness. Carl sat in his easy chair in the darkened room and watched it go. The encounter was over. The climax of ten days of careful planning had been reached. He had achieved contact with a fellow creature and had, in a small way, helped ease its struggle for survival. Their eyes had met and, on that basic level, they had bridged the gap that separates the species.

Carl was too depressed to get up, so he fell asleep in the chair.

Carl sat in the conference room, staring at the clock as it moved backward.

"I think I have a problem with 'gallbladder.'"

Carl stiffened.

Kit went on. "I think gallbladder's a joke organ."

"How do you mean?" Carl asked.

Kit lifted a page from the script, which was already bloody with corrections in red ink. "Okay so, he says, 'Then where's Pablo?' and Joanne says, 'Probably chewing the gallbladder out of Mr. Upmann.' Don't you think gallbladder sounds like a joke organ? It's like 'spleen,' it doesn't sound real."

"Well, they are real, Kit. I mean, people do have spleens and gallbladders."

"But what do they do?"

"I'm not a doctor, I don't know. They purify something or filter something. I know they're there."

"I think maybe we should come up with another organ."

Carl glanced away from Kit, trying to conceal his resentment. They'd been rewriting the script since the disastrous rehearsal that afternoon. At ten-thirty the other writers had left, thinking that the work was done. All Carl and Kit had to do was proof the damned thing, and somehow Kit had made that simple task take two and a half hours. Now he was suggesting that they spend an undefined period of time trying to come up with a more serious organ.

Carl tried to be reasonable. "Look, why don't we see it on its feet tomorrow? If it sounds too jokey, we can fix it then."

"Or we could fix it now." Kit's voice had a calm, rational tone to it that made Carl want to feed him a beer bottle.

"Okay, what organ do you like?" Carl asked.

"Well, it's not a matter of liking. I don't know . . . Liver?"

" 'Chewing the liver out of Mr. Upmann'? That's not funny."

"Well, don't get irritable."

Kit was hurt. Carl scratched his head vigorously. "I'm sorry, it's just late, and we're going to see this thing three more times before we shoot it, and I think we ought to hear 'gallbladder' at least once."

"All right, if you feel that strongly about it, next page." Carl turned the page. "I'll see you back on that tomorrow night," Kit added.

Carl turned the page back. "Okay, how about kidney?"

Kit nodded. "That's not bad. Do you like kidney?"

"I like gallbladder better."

"Honey, you got to learn not to get married to jokes."

Carl stifled his scream with a bite of cold pizza and swallowed it, gagging. "How about 'lymph nodes'?" he asked.

Kit considered. "Chewing the lymph nodes out of Mr. Upmann." He laughed his barking laugh.

"Chewing the lymph nodes out of Mr. Upmann," Carl repeated, laughing his hissing laugh. They both repeated it a couple more times, still laughing, and Kit wrote it down.

"You see, Carl," Kit said, "if you really push yourself you can come up with the right joke."

Carl glanced around the room for the right beer bottle to feed Kit. Maureen would deliver the line tomorrow and, if it got a laugh, they'd see it again on Monday, when it would get less of a laugh. By Tuesday they'd all be tired of it, forget it was ever funny, and decide to come up with another joke. Even if it survived that long and they shot it Tuesday night, even if the studio audience laughed at it and they didn't cut it out in editing, even if it did make it on the air Friday night at eight-thirty, there was still the certain knowledge that in several million of the 26 million households that watched it, someone would burp, rustle the newspaper, or leave to make a sandwich at the moment the joke with the perfect organ was delivered.

"Or, I don't know," Kit wondered, "is lymph nodes funny or just odd?"

Carl decided the Heineken bottle would do the job nicely. But as he went for Kit with the bottle, Kit became a cat and chased Carl about the room, drooling, while Carl ran from him on chubby raccoon legs.

The details of the dream vanished as soon as Carl's eyes opened and he found himself still sitting in the wicker chair by the patio door. But even as the specifics skittered away like cockroaches from a switched-on light, he seized on enough of them to be annoyed. So now even in his dreams he was sitting in that room, coming up with jokes and scene blows and second-act complications. The same things he did all day, every day.

It reminded him of a time when he was a teenager: he and some friends had spent an endless week backpacking in the Angeles Crest Mountains. Weariness and fatigue so numbed his mind that by the third day, his entire consciousness of the world was narrowed down to nothing more than the putting of one foot in front of the other. Left foot, then right foot, left foot, then right foot, and if civilization had come to an end or lapsed back into stone-age chaos he wouldn't have known or cared. Indeed, he would gladly have brought about either occurrence in return for being able to stop putting one foot in front of the other, endlessly, day in and day out.

But when he'd finally come home and fallen onto his bed and felt the incredible softness of his pillow under his head, what had he dreamed of? Putting one foot in front of the other, left, then right, left, then right. He'd woken up feeling betrayed by his mind, just as tired as if he'd been walking all night.

So it was like that here now. Television had so infiltrated his brain as to rob him of even the release of REM sleep. No more erotic fantasies or bizarre Freudian scenarios for him. And to make matters worse, he couldn't even remember if the dreamjoke he'd come up with had been good enough to put into the script he was supposed to be writing.

Oh, Christ, he hated to hear himself complaining like this. He imagined for a moment that he was a character in a half-hour comedy, maybe a good one, with a killer time slot. Thursday nights on NBC, say. Who the hell would want to watch him? Who would feel any sympathy for a young (well, youngish) successful guy in an exciting (theoretically) line of work, who sat around feeling sorry for himself? So what if he was lonely and without love, with a gnawing indefinable emptiness chewing at his inner soul? Where was the funny? Find the clicker and switch channels.

Carl often hoped that God had a longer and more forgiving attention span than the television audience. Or at least that He didn't have a clicker.

To distract himself from these grim thoughts, he decided to wonder what had woken him up. It might have been discomfort from sleeping in the chair, but his back didn't hurt. He couldn't hear the cat tromping around and screeching as it often did when he was just drifting off.

He heard a snapping sound and sat up fast. There's nothing as loud as a sudden sound in an empty house at night, he thought, as he peered through the darkened window for any sign of the raccoon. Nothing. He lapsed back to normal breathing.

The snap again. But it wasn't quite a snap, now that he listened closely. It was a crack and a rattle and it came from upstairs. He turned toward the stairway, which seemed a long way off.

Crossing to the stairs was easy as long as he didn't hear the sound. When it cracked and rattled again he stopped dead, his heart pounding in his chest. Really pounding, he noted in surprise, picturing it bouncing off his ribs. And yet there was no sense in being afraid. There was nothing dangerous about the sound. He couldn't imagine a burglar up there, rifling through his drawers while dropping marbles at regular intervals.

In the silence he made it halfway up the stairs, two visions fighting for his attention like overheard conversations at a party. In one, his cat was disinterestedly playing with a Ping-Pong ball; in the other, the same ball was played with in the same way by a bloodied serial killer. He laughed, then froze when the rattle came again.

This time he knew his fear wasn't physical. There wasn't anything up there that could hurt him. He was afraid because he recognized the sound but couldn't place it. He only knew that it came from a long time ago and that it didn't belong here now. It was a ghost sound. Like the laughter of phantom children and the bouncing of invisible toy balls in a 1970s horror film.

He ran the rest of the way up the stairs and into his study, the room that used to be his bedroom. The window overlooked the backyard and through it he could see the night sky, heavy with a thick haze that trapped the lights from the city and turned them back in a perpetual twilight. The light made it easy to see the handful of pebbles sailing up toward the window. The larger one struck the glass with a crack; the smaller ones rattled against the sill.

He stood in the doorway, blinking at the window in disbelief. He knew what it was now. Even if he hadn't seen it, he'd have known just from being in the room. The sound was different here; it was welcome, it was waited for, it was the sound he couldn't sleep for praying it would come. It was the sound that was as far from frightening as any he'd ever heard. Except that he hadn't heard it for seventeen years, and it couldn't possibly be real.

His bed had been in the far corner. When he was seventeen he had lain awake in it every night in a sweat, wondering if that sound would come. If it didn't, he fell into fevered sleep in the early morning and twisted through delirious dreams with a harem of women from all parts of the earth. If the sound did come, he crept from his bed, slipped on his bathrobe, and sneaked down the stairs, his dick pivoting wildly in front of him, leading the way she used to say, like a divining rod seeking out her moisture.

He'd open the French doors in the living room with exquisite care and rush out back to find her. Jesse would be standing by the eugenia bushes. He would rush into her arms and they would kiss clumsily, not from lack of experience, but because you couldn't kiss like they needed to and do it with any refinement. Any pretense of refinement was out of the question anyway, with his cock digging into her leg. That was part of the kiss as well, like his hand rubbing her pussy through her jeans. She would moan, and he would tell her to be quiet and not wake his parents. How would they explain what they were doing? he would say, laughing. She would grab his cock and squeeze and say she thought this guy would explain things pretty clearly.

They would run to the greenhouse, stumbling, somehow holding onto each other all the way, and fall on the tarp and make love. His cock would be so hard he wouldn't even feel anything at first, wouldn't even be sure he was in her unless he reached down and felt the join with his hand. Then sensation would come, and they would climb all over each other and kiss and bite and who knows what, because in those days it didn't even matter what you did or even how long you did it because you were so overwhelmed by the sheer miracle of doing it.

Carl was so deep into his reverie, he half expected to see her standing in the backyard when he walked to the window. But that didn't stop him from being surprised when he did see her there.

She was standing below the window in a white summer dress, gesturing to him impatiently to come down. Or someone who looked like her was; it couldn't really be her. But it couldn't be anyone else either.

He opened the window and she spoke to him in a loud stage whisper. "Where the hell have you been?"

"Jesse?"

"Is something wrong?"

"Well . . ." But there wasn't, was there?

"Come on down."

He closed the window and crept out of the room, knowing full well he needn't worry about waking anyone. It didn't hurt to playact a little, and anyway it all had to be a dream. He much preferred this to the one about the conference room.

As he descended the stairs he considered the possibility that this might all be real, feeling a wave of depression and apprehension. If it were real, it couldn't be what he'd been assuming—she wouldn't be here to reenact a night of teenage passion from the seventies. The only thing that could make a normal woman sneak in darkness to the house of someone she hadn't spoken to since the Carter administration was some unusual and urgent kind of trouble.

He hesitated at the French doors, remembering the circumstances of their breakup, and he was more sure than ever that no mere sexual whim would have brought her back here. He drew a deep breath as he opened the door and walked out into the night.

The raccoon had finished every bit of the dried cat food and spilled the dish of water across the patio. There was no one under the window, no sound of anyone around. If it was a dream, when had it ended?

An arm grabbed him around the chest, and another reached between his legs and grabbed him there. He gasped and tried to pull away. Then he heard her laugh.

"It's me, stupid."

She turned him around and kissed him. His mind was reeling from surprise to fear to pleasure, but it was soon calmed by a wave of memory. The thick softness of her lips and the familiar taste of her tongue. Nothing like this could have brought her here, but her hand was running down his chest and into his jeans.

"What are you all dressed for? Did you think we were going on a hike?"

One of the first things he had learned as a comedy writer was not to try to make a joke if he couldn't think of anything funny. So he just kissed her again and let her fumble with his belt. She backed away and touched his lip curiously with her fingers.

"Since when did you grow a mustache?" she asked, sounding genuinely confused.

"I had to do something while I was waiting for you."

He kissed her neck and she giggled. "It tickles."

"You don't know the half of it," he murmured, while nibbling on the tender flesh of her neck.

She gasped. It was a tender gasp, yearning and hungry, and at the sound of it Carl froze and felt his lips tremble on her neck. He knew that gasp so well, and it came from so long ago that he felt his heart grow in his chest. He shut his eyes and tears squeezed from them.

Jesse pulled away to look at him, puzzled. "What is it?"

He laughed. Only two tears had fallen. He was in control. He squeezed her arms, playfully. "It's just so good to see you."

"You silly."

In the old days she had always been the one to frighten him off with the depth of her feelings. Now here she was, laughing at his emotion as if her showing up now were the most natural thing in the world. Didn't she know, or didn't she want to know, that he could stare at her in this darkness all night long? Was it all just a game to her?

She unfastened the top two buttons of his jeans and

reached in. Any resentment he might have been feeling vanished in a surge of goodwill.

"He's happy to see me too."

There's an adorable tone of pride a teenage girl gets in her voice when she realizes she can cause an erection. Grown women never have that tone—they know the potential for pain and confusion too well, or perhaps they're just bored with the whole thing. But a girl still thinks it's a marvel she can have that kind of power, and never thinks of what it might bring on. Jesse still had that tone in her voice. Carl thought his heart would break.

He kissed her again. She flinched for a moment when she felt the bristles of his mustache, but he pulled her close. He ran his hands over her body wildly, wanting to touch every inch, wanting to devour her. She pulled away again, laughing.

"Jesus, where have they been keeping you?"

He moved to her again, and they crawled over each other. It had been years since he'd gone wild on a woman like that, pawing and rubbing even though they were both still fully clothed. There weren't enough restrictions on adult sex to make it this exciting. He was pulling up her shirt when she brushed him off, playfully. "Come on. Not here, your parents will hear."

He could have told her his parents were dead, but he didn't like to change the subject. So they ran to the greenhouse, clinging to each other, just like in the old days. Only they didn't feel like the old days. They felt like now. It was all the things that had happened since that seemed like distant memories.

"What happened to the avocado tree?" she asked as they passed the old stump.

"It died," he said, breathless.

"You're kidding!" She sounded genuinely shocked, and

he thought of telling her that time does pass and she couldn't expect all things to remain the same and that was all a part of growing old gracefully and accepting the passage of the years, but he grabbed her tits instead. She laughed and dashed ahead into the greenhouse.

He was on her in a moment, swinging the door shut behind him and touching every part of her. He stripped every bit of clothing off her and himself, which was an insanely dangerous thing to do, considering his parents might burst in any second. And he couldn't help but consider that. He couldn't help but travel back, using her body as a time machine. He forgot that he'd ever been with another woman and fell back into the patterns of Jesse as if he'd made love to her yesterday, making circles with his fingers and tongue, pressing and pinching and biting in all the magic places. Hearing her gasp and cry out the magic sounds, seeing her white flesh turn ruddy as it blushed and her muscles tightened and her back arched and the sounds stopped, even her breath stopped, and she pushed herself up at him and his mouth filled with her taste. Finally the sigh and the shudder and she fell back to the earthen floor of the greenhouse. Tears came again to him, and this time he couldn't stop them. He rubbed his face against her and mingled his wetness with hers.

She twined her fingers in his hair and shushed him like a loving mother. Then she pulled him up onto her, and it was a long time before they were still.

When it was over, she fell asleep. He realized that he'd never seen her sleep before. There was never that kind of time in the old days. She'd always rush away after a cigarette or two, each time professing to be shocked that she'd taken such chances.

He studied her face. The moon had made its way through

the haze and was falling on her through the skylight. He was relieved to see that she did look older. This was no visit from the Twilight Zone after all. There were tiny wrinkles around her eyes, smile lines at the sides of her mouth, a very slight sagging of the flesh on her throat. Her body had changed too, it was a little broader below, but he liked that. There was a scar on the side of her belly, perhaps from an appendectomy. Its bright redness contrasted vividly with the paleness of her skin. He liked that too.

He nuzzled up to her and tried to pretend that she might like the added inches on his own gut. He felt as if it might be possible to ignore all these details and just close his eyes and go back to a time when they'd both been impossibly young, when they'd wanted each other so much they'd thought they were in love. But what if he did? The morning would still come, her game would be over, and she'd be on her way. Don't pretend that makes you angry, he told himself. What the hell would you say if she wanted to stay?

He opened his eyes and was thirty-five, with a set of keys digging into his back, lying on the hard dirt floor of a run-down greenhouse, powdered with the summer grime of a Los Angeles August, hugging a woman he hadn't seen or heard from in sixteen years, wondering what she was doing here. Women are always complaining about men falling asleep after sex, but Carl preferred that to staying awake and thinking.

He shifted a bit, slipping the keys to a less painful location. She awoke suddenly—she gasped as if she didn't know where she was. Then she nuzzled up to him, contented.

"I fell asleep," she apologized.

"I took it as a personal compliment."

"Silly. What time is it?"

He retrieved his watch from under the pile of clothes. "Four-thirty," he told her.

"Shit!" She was up and scurrying around for her clothes. "Why the hell didn't you wake me up? Mom's gonna kill me."

"How *is* your mom?"

"She's gonna kill me, that's how she is." She stopped for a moment and rubbed her side. "You must have been a little rough on me, friend. I think you broke a rib."

He found her white sun dress and handed it to her. She looked at it, puzzled, as if she'd never seen it before. "What's that?"

"Your dress."

"Oh, yeah," she said doubtfully. She took it and started slipping it on. "God, I hope I can get home before she wakes up."

"Do you need me to drive you?"

"Oh, right, you're going to wake your dad up and ask for the keys."

"I have my own car, Jesse."

"Since when?"

"I don't know, 1980?"

She looked at him in angry annoyance. "Stop being weird."

She brushed by him and headed out into the yard. He followed her. She was heading for the gate, so he called out, "I told you I was driving you home."

"Keep quiet! Do you want to get us killed?"

He took her arm and led her to the patio and into the house. He flicked on the light and his eyes ached with the brightness. She snapped at him, "Carl, what about your folks?"

He turned and faced her. Just because she still lived with her mother, why should she think he did? Why should she think he still lived here at all? Unless some mutual friend had told her. But then she would have heard that his parents were dead. And no matter how much she wanted to play her stupid game, that was hardly something to joke about. "They're not here," he said sharply.

"They're not here!" She seemed suddenly angry. "Then why the hell did you drag me out to that old greenhouse if your parents weren't here?"

"Isn't that what you wanted?"

"Why the hell would I want to lie down in the dirt when I could have a bed?"

He was getting sick of this. "Look, what are you trying to do?"

"I'm trying to go home so I can get some sleep before I go to class."

"You're taking classes?"

"What are you talking about? Of course I'm taking classes."

"Are you going to college?"

"I don't know. I haven't decided." She stopped suddenly and stared at his seventy-inch projection TV. "Christ, that's a big TV. What are these things?" She was examining his home entertainment center.

"You know, CD, VCR, laser disc player."

But she wasn't listening, she was looking around the room in confusion. "Where'd you get all this furniture? Everything's different."

"Of course everything's different. What the hell did you think, everything was going to stay the same?"

"But . . ." The confusion on her face was undeniable. Carl decided to cut the crap.

"What are you trying to pull? Is this a game? If you want to fuck me once and never see me again, just tell me!"

She backed away from him, hurt and afraid. "Why are you saying that? You know how I feel about you."

What could he say? "No, I don't. I don't know anything."

She shook her head, trying to brush it all away. "I don't like this, let's not do this. Just take me home."

He gathered up his keys and wallet from the mantelpiece. "Where do you live?"

She turned on him, screaming, "You know where I live!" She was shaking with an anger and frustration that was close to tears. He hurried to her in surprise and held her. Feeling her warm body sobbing against him, she was the little girl again and he was her boy. He'd been right when he first saw her, something was wrong. Why wouldn't she tell him what it was? "Are you okay?" he asked.

"I'm okay," she whispered; then, with a nervous laugh, "Good thing your parents aren't here."

"Yeah."

"Where are they?"

"They're dead, Jesse."

She pulled away from him, wiping her nose with the back of her hand. "That's not funny," she said as she headed out the side door.

She stopped in the driveway, staring at his moss-green Jeep Cherokee Limited with the gold trim.

"Where'd you get this thing?"

"I stole it," he told her.

She climbed up into the passenger seat, laughing under her breath. "Jesus, a fancy *Jeep.*"

They drove along in silence. Carl figured from her outburst that she still lived in her old house, but that hardly made his question anything to get angry about. Nowadays people don't live in the same state they grew up in, much less the same house.

That, however, was the least of the mysteries of the evening. For the life of him, he couldn't figure out what she was up to. She lived at home. Perhaps she was divorced recently. Feeling unhappy with life. Wanting an evening of youth. But how would she have been so sure where he lived? Well, he thought with a laugh, she could have done something damnably clever like look him up in the phone book.

So she's sitting at home with her elderly mother, watching late-night TV, feeling the urge. She looks him up, sneaks to his house (How? She didn't seem to have a car. Did she really walk the mile to his house? Did she ride her bike, like she used to in the old days?), throws her pebbles, and just assumes that he'll play along? It was crazy. But he did play along. And could he honestly say he was sorry he had?

So maybe he should stop complaining and enjoy what had happened for what it was. Maybe she was right. Maybe the only way for it all to work was to pretend that no time had passed.

"Is that Springsteen?" she asked.

He hadn't noticed, but "Streets of Philadelphia" was playing on the radio.

"Yeah."

"He sounds so depressed."

"Yeah, well, social commentary mode."

"Is it new?"

"Not really."

"How did I miss it?" Her brows were furrowed. She glanced at the green dashboard lights—the clock, the outside temperature gauge, the directional indicator, the day of the week, month, and date. "Christ, it looks like the *Enterprise* in here. What's with all these numbers?"

Carl's lips tightened, reflexively. He'd always felt self-conscious about owning a luxury automobile; it was such a show business cliché. That was why he owned an expensive four-wheel drive vehicle, as opposed to a BMW or a Mercedes. That was why ninety-eight percent of the people in show business owned expensive four-wheel drive vehicles. Now he felt she was calling him on his pretentiousness. "It has a few extras."

"I guess." She was looking over at him now, as if trying to puzzle something out. "You look funny."

"Okay, well, thank you." Maybe he should have just let her walk home. This was taking spoiling the mood to absurd lengths.

"Maybe it's the mustache," she said doubtfully. "It makes you look older." She looked at him more closely. Though Carl wasn't self-conscious about his looks, he knew he wasn't movie-star handsome. Still, his sandy hair and dark eyes had a quirky charm about them, and during his confident moments he imagined himself looking like one of those not-quite-perfect actors (say, Tom Hanks or Nicolas Cage) who, through sheer force of will, turn themselves into matinee idols. This wasn't one of his confident moments. "It makes you look a *lot* older," she went on.

This was getting more lovely by the minute. "That's why I grew it. I'm going for the wizened look."

"Stop being weird." And when she said it, her tone matched so exactly his memory of her voice saying those words, that even though they were her favorite expression of annoyance, he felt comforted. Besides, back then hadn't he always known how to joke her out of her moods? How did I do that, exactly? he wondered, his own mood souring again as he realized that he couldn't for the life of him recall. Some boyish charm, he supposed, that he'd long outgrown.

He had to drive up and down her street twice before he realized that her house wasn't there anymore. Somebody had torn it down and put up a white angular monstrosity that filled the lot with only inches to spare.

He pulled over and asked her, confused, "Am I in the right place?" Then he looked over at her and saw the horror in her eyes.

"Where's my house?" she asked, her voice small with fear. "There's the Sterns' house, there's the . . . Jesus, where the hell's my house? Where's my house?"

Carl reached out to hold her, but before he could reach her she was out of the car. He leaped out to follow her. She was pacing the dark street, staring at the impossible building in front of her.

"I know this is the right place. How could it be gone? I was just there. How could they take it away?" She was seized with a horrible new thought. "Mom and Dad . . . and Nicky, are they okay?"

She broke into a run, heading for the house. He grabbed her and she staggered to a stop. "I gotta get in there." She was trying to pull away. "I have to find out if they're in there."

"They're not in there," he told her.

"How do you know?" she asked, and suddenly he seemed to look as threatening to her as everything else. "Do you know something about this?"

"No, but it's obviously something very serious, and you can't go off and do something that might be . . . dangerous. Right?" He was vamping like a corrupt politician, but it was the only way he could think of to calm her.

She looked back at the house, warily. "Yeah," she agreed.

He took her back to the car as slowly and carefully as he could and sat her in the front seat. "Now let's think about this. When did you see the house last?"

"What kind of question is that? This morning."

"And what did you do this morning?"

She was annoyed. "I don't know . . ." He could see her realize the truth of what she said. "I don't know. That's funny, I can't remember." She tried to shrug it off. "Just what I always do, got ready for school."

"What school?"

"What do you mean? Our school."

He took both her hands and moved close to her so he wouldn't have to ask the question too loudly. "Jesse, what year is it?"

"What kind of question is that? It's 1978."

"And how old are you?"

"Seventeen. Are you okay?"

He took her in his arms and kissed her once before he turned on the car's interior light. "Look at me."

She looked at him in annoyance, but she kept looking. She looked for a long time.

"You don't look so good."

"I look older." He let go of her hand long enough to press the button that locked all the doors. "Honey, I'm thirty-five." She snatched her hands away. "Your house isn't there because somebody tore it down. I don't know where your parents are."

"Is this some stupid joke? I'm going home."

He pulled down the visor on the passenger side and slid open the mirror. The mirror light set her face aglow and she stared at her reflection in fascination. She seemed to trace each new line with her eyes. Then the full force of it hit her. She slammed the visor up and reached for the door. She couldn't open it, she couldn't even find the handle. She flung herself in a fury at the ceiling of the car. Carl tried to grab her, but she lashed out at him, smacking his nose and cracking his head against the window.

She tried to climb into the back and he grabbed her again, pinning her arms. She flailed about, slamming his knee into the steering wheel, gouging his shin with her heel. She kicked open the glove compartment and screamed a long wild howl before she began to cry.

He held her while she wept, feeling warm blood flowing from his nose, feeling the aching in his shin and the back of his head. He'd had no idea she was that strong. She finally stopped crying and curled up next to the passenger door, silent, breathing heavily, like a wounded animal.

He was panting himself, watching her, waiting for her to move. But she didn't.

So he drove her back to his house. He couldn't think of where else to take her.

He pulled into his driveway, the eucalyptus shadow long forgotten, and as he shut off the car he sighed and fell back on his seat, wiping the blood from his lip. He could smell her scent on his fingers, just as he had after the long hours they'd spent parking at the Starlight Bowl. And this was how he'd felt then, too; breath short, pulse pounding in his head, body slick with sweat. But for different reasons.

He looked over at her and took a sharp breath when he saw that she was looking up at him, her eyes bright in the darkened car.

"What year do *you* think it is?" she asked.

2

Searching through the pockets of long unworn jackets; rooting through the musty corners of cluttered drawers. Finding a cigarette was a task difficult to the point of impossibility, but he'd thrown himself into it with enthusiasm since it at least gave him something to do. A way to be of use. A reason to leave the room.

She was down there below him in the living room. Sitting on the sofa, gripping the armrest as if it would hold her steady through this very rocky landing. And didn't she look like the victim of the worst case of jet lag on record? Pale, shaking, sweating, slightly nauseated, and discombobulated beyond comprehension. Forgetting to set her watch forward seventeen years. But she had traveled from where to here?

No—he rattled through the bookshelves in the study—those were the places his mind was not ready to go yet. That's why he was dismantling the upstairs to find her a pack of cigarettes he knew wouldn't be there.

Getting her into the house hadn't been the ordeal he'd feared. He'd expected resistance, anger, hysteria . . . well, given the circumstances, he'd expected pretty much anything. Instead she was compliant. Docile. As if she didn't much care where he put her. He'd have preferred another bout of violent hysteria.

The one thing I couldn't bear, he thought, as he put her on the sofa and sat opposite her, is the notion of her becoming some retarded, broken thing. He watched her, as she sat stock-still, staring at the floor, and he thought that whatever might have been wrong with her earlier in the evening, she'd seemed alive and fully herself. He prayed that this stunned condition was just the result of shock at finding out . . . finding out?

That's when he realized that he was just sitting still and staring himself. Maybe she was in shock, but he wasn't coping with the situation too well either.

He shook himself out of it and spoke, just to hear himself say something. Nothing original, nothing helpful. He just asked if she wanted anything. She looked over at him dully and muttered that she needed a cigarette.

It was when he said he didn't have any that she started to come back to herself. Her irritated self. "C'mon, you always have a cigarette." And when he told her he'd quit last year, that was when she really shot out of her funk, lashing at him, "You didn't quit last year! You're the one who started me smoking. Now get me a cigarette!"

Well, it was something to do. In fact it was the only thing on God's green earth that he could think of to do. So he took apart his bedroom, and now he was taking apart the study, and all he knew was that he couldn't go back down there till he found a pack. Even if it meant climbing out the window and sprinting to the market to buy one.

He glanced out the window to the grass below. In that square of light he'd first seen her. When? An hour and a half ago? Impossible.

There was a half-empty pack of American Spirits, crumpled and brittlely stale, behind the four volumes of Anthony Powell's *Dance to the Music of Time.* He carried them downstairs in a sweaty palm, knowing, absolutely *knowing,* that when he walked into the living room she'd be gone, as if she'd never been there.

She was there.

She was sitting cross-legged in front of the TV set, feeling around the edges of the black console, looking for a knob or a dial. "How the hell do you turn this thing on?" she snapped at him.

He picked the remote up from the coffee table and switched the set on. Headline News was giving the sports scores. She didn't pay attention, though; she was walking over to him, looking at the remote. It is a giant wanking thing, Carl thought, looking at it with fresh eyes. Huge black dial, covered with rubbery buttons, each lit from within. Mr. Spock's tricorder had looked simpler.

Jesse took it from him and turned it over in her hand. She pointed it at the TV and turned the dial, which did nothing but start the VCR rewinding on the bookshelf. She started at the whirring sound, then looked back to the remote. Carl reached over and pressed the SCAN button to switch the channel. She pressed it now, flipping through the channels. After ten she stopped.

"How many channels do you get here?"

"About three hundred." She just stared at him. "I have satellite," he explained.

"You have a satellite," she said, her voice dripping with sarcasm. She tossed the remote onto the sofa in disgust. "This is such bullshit."

She glanced back at the set. She'd landed on MTV and the veejay was interviewing a set of female teenage rap artists.

"How do you feel about full frontal nudity in magazines? You wanna see the guys straight up?" The interviewer looked to be about nineteen; the singers looked younger.

"Oh, yeah," the girls laughed, "you wanna see what they got."

"I wanna see how it's hangin'," another added.

Jesse glanced back at Carl, dubious. She grabbed the pack from Carl and shook out a tattered cigarette. She held it to her lips and looked at him for a match.

He smiled wanly; no matches. She marched past him into the kitchen. He pulled out a smoke of his own, shut off the TV set, and followed her.

She had one of the burners on and was leaning on the counter, her eyes scanning the front page of the day's newspaper. "Ex-POW Picked as Ambassador to Vietnam," she murmured, cigarette dangling from her lip. "President *Clinton* on Friday announced his choice . . ."

She leaned over, stuck the tip of her cigarette into the blue gas flame, drew deep, then released a hacking cough, tossed the newspaper aside, and walked off into the den. He lit his own cigarette in the burner, coughed his own hacking cough, and followed her.

Well, think of something to say, he told himself. There's always an appropriate comment for a particular situation. So, how do you enjoy being a total, gibbering madwoman?

He found her standing in the middle of the den, looking around her in anger.

"Why isn't this the bathroom?" she asked.

"Dad added on. It's through there."

She walked on into the bathroom and switched on the light. He moved closer to her, watching her through the half-opened door as she took another drag on the cigarette.

"This thing is gross." She coughed a few more times and tossed the cigarette into the toilet.

"All natural ingredients."

She shot him an angry glance, then leaned over the sink and peered at herself in the mirror. Her lips were tight, as if she were bracing herself, determined not to react as she had in the car. Determined not to be frightened by the face staring back at her.

How different does she look? he asked himself. To him she seemed much the same. Certainly, if he'd just met her walking down the street, he would have said, "Jesse, you haven't changed a bit." There were signs of age—the slight crosshatching around the eyes, the inevitable coarsening of the skin; still, she seemed remarkably youthful.

But there was an indefinable change, one he could only see if he brought her old face before him in his mind's eye: that had been the face of a child, this was the face of a woman.

She touched her hair; it hung to her shoulders, but it was shorter than it had been in those days of long straight Marcia Brady hair. It was still, as he'd told her then, the color of straw in the sun. Not that he'd ever seen such straw, but the voice of love needs no research.

She turned around and leaned back on the sink, thinking.

"So you're telling me you're how old?" she asked.

"Thirty-five."

She breathed out. "That makes me . . . ?"

"Thirty-four."

"Is that how old I look?"

He hesitated. "You look good."

"I'm not asking for a compliment, Carl." She took a turn around the bathroom and sat down on the edge of the tub.

"So you're telling me suddenly it's the nineteen nineties?"

"Well, not suddenly, but, yeah."

"Then how come last weekend we went to see *Rocky Horror* at the Rialto?"

"Was that really last weekend?"

She thought back, looking a little vague and a little scared. "Well, it was *recently*."

"It was seventeen years ago."

"That is bullshit! You picked me up in your dad's Volare. You had that Linda Ronstadt cassette on where she sings "That'll Be the Day." You wore that stupid plaid shirt. I had on the yellow blouse with the big collar and the buttons down the front for easy access. We stayed out necking too late and you drove through a red light getting me home. Don't you remember?"

"I . . . I remember nights *like* that." He braced himself to state the obvious. "Jesse, I think . . . maybe you're not well."

She stood up and faced him. "How do you know it's me? How do you know you're not hallucinating?"

"Okay, we're both in denial."

"What?"

"Sorry, it's a new cliché."

She brushed past him and walked back into the den. He moved with her.

"All right. If I'm hallucinating, where did this room come from?"

She looked around, weakening. He could see she was going to have to accept reality soon, but she hung back at the edge of disbelief like a child on her first dive off the high board. He pressed on.

"How come I look older? How come you look older? How come your house is gone?"

She was still fighting it, and how could he blame her? How could she accept reality when reality was so impossible?

He looked around the room for some other evidence of the passage of time. Some futuristic gadget that would convince her that it wasn't "then" anymore. He took a CD out of the music rack and tossed it to her.

"What's that?" he demanded.

She looked at it, puzzled. It was a Pam Tillis album from a few years back. She turned the plastic case over and over in her hands, as if it were a Chinese puzzle box. She pulled on it and it came open, revealing the red CD inside. She grabbed it and yanked it out and turned it over, the light making rainbow beams on the silvery surface.

"Come on," he went on, "everybody has these, you must know what it is."

"Okay, what is it?" she asked, petulantly.

"It's the new way to play music. We had to buy all our albums over again, don't ask me why."

He crossed to the console and pressed the OPEN button. The drawer in the CD player slid open silently. Jesse was looking at the label side again, reading the release date.

"1991."

"Put it in."

She dropped the CD into the drawer. He pressed PLAY, and she started when the drawer shut itself and the disc whirred. She listened intently as the steel guitars started whining through the speakers.

"Christ," she muttered, amazed, as the digitized sound from the Dolby speakers engulfed her, "you listen to *country* music now?"

He laughed. She hadn't lost her sense of timing. "Is this your idea of a joke, Jesse?"

"It's *somebody's* idea of a joke." She walked back and sat down on the fat sofa. "So it's seventeen years since yesterday and somebody I never heard of is president and your acne has cleared up . . ." She looked up at him for help. "What the hell happened?"

But he had no help to offer. "I don't know."

"No, come on, have I been in a *coma* all this time, or what?"

"I don't know."

She was exasperated. "How can you not know?"

"We kind of . . . lost touch with each other."

For the first time she looked hurt. "You mean we broke up?"

Oh, Jesus. He shifted on his feet, feeling the guilt wash over him. "Kind of."

"How come?"

He made a face. "You know, we've sort of been through all this."

"*I* haven't! When have we been through this?"

"Our senior year."

She was appalled. "We didn't even make it through our senior year?"

"That's a tough age," he said weakly. But by then she was on her feet again, pacing in circles, her mind working.

"So I had a senior year. So I graduated?"

"Yeah."

"How'd I do on the SATs?"

"I don't remember. Pretty good, I think. You went to Berkeley."

"I went to college? So I had a life, I kept doing stuff." She looked at her hands. At the tan mark on her ring finger, left hand. "Christ, am I married?" She looked up at him, scared. "Do I . . . do I have kids?"

"I don't know, I don't think so. I think I would have heard. I don't really keep in touch with the old crowd."

Her face was blank and vulnerable now. "And you don't know where my parents are?"

"No. People retire, move away."

"What about your folks?"

"I told you. They're dead."

"Really? Oh, Carl . . ." They both fell into silence, neither of them wanting to think about the possibilities seventeen years could bring to those she loved.

"What about Nicky?" she asked in a small voice. Her little brother, six years old when they were dating. He'd be twenty-three now.

"I'm going to call Becky Holtzclaw"—she moved to the phone—"I know *she* kept in touch."

"Jesse, it's four-thirty in the morning."

She replaced the receiver in frustration. "Well, what do you want me to do? Go to sleep?"

"Why not? You can take the bed, I'll stay down here on the sofa."

She blew up at him again. "Well, thank you for being a gentleman, but you already *fucked* me in the greenhouse! If we broke up, what the hell was that about?"

He squirmed, guilty; he'd known it would come back to that. "I thought you wanted it."

"Of course I wanted it. I'm your girlfriend. But you . . ." Her anger and the situation seemed impossible for her to put into words. She muttered under her breath, bitterly, "Oh, you haven't changed."

His mind, searching for a way to change the subject, settled on aggravating a small pain in his upper back, the result of wrestling in the dirt floor of the greenhouse and rolling over on those damn keys.

Keys?

"Wait a minute."

Before she could answer, he was out the back door, racing through the night, stubbing toes and barking shins on a variety of unknown objects, scrabbling on the earthen floor of the greenhouse for the keys.

"These are your keys," he said triumphantly, once he made it through the darkness back to the house.

"Never seen them before in my life." She held them in her hand and stared at them, as if they might explode or pop out a jack-in-the-box head at any moment. Two keys on a leather strap; one a plain house key, the other a large car key with a BMW emblem embossed on the black rubber.

"Well, they're not mine," he said. "They *must* be yours." He hurried to the window and looked out at the street—no unfamiliar Beemer was sitting in front of his house. "How did you *get* here?"

"I don't *know*!" She threw the keys to him, angrily. "Look, you're just confusing me. Give me another one of those gross cigarettes." He passed her the pack and she headed into the kitchen. "You have anything to drink?"

"I could make some coffee," he said, following her.

"I hate coffee. Since when do you drink coffee?"

"Since my face cleared up."

She stopped and laughed. Their eyes met in a friendly glance. Their sense of humor had always been their strongest connection, he realized. Stronger even than sex. It had been that he had missed most when she disappeared from his life.

With that friendly glance came a moment of relaxation. The lines of age seemed to fall away from her face, replaced by a look that was very young, very innocent, very vulnerable.

"This is real, isn't it?" she whispered.

And he felt her age double over onto his until he thought he would collapse from the weight of years. Who was he to say what was real anymore?

3

In her dream Jesse was deaf and blind and her world was nothing but scent. Night-blooming jasmine by her window, hot asphalt from the street, cinnamon and syrup on French toast, the milky smell of her mother's rosewater, acrid smoke from a summer fire, the cookie dough perfume of her baby brother's newly washed head, the musk of Carl from a sweater of his that she kept hidden under her mattress, someone's cigar she knew but could not place, a pervasive aroma of mint and lemon, and again, maddeningly elusive but wafting through it all, like hot wind, the saltwater scent of blood.

Carl watched her sleeping in his bed, her face blank, her breathing slow and peaceful. Sleeping Beauty lay in her glass coffin for a hundred years, if he remembered right, before she was awakened by a kiss. What must she have thought when her eyes fluttered open on a new century?

Jesse rolled over, her head burrowing into the pillow. It was that quiet instant before dawn, when the sky turns a purple that seems darker than night. Carl had floundered on the sofa for over an hour before he'd finally fallen asleep. A few minutes later, the cat, confused by the new sleeping arrangements, had expressed its anxiety by coughing up a furball somewhere in the room where he slept. This was not a sound conducive to relaxation. He tried to place it in the room so as to avoid the unpleasant surprise of finding it with his bare feet in the morning. But the sound seemed to move around the room, like some kind of disgusting Surroundsound demonstration, so he never could locate it, and the effort left him wide awake. And thinking.

So he'd crept upstairs to peek in on her, like a new parent checking to see if his infant is sleeping soundly or has its head stuck between the crib rails.

What am I to do with her? he thought. She carried no ID with her, nothing to give him a clue to her address. There was no listing for her in the phone book, or for her parents or brother. That fading tan line on her ring finger might mean she was married or divorced. She was in good health, as near as he could see, clean and well taken care of. She obviously hadn't been wandering the streets.

Was it a temporary attack, he wondered, something like a stroke? When she wakes up, will she be fine? Back to her normal self? Whoever that might be.

Or had she been in an accident? She showed no sign of physical injury. He couldn't think of a tactful way to check her for lobotomy scars. Despite his earlier worries, she didn't seem crazy. Her behavior was perfectly sane, given the perfectly insane situation she found herself in.

Carl had seen enough TV to know about amnesia. He remembered *Shenandoah* and *Coronet Blue,* with Robert Horton and Frank Converse searching for their forgotten identities through series that were always canceled before they could be found.

This was different though. Jesse knew who she was, remembered every detail of her teenage life as if it were yesterday, indeed believed it was yesterday—but everything since then seemed to have been erased.

There was an adult, responsible way for Carl to handle this, he was sure. People must be looking for her; her family, her husband perhaps (Carl winced a little at the thought). He just had to find them. But how? Was he supposed to put notices on telephone poles, like a child who's found a stray dog? And if this theoretical husband of hers saw the notices and came to "claim" her, she'd have no idea who he was. How would she cope?

But was that his problem? Was he his ex–high school girlfriend's keeper? Surely, the sensible thing was to call the police or some social service organization. They'd take care of her in some nice state institution while the authorities located her home. There, that was the straightforward, logical plan.

So why wasn't he moving? Admit it to yourself, his bullshit monitor told him, you *are* like that kid with the stray dog, pestering his mother, "Can I keep it, can I keep it?," looking for excuses not to call the pound.

Oh, don't be so hard on yourself, said another voice in his head, this voice coming from his chronically ineffective defense team. It's only natural that you'd be deeply affected by seeing this woman. She wasn't just your first lover. More than anyone else, she'd been the one who encouraged him to write, reading his lousy short stories, third-rate imitations of Harlan Ellison and Richard Matheson, and urging him to shoot higher, to push harder, to write for the theater; she gave him the guts to go on and write third-rate imitations of Edward Albee and Harold Pinter. And if eighty percent of his creative impulse came from a desire to impress his way into her flared jeans, well, wasn't that what art was all about?

Yes, no doubt about it, he was glad to have her here, this visitor from the less innocent days of his youth. Not forgiving his sins, perhaps, but forgetting them with sweeping efficiency. So what are you thinking, his bullshit monitor shot back, that this is a second chance? A path back to an artistic integrity you never really had? Someone to fill the void in your life?

He cursed himself for a pathetic fool and went downstairs with every intention of calling the police right then. But it was early, wasn't it? And she needed her sleep, didn't she? And he owed her at least a nice breakfast, didn't he? And if he couldn't effectively argue with his bullshit monitor, he was at least very adept at telling it to shut the fuck up.

Brring!

He jerked awake to the blaring sound of Saturday morning cartoons mixed with his doorbell ringing. He sat forward, heart thudding in his chest, and switched off the set just as Pinky and The Brain were failing once again to take over the world.

He didn't even have a moment of blissful disorientation in which he wondered why he was sleeping on the sofa or whether last night's events had been only a dream. As soon as he woke up, reality came falling down on him like the gold brick that had just squashed The Brain as flat as a pancake.

The doorbell rang again. He checked his watch. It was after nine. Kit. Work. Unbelievable.

He flung open the door to find his partner standing on the stoop, laptop slung under his arm, the remnants of a hangover rouging his eyes. "My God," Kit said at the sight of Carl, "you look like I feel."

Kit. Work. Script due on Monday. Carl just shook his head. "Can't today. Personal life."

Kit just walked on in. "The season grows long, Carl, there's no time for a personal life."

Carl thought about blocking his way, but then he was seized by a hopeful inspiration, so instead he pulled Kit in and took his bags. "Maybe you can help me."

Kit said that he lived to serve, so Carl told him to wait there a second and he'd be right back. He raced upstairs and peeked in on her again.

She must have been exhausted, because she still lay on her stomach, breathing softly and steadily, the sheet entwined between her legs. She was wearing his blue pajamas, the ones Amanda had given him. They were bunched up slightly on her left leg; the waist was twisted around her, covering her haunches in rolling, silky ripples. There were few things in the world as erotic, Carl thought, as the sight of a woman sleeping in your borrowed pajamas. It said so much about intimacy and friendliness. Not to mention lack of planning.

He was surprised and a little ashamed at his own arousal. What right did he have to be attracted to her? Perhaps he'd had a claim on her once, but he'd forfeited it long ago. And yet what woman had ever looked as comfortable sleeping in his bed?

Too bad he hadn't been able to join her.

"This is a wonderful story, Carl. Please don't tell me it's true, it would spoil the magic."

Over coffee, Carl had related the whole story, skipping delicately over the greenhouse episode. "It's true. Can you do it?"

Kit pursed his lips, thinking it over, the way he thought over a plot point in a story conference.

"Maybe you don't think you've given me a lot to go on"—he wanted to be impressive, so Carl let him—"but just the name, you'd be surprised how much you can find out from just the name. For instance, nobody ever thinks of something as simple as checking the phone book."

Carl told him he'd checked the phone book.

"Yeah, well, you would, you always take the fun out of everything. No luck?"

"Not listed," Carl said.

"How 'bout your high school alumni organization?"

"Didn't think of that."

"Thank God for small favors. I'll start there."

Kit unwrapped his long fingers from the coffee mug, stretched his lanky legs under the kitchen table, and pulled out an embossed leather notebook, one of his many affectations. Carl's eyes kept drifting to the new color of his partner's hair—Jean Harlow platinum blonde. Kit was a homosexual of the old school, far too flamboyant to be acceptable in today's politically charged gay community. Once or twice they'd even cast him in episodes of the show, playing a gay character, and their gay casting director had objected that Kit was too much of a stereotype. But he'd been through the wars, Kit maintained, and he'd earned the right to be a queen.

He was in great shape, thin and improbably tall, with only his oddly bulbous nose betraying his forty-odd years. They'd met at Paramount, when Carl was delivering sandwiches and Kit was running the research department. They shared no interests and couldn't have been more different temperamentally, so they decided they were ideally suited to be writing partners. For nine months they worked after hours at Nickodell's, scribbling on legal pads in a booth in the corner. After eleven unsold scripts they started getting work and they hadn't looked back since. They didn't resent each other half as much as most partners, though of course, each secretly knew the other was dragging him down.

It was Kit's expertise in the research department that had prompted Carl to ask for his help now. Kit had always bragged that he could find the answer to any question within an hour. Carl had decided to put him to the test.

There really wasn't much information. Jesse's dad had been in real estate, but Carl didn't know what firm. Her mother had been a grade school teacher. "Would they be retired now?" Kit asked. "How old were they?"

Carl shrugged. "You know how it is when you're a kid, grown-ups are just old."

"What about the brother? Any ideas what line of work he might have gone into?"

"He was six. He wanted to be a fireman." Carl thought about Nicky. Always tagging along, especially when Carl wanted Jesse to himself. But even as a teenager, when one dislikes children so intensely because one is afraid of being mistaken for one, Carl had liked Nicky. The kid knew how to laugh at Carl's jokes. And he was such pals with his sister. Jesse didn't play with him out of an embarrassed sense of duty, but for the sheer fun of it. It looked like so much fun that Carl couldn't help but join in, relaxing his constant effort to appear world-weary in the exhilaration of a wild game of capture-the-flag.

Nicky would be a man now, and Jesse wouldn't recognize him if she saw him.

"Okay, I'll find them or him or whoever. You could do it yourself, but it'll be good for my ego." He slapped the notebook shut and slipped it back into his linen jacket. "So do I get to meet her? I'm imagining something very pre-Raphaelite. Very Ophelia floating down the river."

Carl figured it was time to get her up anyway, so he told

Kit to wait right there and Kit said, fine, anything to put off working.

Kit sipped his coffee and listened to Carl walk up the stairs. Heard Carl's footsteps hurrying around upstairs. Listened to him calling "Jesse" over and over. Heard him troop down the stairs and hurry into the kitchen, with a dumbfounded expression on his face.

"She's not there," Carl said.

"Did we mix some pharmaceuticals contrary to doctor's orders last night?"

Carl turned and hurried into the living room. Kit sighed and got up to follow.

He came in to see Carl standing in the middle of the room, looking out through the patio doors to the backyard.

She was standing there, sunlight falling on her yellow hair, blue pj's hanging a little too loosely on her slight form, staring up at the sky like a supplicant.

"*Very* pre-Raphaelite," Kit said. He took in the expression on Carl's face as he looked at her. "Careful, buddy. You're worse than I am. You've always been attracted to the damaged ones."

"Look at that," she said to Carl, as he approached her.

He looked up. Two hawks were circling high above the hills to the north. They always came out in the mornings, to soar and play games and occasionally drop as fast as a stone to earth in search of prey. Carl loved to watch them. They were part of his backyard family, along with the raccoon, and the dove that just sat in the birdbath on hot days, and the escaped canary that spent most of its time hiding near the feeder. He liked to imagine that the hawks were sparring, wisecracking lovers—a feathered Nick and Nora Charles. Jesse was the only other person who'd ever noticed them.

"They're beautiful," she said.

He wanted to slip his arm around her and watch them wheel, but he asked her if she wanted breakfast instead. Did he have any Cap'n Crunch cereal? she asked. Sorry, he was fresh out.

Kit joined them, offering his hand. She wrapped the pajama shirt around herself, a bit self-conscious about her state of undress.

"I'm Kit."

"How ya doin'?"

"Fine. So Carl tells me you can't remember anything since 1978."

Jesse blanched. Carl flinched. Kit prided himself on being able to find the wrong thing to say for all occasions.

"You didn't miss much," he went on. "Think what she's been spared, Carl. The complete works of Madonna. The careers of Andrew Lloyd Webber and Quentin Tarantino and Newt Gingrich. 'Where's the beef?' 'Don't take the car, you'll kill yourself.' 'I've fallen and I can't get up.' Video games. Running shoes. Call waiting. Post-it notes. Roller-blades. The Gulf War. AIDS. I tell you, Jesse, if you could bottle this, you'd make a fortune."

4

$\mathcal{J}$esse sat with the phone in front of her, staring at it as if it were an alien thing. In many ways it was, of course. Everywhere Carl looked, he was now aware of how many small things had changed in the past seventeen years. Phones used to be solid, heavy, and simple. This thing was sleek, fragile, and confusing. Covered with redial buttons and memory buttons and remote message-checking buttons, speakers and microphones, a little screen where LED figures displayed the time and date; even the homey old Ma Bell logo was gone, replaced by the AT&T Deathstar globe.

It was almost noon, and from the moment she'd gotten up she'd been saying how she wanted to use the phone, to call her people, to find out where she belonged. But she'd put it off for two hours now, having breakfast, talking with Carl and Kit, finding excuses. Carl knew why. She was scared.

And who wouldn't be? She might find her life on the

other end of that line, but what if she didn't like it? She couldn't send it back.

"Who are you going to call first?"

"I don't know."

"We could wait. We could see what Kit comes back with."

"It doesn't make sense to wait."

Jesse and Kit had hit it off remarkably well, somewhat to Carl's annoyance. Kit was a trusted friend, but his vaunted wit had started to cloy for Carl years ago. Indeed Carl spent most of his time trying to break through that witty veneer, to circumvent it, to get to the "real" Kit, as it were. Kit found this behavior of Carl's irritating in the extreme. "I built this character for a reason," he'd say. "If I wanted people to know me, I wouldn't have bothered."

But Jesse found him vastly amusing and, Lord knew, she needed to be amused. So they ate Carl's scrambled eggs and hash browns while Kit related his Improved History of the Late Twentieth Century, in which Bill Clinton was the first president elected on a purely cunnilingual platform and George Bush and Saddam Hussein settled their differences in a "very special episode" of *American Gladiators*.

She laughed at every joke, in that gasping breathless laugh Carl knew so well. Of course, she didn't get half the references, but she knew he was being outrageous and she'd always loved that.

"I have to say," she said, looking around the room, "I'm a little disappointed. Where's all the cool technology? I mean, shouldn't the future look a lot more like *The Jetsons* than this?"

"It's been a letdown for all of us," Kit agreed. "Pretty much the only real advance in the past twenty years has been those SnackWell fat-free cookies. Oh, and the Internet. That's a system that allows boring people with behavioral problems and bad hygiene to have a social life."

"A 'virtual' social life," Carl overlapped.

Kit nodded. "Yes, and we've also learned to add the word 'virtual' in front of every phrase, whether it means anything or not."

"But come on," Jesse persisted, laughing, "where are the flying cars and the transporter machines?"

"Well," Kit explained, patiently, "the transporter machines made the flying cars obsolete. But they didn't last either. Someone was always beaming in on you while you were having dinner, or taking a shower. It got very annoying. So in the end people just settled for 'call waiting.' "

"Interesting," she said with a smile. "Gimme another one of those cigarettes with the Indian on them."

"That's another thing," Kit warned her. "They're not Indians anymore. They're Native Americans."

She pulled out the last smoke, shrugging, annoyed. "I know that."

Carl thought this might be significant and asked her how she knew the term.

"Mrs. Hobson always called them that." Mrs. Hobson, their ninth grade social studies teacher, politically correct before politically correct was cool. "You know, Native American, Afro-American."

"Now it's African American," Kit interjected.

"Why?"

"Just to keep us on our toes."

"Guys, come on." Carl spoke in the same tone he used to scold the writing room when they'd spent too much time off on a tangent. "We have to start focusing." Carl pushed his half-finished eggs aside. "Now, I'm going to labor the obvious here."

"He's good at that," Kit told her.

Carl ignored him. "You don't remember *anything* about the last seventeen years?"

She shifted in her seat; clearly it was easier for her to joke about the situation than face it. Who could blame her for that? "I guess not."

"Nothing?" Carl went on. "Nothing about the world at large? You don't remember that Ronald Reagan was president?"

She laughed again, then took in their blank looks. "Really?"

"And you don't know these names: Tom Cruise? Mel Gibson? Michael Jordan? Margaret Thatcher? David Koresh? Jeffrey Dahmer?"

"No. Were they in a band?"

"You should have heard them," Kit said.

Carl shot him a look, then went on. "What about your personal life? You have no memory of a job?"

She was thinking now, trying to piece things together. But in the end she just shook her head.

"When you get up in the morning, what do you do?"

She laughed, but it was a different kind of laugh now; embarrassed and a little helpless. "I go to school."

Carl sat back, trying to find a new tack. "Okay . . . what month is it?"

She looked at him, face blank. She glanced out the window. "I don't know. Looks like spring or summer."

"Don't just guess. It's August. Do you remember that it's August?"

She was concentrating now. He saw furrows on her brow that he'd never seen before; signs of age and worry.

"I . . . I'm not sure."

"What's the last thing you remember? I mean, before you came here?"

She shifted in her chair, uneasy. "Just the usual stuff. Going to school. Hanging around."

"But specifically. Like, yesterday morning, what did you have for breakfast?"

"I ... I'd usually have, you know, Cap'n Crunch or Life—"

"But specifically?"

"I don't know!" She snapped at him, then sat back, shaking her head. "It's weird. It's just, it doesn't *feel* like anything's wrong, but ... when I try to pin things down, it all kind of squirms away."

"That's all right. I'm sorry, I didn't mean to push. Do you want to stop?"

She gave a nervous laugh. "No, let's keep talking. Let's find out how sick I am."

"All right ... What about last night? How did you get here? Did you walk? Did you drive? Did you bicycle?"

She thought for a moment, then shook her head. "You know, the thing is, I'm not even aware I don't know these things until you guys bring it up. I guess some things you don't question. You figure they're so obvious, you *have* to know them." She sat forward on the edge of her chair and looked at Carl. "I don't know how I got here. I mean, I remember walking down your street, but it's not like I suddenly appeared there and wondered, How did I get here, what am I doing here? I was just on your street at night and when I'm on your street at night I'm coming to see you. So I came to see you.

"Before that ... just a general sense that life was normal, and I was in school and ..." Another nervous laugh and a glance down at her plate. "Jesus, this is really sad, isn't it?"

To Carl's surprise, Kit spoke up quickly, with real concern in his voice. "No, we're just figuring this out. It's probably just temporary. If you see the right thing it'll all come back to you. You know, like Proust and that cookie."

Jesse looked puzzled. "Are those the fat-free ones?"

Kit politely ignored her confusion. "Let's say you lost your memory, I don't know how. You're wandering around and you see Carl's house and that triggers your memories about Carl. So maybe if we could take you where you live or work, maybe you'd remember all that too."

Jesse mulled this over. "Maybe . . . I don't know. I mean, it's not like I only remember Carl and this house. I remember my whole life . . . up to a point. I don't really even remember everything about Carl." She looked over at him. "I don't remember why he broke up with me."

Kit looked at him, offended. "You broke up with her? You pig!"

Carl went on the defensive. "How do you know *I* broke up with *you?*"

"Well, I would never break up with you. Unless you did something really creepy. What did you do?"

"So either way it's my fault?"

"Well, it was, wasn't it?"

Carl sighed. "Can we go into this another time?"

Kit took that as his cue to leave. He left, swearing, with unaccustomed seriousness, to be back in two hours with her life story. One quick reminder that Carl wasn't good enough for her and he was out the door.

They were both sorry to see him go, and only partly because they liked him. Being alone together wasn't as easy as it had been last night. Too many questions had been raised.

She glanced over at him. "So you work together, huh? What do you do?"

Carl told her that they wrote for a television series.

"So you did it?!" she said, overjoyed. "You're a writer!

Jesus, Carl, I told you you could do it, you never believed me!" Then, a little more doubtfully, "Television, huh?" She had always been his greatest fan—and his most merciless critic.

"It's a good show," he said, only a little defensively.

"I'm so happy for you." She walked a few steps back to the kitchen. "Sometimes I feel like I'm looking at a crystal ball into the future. Like I'm going to be able to run back to school tomorrow and tell you, 'Carl, don't worry, it's going to work out for you.' But this isn't the future, is it? It's supposed to be now."

Carl took her arm and led her to the stairs. "Come on, I want to show you something."

After his mother had died, Carl's father had moved out of their bedroom and into the old playroom. Just carried all his stuff across the hall one day and settled in. Maybe he'd thought the move would only be temporary, for he didn't change the room at all. It was still set up as it had been in Carl's happiest childhood years, when he'd been six or seven and he'd spent his off-school hours with his father building H.O. trains and relief maps of California and volcanoes that erupted with baking soda lava. The long table was still under the window, where they'd rushed home from their working days, to assemble Aurora Famous Monsters kits of Frankenstein and The Wolf Man and the pre–Michael Crawford Phantom of the Opera. The dusty models still lined the upper bookshelves, with real cobwebs accenting the plastic ones. The monsters towered over the more mature creations of his preteen years; World War II battleships and fighter planes, the *Monitor* and the *Merrimack,* and fragments of the U.S.S. *Enterprise,* destroyed in a Klingon-inspired Frisbee attack.

It had been strange, in the year Carl and his dad lived

alone in the house together, to see the Old Man in the
mornings, sitting on the edge of the little bed, his spotty
head framed by Daniel Boone wallpaper, looking lost and
small. Carl, newly homeless after his breakup with Amanda
and knowing that his widowed father needed to be kept
company (and needing company himself, if he'd been able
to admit it), was forced to take his mom and dad's old room
when he moved back into the house—to sleep in their old
bed and listen to his dad snoring under a fading poster of
the Man from U.N.C.L.E. Carl considered it a personal victory that he didn't take to drink that year.

Once Carl had tried to rearrange the playroom, shift the
table away from the window, order a bigger bed, but his dad
seemed reluctant, so he dropped the idea. Dad found the
place comforting. It had seemed strange to Carl that the Old
Man should be nostalgic for a childhood other than his
own. Of course, for Carl that had been a golden time
(wasn't that what childhood was supposed to be?) but he'd
never thought of what it had meant to his father.

And how had that era ended? Was there a turning point, a
last day? A last aircraft carrier, unfinished on the bottom
shelf? Was there a day where they worked on it and then
put the glue away forever? Had either of them recognized
that this was their last trip to the navy yard? Their last visit
to Frankenstein's laboratory?

He supposed it had happened as it did with all boys; he'd
started to grow hair in unexpected places and to look for his
heart's desire anywhere but in his own backyard. Leaving
this room without a backward glance. Leaving the Old Man
like Puff the Magic Dragon in his cave. Without further
excuse to build model kits or to play ball. Maybe that, Carl
wondered, was when the Old Man had started to grow old.

He had been, at that time, one year older than Carl was
now. Carl himself had no children, nor any prospect of any.

But then, like the rest of his generation, Carl was determined not even to grow up, let alone old.

A box in the back of the playroom closet held all the personal correspondence Carl had saved. There weren't many letters, since his epistolary period had been short—the first years of college when one fancies oneself an intellectual and there are old high school friends to keep in touch with.

He rooted out the envelope he needed, smelled the musty paper, took out an old photograph, and handed it to Jesse. She looked at it, puzzled. She turned it over and looked at the back; it was developed in the days when Kodak always put the date on the back.

"1980 . . . So this is two years from . . ." She hesitated and he knew it was because she was going to say "two years from now."

"That's you at college," he explained.

The picture showed her with long hair and a peasant blouse, standing in Golden Gate Park. Two other girls were standing with her—one with a head of wild curly hair and a snub nose; the other, with long straight black hair, smiling through crooked teeth. Their arms were around each other with easy familiarity and their faces were glowing with laughter.

"Do you recognize either of those girls?"

She stared at the photo for a long moment, then sat back on the bed. "I'm waiting for something to click in my head, but it's not going to happen. Who are they?"

Carl thought for a moment, then pulled the letter from the envelope and handed it to her. She unfolded the small lavender sheets and read out loud.

" 'Carl, I s'pose you're surprised to be getting a letter from me, but not nearly as surprised as I am to be sitting here writing it. I can think of a whole bunch of reasons not to write to you, but I guess if I'm going to still be thinking about you, I might as well find out how you're doing. So how are you doing?'" Jesse gave a snort at her own lame joke and read on. "'I'm including a picture of me and my new best friends, Holly Martin and Lorraine Perdomo.'"

She pulled out the picture and looked at it, then read on in silence, and Carl resisted the temptation to read over her shoulder. No need to. He remembered receiving the letter, reading it once, then stuffing it into the back of a notebook. He read it again a few years later and wondered why he hadn't answered. But too late then, too late.

"'I talked to Becky the other day,'" she resumed, "'but she didn't know what you were up to. I guess you're not keeping in touch with the old crowd much either. It's funny how quick you make new friends and forget the old ones. (How does that "silver and gold" song go?) I already feel like I've known Holly and Lorraine my whole life. So I guess that means I've lived a whole life since I saw you last . . .'" She looked up at him, then back to the letter. "'I just had to go to Lit class and when I came back I read over the beginning of this letter and I almost threw it away, but I figured I'd never write it again, so I didn't. But about that part where I say I think about you; I don't want you to think I'm pining away, or dreaming about you or that kinda shit. It's just that you were a big part of my life and you always will be, so, you know, don't be a stranger. Or be one, if you want to. Or maybe I will throw the letter away. Write back if you feel like it.'"

She lowered the page, lost in thought.

"Anything?" he asked.

She looked up at him. "Did you write back?"

Well, it was hardly the time to go into that. "Sure. We exchanged a couple of letters, but you know . . . you don't keep it up."

"Do you have any of my other letters?"

See, one lie leads to another, he told himself. "No, I only saved this one."

She stood up, looking at the picture. "Funny. These are supposed to be my best friends, and I don't even know which one is Holly and which one is Lorraine."

She looked out the window at the lavender haze of jacaranda blossoms in the street, tapping on a weathered Alfred E. Neuman decal on the glass with her index finger. "I guess I better go call Becky."

And still she delayed.

Checking out the little LED display window on the phone.

"Is that where the picture comes on?" she asked.

"No picture."

"Big TV writer and you don't have a picture phone?"

"Nobody has 'em. They never caught on."

She sighed. "No picture phones. The nineties are a real letdown."

"You're not the only one who feels that way."

She picked up the small handset and reached a finger out to punch in a number.

She hung up again.

"What if Becky doesn't live there anymore?"

"It's a start. Maybe her parents are still there. They can give you her number."

She reached for the phone again. Again she stopped.

"What if . . ." she hesitated, then pushed on, the words tumbling out, "what if, you know, something really gross happened to me and I'm blocking it out and that's why I can't remember anything."

The worry had obviously been bottled up inside her and now that she'd let it out, she sat back, a little embarrassed, but visibly relieved.

"That's stupid, isn't it?" she said.

But he'd been wondering the same thing himself. Hadn't they seen that plot turn in a hundred movies and TV shows?

"I mean, what if I, you know, witnessed a murder or was gang-banged or something? Or what if I killed somebody, even?" She laughed a little, knowing how melodramatic she sounded. "And maybe I don't want to know about it, so I . . . made myself forget."

Carl stood up and took a turn around the room, thinking it over. "I don't know, but . . . I don't think it really works that way. I think that's only in stories. I mean, I guess I've read about people forgetting particular incidents or moments because they're traumatic. But I don't think something like that would make you block out seventeen years."

"But you don't really know, do you?"

Carl had to admit that he didn't.

"I think I'm afraid to find out." She stared at the phone as if it were a baleful machine. Taking a breath, she picked it up and punched in the number. After a moment, she glanced at Carl. "It says it's been disconnected or is no longer in service."

Carl remembered that Becky lived in Silver Lake. "It's a different area code now. You have to dial 213 first."

She frowned and redialed. She started, as if stung by a bee, and hung up fast. "Somebody answered."

"Well, don't you want to talk to them?"

She laughed. "I guess not. I'll try again."

She picked up the receiver; Carl reached over and pressed the REDIAL button. Her eyebrows rose as she listened to the phone dial by itself. "Cool," she said. She caught her breath and spoke into the phone. "Hi, is this the Holtzclaw residence? . . . Well, do you have their number? . . . Well, thank you."

She hung up, disappointed and relieved at the same time. "They're not there. They never heard of the Holtzclaws."

"You want to eat first, or do you want to keep trying?"

She wanted to keep trying. He told her to dial 411 for Information.

She dialed, listened for a moment, and looked up at him in surprise. "A tape recording just asked me 'what city'?"

"So tell it."

She spoke into the phone, tentatively and a little too loud, like his grandmother, who'd always thought you had to yell when you talked long distance. Then she said the name Holtzclaw, and looked up at Carl. "How does it understand me?"

"To tell you the truth, I have no idea."

But then an actual human came on the line and told her they could find no listing under that name. It took three more tries before she reached anyone. Cathy Delorenzo's old number was no good. There was a Sidney Norton in Thousand Oaks, but it wasn't the one who'd been Jesse's lab partner in Mr. Alpert's class.

But someone answered Susie Judd's number.

". . . Yes?" Carl watched Jesse's face, seeing that something was happening. "This is . . . Is this the Judd residence?" she asked.

Carl asked her if she wanted to be alone. She thought for a moment and then nodded, so Carl went into the kitchen to make them some lunch. He understood that this was a tense moment for her, and the last thing she needed was him staring at her, trying to read from her expression what was being said on the other end of the wire. She deserved her privacy. But he hit the MEMO RECORD button on the kitchen phone so he could tape the call and listen to it later. A crude invasion of her privacy, he knew, but he couldn't bear the thought of missing out on the call entirely.

He pulled out the low-fat turkey and tofu cheese and was spreading the nonfat mayonnaise on the thin-sliced whole wheat bread when she came in.

She had an expression on her face that he'd never seen before.

"Well," he asked, "what did you find out?"

It took a moment for her to answer.

"I'm dead," she said.

5

"*H*ello."

"... Yes?"

"Hello?"

"This is ... Is this the Judd residence?"

"Yes. Who is this?"

Carl kept his eyes fixed on Jesse's stony expression while they both listened to the answering machine's playback.

"Is Susie there?"

"Susan's living in Boston now. Who is this?"

"Mrs. Judd?"

"Who is this?"

"This is Jessica, Mrs. Judd."

"I'm sorry?"

"I'm an old friend of Susie's."

"Susan's living in Boston now."

"Jessica Holland, Mrs. Judd. Do you remember me?"

"... You're looking for Jessica Holland?"

"... Yeah, do you have her number?"

"Who is this?"

"I'm an old friend of Susie's . . . and Jessica's. Do you know where she's living now?"

"Susan's living in Boston now."

"What about Jessica?"

"Jessica Holland?"

"Yes. Do you know where she lives?"

"Oh, dear . . . Who is this?"

". . . Becky Holtzclaw."

"Becky. How *is* your mother?"

"Just fine, Mrs. Judd. What about Jessica?"

"I was so sorry to hear about your father."

". . . Thank you. Do you know what Jessica's been up to?"

"Jessica Holland?"

"Yes."

"Oh, dear. I thought you would have heard. Didn't you ever talk to Susan?"

"She's in Boston."

"Would you like her number?"

"That would be nice, Mrs. Judd. But I need Jessica's first."

"Oh, dear. Jessica died, dear. It must be two months ago. I just can't believe no one told you. Some kind of boating accident, I think . . . Oh, I hate giving bad news . . . Becky? . . . Are you there? . . . Oh, dear."

Click.

The machine cut off, ending the playback, and the tape rewound itself.

Jesse sat across the kitchen table, looking exhausted from reliving the conversation. Carl had never been good at letting silences hang. Better to blurt out something stupid than keep staring at each other across such a bleak divide.

"What do you think?" But did he have to say something *that* stupid?

"What do I *think?* What the hell am I supposed to think? Somebody just told me I've been dead for two months. Jesus!" She passed a hand over her brow, then paused to look at it. "I don't feel like a ghost."

Carl, in one of those embarrassing outbursts of sincerity he always regretted afterward, reached out and grabbed the hand she was studying. "No, you don't," he said.

She gave him a surprised look, then burst out laughing and snatched her hand away. "Don't get weird on me, Carl." Thus it always ended. Time to pull back and be rational and pretend that didn't just happen.

"Look, you can't take this seriously. She sounded all confused. She didn't even know who you were."

"Carl, *I* don't know who I am."

He snuffed the impulse to seize her hand again and say that he knew who she was. Too mushy. "You do, too. This is just some senile lady who doesn't know what the hell is going on."

"Like me?"

"Knock it off! You never felt sorry for yourself before, don't start now."

"How do we know? Maybe I felt sorry for myself through the entire 1980s. Maybe that's why I drowned myself."

Carl bolted to his feet, and the kitchen chair slammed down on the linoleum floor. "Shut up! You don't know what happened. I know this is all pretty crazy, but you're not dead." Now, he thought, he could grab her and kiss her deeply and show her how alive she is. Or he could turn it into a joke. "Trust me, dead people don't fuck like that."

She burst out laughing her beautiful laugh. Good choice.

Whatever else happens in life, sandwiches still have to be made. He could hear her up in the shower while he pieced together the bread and lunchmeat, and the more he tried not to picture her body slick with soap, casting off splashes of sparkling water, the more crystal clear the image became. Last night's teenage fantasy must still have been lingering in his libido, for he was unable to stop himself from imagining what they would have done two decades back if they'd had the house to themselves like this. Not one room, not one piece of furniture, would have retained its innocence.

Well, that was then and this was now, so get your mind off the soapy parts and back on lunch, he told himself. But isn't she still available to you? asked the little devil perched on his left shoulder. Just yesterday, in her time frame, he was still her boyfriend. The end of their relationship was a mystery to her. If the mystery remained unsolved (and he didn't seem too anxious to solve it for her), perhaps they could pick up where they left off. So what was he contemplating—walking in on her, flinging the shower curtain aside, and joining her under the stinging water?

Lost in thought as he was, he didn't notice the water shutting off, so he jumped when she walked into the kitchen, plucking at his Paramount Studio sweatshirt, which she was wearing over his CBS sweatpants, and holding her dress in her right hand. "Do you mind? I want to wash this dress. I have no idea how long I've been wearing it."

No problem at all, he said, in fact he'd be happy to pop it into the machine for her, anything to get him out of the room before she noticed the erection throbbing down his left leg. He grabbed the frock, skirted out of the room sideways, and was out the door before he heard her smirking voice. "Do you always enjoy making sandwiches that much?"

Sometimes acting like you didn't hear is the only dignified response.

He'd regained control over his body by the time he came back in and found her at the table munching on the sandwich and looking unhappily at the jar of nonfat mayo and the packet of lowfat turkey. "This tastes like crap. Don't you have anything with flavor?"

"They don't do flavor anymore. It's not good for you."

She shrugged, and he joined her in the chalky repast. Checking his watch, he told her he was going to beep Kit and see if he'd found anything.

"You're going to do what to Kit?" Jesse watched him, puzzled, as he punched an inexplicably long combination of numbers into the phone and then hung up without once speaking. Taking pity on her confusion, he explained the modern marvel of the electronic leash. "Man, these phones," she said, "you can do everything but have sex with them." He refrained from telling her that he'd done that too, in his time. Instead, he had an inspiration.

Leading her upstairs, he slid open the lid of his rolltop desk, revealing his pride and joy, a new NEC Versa 6200MX Pentium Processor. She wasn't impressed though, only confused; an IBM Selectric typewriter was state-of-the-art to her.

If she *had* been involved in some sort of boating accident that Mrs. Judd's confused mind had turned into a fatality, Carl explained to her, it might have made the paper, in which case he should be able to find it through the Times-Link on America Online. Logging into the *L.A. Times* website, he gave her a cursory explanation of the information superhighway and punched in the keywords *Jessica Holland.*

"That's assuming I didn't die under my married name."

He shot her an annoyed look, not sure if he was more irritated by her insistence that she was dead or that she was married.

While the machine muttered and purred, gathering its thoughts (Carl always pictured a tiny Jeff Bridges from *Tron,* riding a messenger's bike around a badly fluorescent-lit maze, plucking information from little shoots and stuffing it into his shoulder bag to fetch it back to his modem), Jesse ambled over to the old upright piano next to the bookshelf and plunked her finger down on middle C.

"Grandpa left me that," Carl told her.

She snatched her hand away and the note was cut short. "I suppose he's dead, too?"

"Too?" Was she still including herself in the rolls of the dead?

"I mean, like your folks," she explained, sensing his confusion.

Carl nodded. She came over to him and sat on the desk next to the PC. "How long ago?"

"Dad, just last year."

She looked down at the monitor. "Would this thing know if my parents are still alive?"

Carl shifted in his seat; he guessed he hadn't explained the limitations of the Internet as well as he'd thought. The doorbell rang downstairs and he hurried to answer it, leaving Jesse to wait for the machine's answer.

Kit was at the door and the half-puzzled, half-sickened expression on his face told Carl what his investigations had uncovered.

"Uh, this is kind of awkward," said Kit, stymied as to how to deliver his bizarre information.

Carl let him off the hook. "I know. She's dead."

"But she wears it well," Kit quipped, immediately bouncing back now that the weight of bad tidings was off his shoulders. "Good idea to lose the mustache, by the way. It takes years off you."

Carl nodded and listened while Kit launched into the rest

of his story. Before he could half begin, they heard the music from upstairs; someone was playing Grandpa's piano, not professionally, but competently, picking out "It Never Entered My Mind" simply and mournfully, and the tune seemed to pull both of them to the bottom of the stairs.

Carl called up, "Jesse?"

"Come on up," she hollered back. "I just read my obituary."

They found her fingering the piano keys, making a few mistakes, but going back and getting it right. A sweet sound, subtle and mature. Carl was surprised she even knew the song. He himself hadn't discovered the majesty of jazz and American popular song until well into college, when he'd dated a music major who fancied herself the white Sara Vaughan. So much of his taste and education had come from old girlfriends, Carl sometimes felt that he was little more than a collection of the attributes of his discarded loves.

But wait, he told himself as she finished the piece, her knowing the song was not the surprising thing. "When did you learn to play the piano?" he asked.

She turned around on the piano bench and spoke in a quiet voice, as if not wanting to break the mood. "Never. I never played before." She gave a little half-smile. "I'm a talented ghost."

Jesse had loved to sail, a preoccupation Carl had always found annoying. Southern Californians are, by birthright, obliged to love the ocean and the beach, but Carl was uncomfortable there. Hot sun tightened and pricked at his skin; lying in it made as much sense to him as voluntarily relaxing in a swarm of mosquitoes. Sand was useful as a tool for planing wood; letting it actually touch one's skin and collect in sensitive crevices as a form of recreation seemed contrary to the most rudimentary concepts of proper hygiene. And sailing, combining all these irritations with hard physical labor and rope burns, was a trial Carl found hard to endure.

But Jesse loved it and for her sake, and for the sight of her in a skimpy two-piece bathing suit, he had been willing to put up with it. And she was beautiful on a boat. Not because of the swimsuit—after all, he'd seen her naked, and nothing could compete with the wonder of that. The beauty came from the wind in her hair, the sunlight reflected in her eyes, the sweat glistening on her body smelling of cedar and milk. At times he caught sight of her on the deck and he was filled with a love for her that he could not understand. It had nothing to do with lust or friendship and it made him feel unspeakably sad because he was too stupid to know what to do with this feeling. He would know when he was older, he had told himself. He was older and had not felt it since.

So it was worth the sunburn and the bloodied palms and the pulled muscles and the constant refrain of her father snapping, "Not that rope" at him whenever he was given a task, and her little brother laughing joyously at all his mistakes, just to see her in her glory. She was a sea creature then, and he was a poor landlocked mammal condemned to strain for glimpses of her through the surf.

She'd drowned in June, two months ago.

She'd gone sailing with her husband (Carl squirmed when Kit used the word) and brother-in-law, and the ship had been wrecked in a sudden gale. The husband and brother-in-law had survived and had searched for her desperately with the help of the Coast Guard, but it was no use. After a week the search was called off. The body was never recovered.

Carl and Kit looked at the body sitting in front of the computer monitor, reading its short death notice over for the umpteenth time. She spoke the last line aloud. " 'Mrs. Holland-Ackerman is survived by her husband, Martin, and her brother, Nicholas.' 'Survived by,' that's got a nasty ring to it," she muttered. "Does that mean I never had any kids? Why didn't I have kids?"

It made Carl's skin crawl just a bit, hearing her talk about herself in the past tense. "Well, maybe you just haven't gotten around to it yet. There's time. I haven't had kids. Kit . . ."

Kit picked up his cue. "I haven't had kids."

All at once she was on her feet, lunging at the machine as if the sight of it was suddenly revolting to her. "How the hell do you switch this thing off?" Before Carl could log off, she yanked the cord from the surge box, and the screen went blank.

"That's not really good for it," Carl said.

"Fuck the machine, Carl. Do you have another one of those cigarettes?" But she'd smoked them all. She swore at the thought of going without, then laughed at her own anger. "I suppose if I was really a ghost I wouldn't need a smoke this bad."

Kit made a little tut-tut noise, followed by a sing-songy, "I don't know."

Jesse looked at him with an interest that made Carl roll his eyes. "You don't?" she asked.

"Well," Kit went on, "I've heard that before some spirits pass over to the other plane, they sometimes go through a period of denial, where they still feel all the old cravings of their corporal form."

My God, Carl thought, was that a look of comprehension on Jesse's face? "You 'heard' that, huh?" Carl asked. "Who did you 'hear' that from, Casper?" He turned to Jesse, determined to wipe that open-minded look off her face. "Please don't listen to Kit, he's one of those people who was disappointed when the world didn't end after the Harmonic Convergence."

"The what?" Jesse asked.

Grabbing her hand, Carl held it tight, then patted her cheek, a little too hard. "Feel that? Alive, okay?" He grabbed Kit's hand and placed it on hers. "There. No ectoplasm. Can we move on to the next topic? Are you convinced?"

Kit pondered. "As far as my objective senses are concerned, sure."

Carl loosed an explosion of air and refrained from thudding his head against the wall.

"I don't know, Carl," Jesse said, "it might be the most convenient explanation for everyone involved."

"All right. But being dead still doesn't explain why you don't remember anything."

"Maybe she had a head injury," Kit offered.

"A ghost with a head injury?"

"Hey," Kit said defensively, "I'm just spitballing ideas here."

Jesse looked at Carl, almost challenging him. "So what do you think happened?"

"Obviously, you made it to shore somehow. Someone rescued you or something. And you had a brain trauma that's affected your memory."

"Okay," said Kit, in the same studied, critical tone he used when they were coming up with stories for the show, "where has she been for the last two months?"

Carl shrugged. "I don't know."

"When you found her, did she look injured? Was she in a coma? Was she filthy, dirty, did she reek of the streets?"

"No."

"Then someone's been . . . taking care of me," Jesse spoke up, half to herself, "or I've been taking care of myself."

"But not calling your husband," Kit reminded her.

"This is a creepy thing to have to ask but . . . tell me about my husband."

"He's the guy that started that Fifth Sun Chocolate Company," Kit told her.

"Never heard of it," Jesse said. "But I love chocolate."

Fifth Sun had been one of the many pseudocounterculture food conglomerates that flourished in the eighties and nineties (Ben and Jerry's, Häagen Dazs, Republic of Tea, Starbucks, etc.), all socially relevant ways to feed your face. Fifth Sun claimed, Carl recalled, that they made their chocolate from cacao beans harvested by real Maya Indians and used "a portion" of their corporate profits to help the Indians protect their rainforest land from evil Western conglomerates. Fifth Sun had ridden the double waves of environmentalism and chocoholism as far as they could go and had floundered in the lactose-intolerant nineties.

"He sold out to General Foods about five years ago," Kit went on, "but he did pretty well. Lives in San Marino."

Jesse gave a visible shudder. "Jesus, San Marino. No wonder I didn't call him. But I don't have kids, huh?"

"No," said Kit.

"Okay." She nodded, as if she weren't at all certain how she felt about this yet. "That's good, because that would be way too weird."

Carl had the phone book in his hand and was leafing through it.

"What are you doing?" Jesse asked.

"Finding his number." She looked at him as if he'd just suggested some unhealthy sexual practice. "Jesse, you're going to have to talk to him eventually."

"Oh, Jesus." Jesse looked stricken; she turned to Kit to rescue her from this appalling prospect.

"Over the phone?" Kit looked dubious. "It's going to be kind of a shock, don't you think?"

"Well, I don't know how I can break it to him gradually. I could start by telling him, 'Your wife's a little less dead than you thought,' and then work up from there."

"Well, you can't just blurt it out. You can't just have her ring him up and say 'Howdee do.'"

"Kit's right," Jesse said eagerly, clearly clutching at anything that would delay the inevitable. "Let's give this some thought. There ought to be something we can do to prepare him."

Carl sat down on the couch, defeated by the thought of it. How do you prepare someone for a resurrection?

6

The dress, cleaned and ironed to the best of her ability, was one of the rayon frocks so popular a few years back. It draped around the curves of her body in a carefully un-studied way and gave her the charming, old-fashioned look of a neorealist Italian peasant woman, sunning herself in the landlord's vineyard, while showing off enough arm and leg to tempt the rich man's callow young son, bringing them both to a tragic but photogenic end.

She plucked at the front of the dress, giving her hair the hundredth swipe with Carl's brush. "My tits have gotten huge, have you noticed that?"

Carl leaned against the doorjamb, watching her. "You know, that's one of those questions for which there is no gentlemanly reply."

"It makes me look fat. Is fat 'in' now?"

"Oh, yes," Kit called from the other room, "you can't even be a supermodel unless you weigh at least three hundred pounds."

"Shut up, Kit," she yelled back with easy familiarity. Then she looked over at Carl. "What's a 'super' model?"

"Same thing as a model. You know, like a superstar is the same thing as a star."

Smoothing the dress across her hips, she checked herself again in the bathroom mirror, then turned to him, the hopeful expression on her face making her look younger than he had ever remembered. "What do you think?"

Well, that was a hell of a question. Her eyes, wide and expectant, were the kind that changed color in different lights. Right now they looked like an astronomical photograph of a smoky nebula; a field of hazel and, floating in it, a shock of green that radiated out from the pupil, the same shade as the green flash he'd glimpsed once in a sunset off the coast of Florida. "You look fine," he said.

"Yeah, right," she replied, capturing perfectly (but then how could she help it?) the sarcastic tone of a petulant teenager. "Look at that." She stroked the flesh just below her collarbone. "It's alligator skin. Didn't I know enough to keep out of the sun? What a moron. And what's this!" She held up her arm, appalled at the inevitable sagging flesh. He could have added to the list, if he'd wanted to: various skin tags he'd noticed, cellulite on her hips, grooves under her eyes. Instead he said, "Hey, even Sharon Stone uses a body double."

"Who's Sharon Stone?"

"Hear! Hear!" called Kit from the other room.

"I don't suppose you have any makeup, do you? Well, I guess this will have to do."

"I think . . . with or without makeup, he'll be happy to see you."

She pursed her lips and shrugged. They'd found Martin Ackerman's address in the book and decided to confront the matter head-on. They would drive there. Carl would go in first, to pave the way as best he could, then it would be Jesse's turn. Not much of a plan, perhaps, but they couldn't think of any reason *not* to do it that way. That was, presumably, her home, and that's what one did when one was lost, wasn't it? Go home?

"This is so weird." She was still examining herself in the mirror. "It's like some nightmare version of the Mystery Date board game. Open the little door and there you are, *presented* with your mate for life, without having any say in it."

"But you *did* have a say in it, right? I mean, you married the guy."

"I guess. I hope I knew what I was doing." She ran her fingers through her hair one more time. "Crappy haircut. Oh, what difference does it make? I've probably got a tumor in my head the size of a grapefruit and my brain's about to explode anyway." She turned to him with a bright smile. "What do you think?"

That question again.

If she'd expected to see wonders from the New York World's Fair City of the Future on their drive through Glendale, she must have been sadly disappointed. Brand Boulevard, as it flashed by them on the way to the freeway, was simply a dingier version of what it had been in the seventies. True, the Galleria had grown, funguslike, to encompass another city block. True, a multiplex cinema had opened off Central, but all they could see of that was its victims, the boarded up single-screen movie theaters, sprinkled along the avenue like a witch's rotting teeth. But there, up ahead—spanking new corporate headquarters lined the freeway entrance, sky-scrapers of red granite and black glass.

"What do you think?" he asked her.

"Ugly in a different way," was her review of seventeen years of civic planning.

She seemed more interested in the kids that strolled by, the "other teenagers," as she must have thought of them. She laughed a sputtering laugh at the boys' baggy, sagging trousers and voluminous shirts ("Who'd date that?") and seemed oddly threatened by the pale girls in heavy Doc Martens, oversized plaid pants rolled up at the cuff, and lipstick the color of dried blood. ("Is that supposed to be attractive?" she asked, no doubt echoing their mothers.)

Through all this was an unspoken hope. Carl was big on unspoken hopes, having been brought up to believe, superstitiously, that to speak a hope was to dash it. Better to let it dash itself, on its own; that way no one else knew about your disappointment and you were saved from embarrassing things like commiseration and sympathy and understanding. And if you'd really played it right and hadn't even spoken the hope to yourself, you might be able to convince yourself that you'd never held it in the first place, that you were positively happy things had turned out the way they did, instead of the way some fool might have *hoped* they would.

In this case the hope, if he'd dared to put it together in his mind, was a simple one: that as soon as Jesse got outside and saw the world around her and the everyday things it contained, her memories would come flooding back to her and all this would turn out to be nothing more than an interesting little mental aberration. It was an obvious hope, one he was sure Kit and Jesse shared as they sat in the leather upholstered seats and watched Glendale speed by them. In fact, none of them said a word about it, that's how dearly they hoped.

But the hope, true to form, must have sensed Carl's thoughts and it skittered to its usual spot on the cliff's edge and threw itself onto the rocks below. Except that it paused once to tease him. When he sped through the yellow light at

Doran, Jesse flinched slightly in her seat and pressed down with her right foot, as if she was hitting the brake. "Careful. I had an accident here once," she said.

Carl glanced at her with interest, daring to let the vaporous hope take shape. "When was that?"

She shrugged. "I don't know, I . . ." She paused, seeming to realize that she really didn't. "I don't know. I . . . I can picture it. I remember the sound and spinning to the side and . . ."

"What happened then?" This was Kit now.

"I don't know."

"Or before." Carl wanted to keep her thinking so the thread wouldn't break. "Where were you going?"

"I don't know. I can almost picture it, but . . . it's like I can't *feel* it. Like I'm watching it happen to someone else."

"Well, what time of year was it?" He was trying to help her build on the memory in any direction, no matter how mundane. But she just shook her head.

"No, it just keeps squirming away. Like when you wake up from a dream and you think you remember it, but just even *trying* to pin it down makes it all evaporate on you." She gave a helpless little laugh. "Even now, I remember telling you about the accident, but the memory itself . . . it's already gone. I can't see it anymore."

The rest of the trip through the arid hills by Eagle Rock and over the Arroyo Seco was spent in sullen silence; none of them were able to openly mourn a hope they hadn't shared. This had seemed the perfect example of the sort of incident that should have jogged her memory. Instead, like an engine that wouldn't turn over, her past had simply made an odd sound and lapsed back into silence.

After that, they were disappointed but not surprised when she didn't recognize her own house.

He couldn't blame her. It didn't look like her house.

A huge, low-slung ranch house, all roof and hedges, hiding its face from the world, it had no trace of her openness, no sign of her welcoming smile. She looked at it with sullen suspicion.

"Nothing?" Carl asked her.

"You sure it's the right address?" she asked.

"Not the sort of place you were planning on?" Kit piped up from the back.

"I was hoping for one of those little places in Laurel Canyon. Or on the beach. Or the Riviera. Or Manhattan. But not San Marino."

San Marino was a bastion of white, monied Republicans. San Marino made Glendale look positively Boho.

"Why would I end up here? And why doesn't it say anything about me having a job in this?" She fluttered the hard copy of her obit in her hand. "What do I *do?* Do I just sit around and do my hair and take care of my hubby like some astronaut's wife?" Carl recognized the reference; she was paraphrasing one of Diane Keaton's lines from *Annie Hall*. Her favorite movie. From last year.

"Maybe you do charity work and have tea with Elizabeth Dole," Kit volunteered.

"Is she one of those 'supermodels'?" Jesse asked.

"I think she's the one that married Billy Joel, right, Carl?"

"I know Billy Joel," she said, pleased not to be in the dark about something and inadvertently reminding Carl of a particularly creative blowjob she'd given him in his father's Volare while "Only the Good Die Young" blasted out of the stereo. It was a thought that contrasted uncomfortably with his current duty of introducing her to her lawful wedded husband.

He popped open his door, climbed down from his Upcountry suspension onto shimmering black asphalt, the skin on his face retreating from the sudden blast of brick-oven heat of the Southern California August, and smiled back at the others wanly. "I guess I'll go in and . . . come back out and get you."

He glanced away quickly, before the look of panic on her face had a chance to slow him down. What kind of goodbye was that? In the emotional scene that was sure to follow, there'd be little chance for a better farewell. So was that the end of their reunion, that one curtailed glance? Why not? He'd certainly had other partings that were even less satisfactory. Hell, he'd never really said goodbye to her all those years ago. Why should this time be any different?

But maybe we'll stay in touch this time, he thought, as he crossed the street. Maybe I'll call her. For God's sake, he scolded himself, am I really thinking this weird encounter might "lead somewhere," as the ever-hopeful romantics would put it? What on earth would his line be? "I know you're married and all, but your current brain damage seems to have opened up some opportunities here. Let's see what happens."

Carl felt as if his feet were slowing down involuntarily as he approached the house, as if his body and mind were having a physical tussle out of a Tex Avery cartoon; his mind was proceeding to the door, but his legs were skedaddling out from under him and sprinting back to the car. Doubts began to assail him. What if she'd been right before? What if something dreadful *had* happened to her? What if she had a reason to block this place from her mind?

Mind slapped legs back into place. "What you're really wondering," mind told body with a bitter smirk, is, "What if she had a reason to come to you? What if it wasn't just a coincidence? What if 'fate' meant you to be together?"

Well, "what if?" body answered back. Bringing her here could still be exactly the wrong thing to do.

With these thoughts jostling in his mind, he was at the

door before he knew it. He swallowed and reached to ring the bell, then hesitated. He pulled Jesse's key ring from his pocket and slipped the house key into the lock. It wouldn't turn. He hurried the key back into his pocket and rang the bell, hoping a maid would answer so he'd have a few seconds to figure out what he was going to say. A large man in his late thirties opened the door. His lips were fleshy and too pink and his eyes drooped like a basset hound's. He wasn't the maid.

"Hello, are you Martin Ackerman?" Carl asked.

He nodded. Carl realized he'd have to come up with another sentence.

"I'm an old friend of your wife's. I was shocked to hear about her death." That much was true. "Could we talk?"

Ackerman looked at his visitor. Carl tried to figure out if it was sorrow or resentment or just boredom that lay behind his eyes. He nodded again and moved to let Carl pass.

There was no trace of her inside the house either. It was a man's space, with heavy, dark, upholstered furniture, a large humidor on an oak end table, a Persian carpet, and dark green fabric on the walls. Leaded windows diffused what little light could slip past the shrubs and roof. It was a room that guaranteed security from skin cancer.

What illumination there was came from three standing lamps, covered with thick shades. Carl congratulated himself on making it to the sofa without stubbing his toe. He tried to tell from Ackerman's expression whether he was expected to sit or not, but either Ackerman had no expression or it was too dim to make out. Carl sat down and noticed that the sofa gave alarmingly. Had someone been sleeping on it?

"Somethin' to drink?"

Carl turned in surprise to see a maid next to him. She was in her thirties, adorable, Hispanic, and almost completely round. He exchanged a few words with her, using the hard-won Spanish that always seemed to amuse Latinas so much. She laughed and went to get the coffee, leaving Carl alone with the problem at hand.

To delay conversation, Carl got up and walked around the room, feigning interest in the art scattered about. He stopped at a reproduction of a pre-Colombian vase, covered with vivid images of men and women with pointed heads and large noses hacking at each others' throats and lounging on cushions. The artifact seemed completely out of place in these staid, middle-class surroundings, and Carl had to remind himself that this was the home of the rainforest chocolate man.

"Is this Aztec?" he asked.

Ackerman looked up without interest. "Jessica told me it was Mayan. Excuse me, 'Maya.' You're not supposed to say 'Mayan' for some reason. All that Mesoamerican stuff on the wrapper, that was her idea. She was a genius at marketing."

Carl turned to him in surprise. "I didn't know she worked for the company."

"Not officially. It was too corporate for her. She wouldn't . . . stoop to that level. But she was a great help to me in the beginning."

Carl saw that was all he intended to say on the subject. Time to move on then. Time to tell him.

"Of course," Carl said, hating the way he started, "I hadn't seen your wife for many years, and then the other night . . ." The other night what? He backed off, tried another tack. "The other night I heard she'd died and, well, like I said, it came as a great shock."

Ackerman agreed that it was a great shock.

Carl agreed with his agreement.

"You didn't tell me your name," Ackerman said. His

voice betrayed no trace of interest. His face, topped by prematurely gray hair, showed no emotion. Was this the numbness of grief or a businessman's poker face?

Carl told him his name. Ackerman looked at him with a hint of surprise. "You knew her in high school, didn't you? Jessica . . . mentioned you."

Carl nodded, his face flushed with heat as he wondered what she might have said. "It was a long time ago."

"Yes," he said. "Then you knew Nicky?"

"I did."

Ackerman took a letter from a desk by the window and handed it to Carl. "This came today."

Carl looked at the envelope. The postmark was Peruvian. "Is he working for your company?"

Ackerman smiled with his thick lips. "I sold the company." Carl had forgotten that; now he wondered how General Foods was treating the Maya. "And no," Ackerman went on, "he never worked for me. He's there with a Catholic relief fund." Carl had wondered what Nicky might be doing now—he could have guessed for a long time and never come up with this. He pulled out the letter and skimmed through it; it was filled with misspellings and bad grammar—evidently Nicky's reading and writing skills had improved only slightly since age six.

To call it a letter was an exaggeration. It was a note, undated and written in haste, informing Jesse and Martin that someone named Father Vincent needed help in the interior and Nicky had volunteered. Since the countryside was "a little less developed than here in Ayacucho" (Carl shuddered at the thought), he was going to be "sort of out of touch for a while. Can't say how long really. Jesse," he went on, "I know things are rough. I also know that they aren't as bad as everyone seems to think. Remember that the Lord is there for you. I know you'd always roll your eyes when I'd say that, but you must believe it. I pray for you. Love, Nicky."

Carl checked the postmark before handing it back to Ackerman. It was dated a month ago. One month after Jesse's "death." "He doesn't know?" Carl asked.

Ackerman slipped the letter back in its drawer. "We've tried to get in touch with him, but it's not easy. Perhaps he'll be happier for a while, not knowing." His tone was flat and seemed to require no reply.

The maid, whom Ackerman now identified as Mari, was with them again, pouring the coffee in a happy bustling way, as if the room were sunny and filled with children. Carl wondered aloud if the American Embassy might be able to help locate Nicky and was surprised by her bitter laugh. Lima was her home, she told him, and she implied that Americans weren't the best people to go to for help there.

She bustled out the door and the room returned to its somber darkness. The wrong person owns this house, Carl thought. Give Mari a place like this and she could make something out of it. He knew how much Jesse would hate this room and supposed that was the reason he wasn't telling Ackerman about his wife out in the car. But keeping the truth back wasn't an option, he reminded himself.

"It's a shame," Carl said, "that they didn't get a chance to see each other before . . ."

"Oh, they saw each other. Or at least he saw her."

Carl looked up, surprised.

"Excuse me, but how much do you know about my wife's death?"

The abruptness of the question startled him. It was as if this were the first time Ackerman had actually spoken to him. "Almost nothing. I guess that's why I'm here. I hope I'm not intruding."

"Of course not. It must be very painful knowing you'll never be able to make your peace with her."

Carl looked away. She must have told him then, he thought, feeling himself blush. He took a sip of coffee to cover his embarrassment and scalded his tongue.

"I suppose some people might have thought her death was something of a kindness, but I . . ." Ackerman stopped when he saw the surprised look on Carl's face. He took a breath, looking like someone who had told a story once too often, and explained.

"It was around Christmas of last year. It's hard to believe so little time has passed. She was going on an errand—I never knew what—and she was in a car accident."

"Was the accident in Glendale?" Carl asked, remembering the intersection at Doran and Brand.

Ackerman looked a little irritated at being thrown off his rhythm. "No. In Pasadena. Someone stopped short in front of her on the bridge and she couldn't stop in time. It wasn't serious, or it didn't seem to be. Just enough to activate the air bag. The witnesses said she was able to get out of the car. A little dazed, they said, but she laughed off their concern. Evidently she called 911 on her cell phone. She even called our answering machine while she was waiting for the ambulance. I listened to the message later. Her speech sounded a little slurred, like she was tired, but other than that she seemed fine. She told me to meet her at the hospital, that she'd been an idiot, but thank God she was all right. That was the last time I heard her voice."

Ackerman sighed and looked up at Carl, a little surprised, as if he couldn't remember *why* he'd started to tell this story to a complete stranger. Ordinary good manners should have prompted Carl to tell him that he didn't have to go into it if it was too painful. But Carl needed to hear.

When he wasn't let off the hook, it seemed easier for

Ackerman to go on than to retreat. "I was at a meeting in Reseda and it took me a while to get word about the accident. By the time I got to the hospital three hours had passed and . . . her condition had changed.

"She couldn't speak. She seemed dazed; barely aware of what was going on around her. She didn't recognize me. She didn't recognize her brother. Didn't recognize anyone. Not that it seemed to concern her. She just sat there, happy for all we could tell, but lost in a haze.

"The doctors were puzzled. They brought neurologists in and did a CT scan and God knows how many other tests. They found, let me see, a diffuse cerebral edema, bilateral posterior cingular hypometabolism, and an insult to her right temporal lobe with possible damage to the hippocampus and cortex." He gave a sad smile. "After awhile, I heard terms like that often enough I could almost pretend I knew what they meant.

"But none of these discoveries seemed to satisfy the doctors. They might have caused her to have neurological problems, even difficulty with her retrograde or anterograde memory. But nothing to produce this condition that the doctors found so intriguing. It's not fair to say that they were pleased, but you couldn't help but sense their enthusiasm as they tried to piece together an interesting mystery."

"And what was her condition?" Carl asked, the coffee mixing with bile in his stomach.

"Just the same," Ackerman said. "Just calm, apparently awake, but not comprehending anything. She might even respond to simple commands or requests. You could get her to sit up, to walk, to dress herself. But she never connected. Not with me, not with her friends. Not with the room around her. It was like she was sleepwalking, or hypnotized. In the end, they decided to call it a temporal lobe seizure, though I could never see how a seizure could look so calm."

"And they couldn't help her?"

"They tried the whole pharmacy on her. Diazepam. Phenytoin. Larazepam. On and on. Nothing worked. My brother insisted we try alternative medicines. Acupuncture. Physical stimulation. Hypnosis, though who could tell if she was under or not? Aromatherapy, for Christ's sake. But there was no change."

He was standing now, looking at the Maya vase, at an image of a woman pouring a long stream of dark liquid from one jar to the other. "Do you know that this is the earliest known representation of the preparation of chocolate? Jessica wanted to put it on the wrapper, but I thought it looked too much like somebody emptying a chamber pot."

"But how . . ." Carl stopped himself before he asked how she recovered. "There was no hope for her at all?"

"Just enough to keep the pain alive." Carl was surprised to hear the word, since Ackerman had shown so little emotion as he told his story. Had feeling been drained from the story by too many tellings? Had time and mourning dulled the pain? Was he of the old school that considered it impolite to share such feelings? Or was he simply, as Carl found himself hoping, to his surprise, a shallow man, unable to feel deep emotions toward Jesse and, therefore, unworthy of her?

"There was always the chance," Ackerman went on, "that she might spontaneously recover. That the matrices of her mind might unscramble themselves for some reason, or for no reason at all, and she might simply get up one morning and pick up her life as if nothing at all had happened.

"That's what made every morning a torture. Getting up and hurrying to her room—yeah, we brought her home. Why not? She was in excellent health. Hurrying to her room and thinking this might be the morning when she'd look at me and know my face . . ." Lines of age seemed to etch themselves in Ackerman's face as he talked, and Carl felt a blush of shame for his earlier judgment of the man.

"In the meantime, the doctors came and the nurses came and they all said the best we could do was keep her comfortable and happy. I don't know how they thought she could be happy like that, unless they meant happy like a well-fed dog or cat, and I couldn't bring myself to think of her as a house pet. Can I get you anything? You look pale."

Carl tried to shrug him off.

"I'm fine. It just must have been very painful for you."

"Oh, yes," he agreed quickly. "It's horrible to say, but I often prayed that the doctors would tell me her condition was irreversible. Then I could have 'gone on with my life,' as people say. That way, even now, I could say her death was a mercy. That it spared her thirty or forty years of zombiehood. But I don't know that, do I? For all I know, the day after she died might have been the day she was going to recover. The day I was going to get her back again." He smiled a quick smile and started for the door. "Well, I have no idea why I told you all this. Perhaps I needed to say it. I don't know if you needed to hear it."

"Nicky . . . it seems odd that he'd write her a letter, if he'd seen the condition she was in. He didn't think she could read it, did he?"

"Nick is one of those people who believe that if you ignore a problem, it will go away. Only he uses the word 'pray' in place of ignore."

Carl tried to laugh. "I don't know if relief work in Peru is ignoring problems."

"Well, that depends on which problems he's ignoring, doesn't it?"

Ackerman opened the door. He was clearly being dismissed. Now was the time to tell him.

"But what happened on the boat? How did she die?"

Ackerman seemed irritated to have to go on, as if this part of the story were hardly significant enough to bother with. "My brother and Jessica were very close. We all used to go sailing together; she always loved it. As I may have hinted, my brother has very little faith in what he calls 'Western medicine.' It always sounds to me as if he's talking about Doc Adams from *Gunsmoke,* but I gather he means all medical practitioners without Oriental or Indian names.

"Some 'counselor' of his, some operator on the Psychic Friends Network probably, persuaded him that all she needed was 'familiar surroundings and love' to make her 'soul heal itself.' It sounded pretty nauseating to me, but after a point . . . well, what would be the harm in trying?

"She'd always loved the sea, so he thought that might be the 'familiar surroundings' "—he spit the words out derisively—"that would do the trick. He was wrong."

"And what happened?"

Ackerman shrugged. "Of course it was ridiculously irresponsible of us to take her out in that condition. As is usually the case, the worst thing that could happen, happened. We were caught in a squall. She became disoriented. We tried to calm her, but we were distracted by trying to stay afloat. The storm was too much. We lost the boat. We lost her."

There was no grief in his voice, just weary discomfort. Or was that just a stage of grief life had yet to reveal to Carl?

He had to speak now. It was either that or head out the door. "Look, I don't know how to say this, so I'm just going to . . . It didn't happen like that."

Carl meant to go on, he meant to say that she hadn't drowned, that someone had picked her up or she'd somehow made it to shore. But there was a startled look and then a stillness in Ackerman's eyes that made him stop.

"What?" Ackerman asked.

"After she was in the water. She didn't just go down like that . . ."

Even then Carl was going to go on, stop this clumsy hemming and hawing, and spit it out. But Ackerman stood and walked to the door and very quietly shut them in.

"How do you know that?" he whispered, when he turned back. His look set the coffee roiling in Carl once more, and he knew they were talking about two very different things.

"I know," Carl said.

Ackerman circled the couch, keeping his eyes locked with Carl's as he moved.

"There *was* another boat," he said. Carl didn't shake his head. He didn't nod. He didn't do anything but try his best not to faint.

"You were in the other boat," Ackerman said; but then he smiled. "No, that's ridiculous. You don't know anything. Get out of here."

Carl spoke without thinking. "I know she didn't drown like you said."

Ackerman regarded Carl in silence for a moment. Something in the large man's eyes was making a knot in Carl's stomach; making him want to throw his hands up to block a blow. Carl had once spent an afternoon doing script research with a professional bodyguard who had talked to him about fear. It was an asset, the man had said, and should never be ignored. When people got attacked or assaulted, they almost always said afterward that they knew something was wrong, that they ignored the signals of danger from their assailant because they figured they were just being paranoid. Paranoia was your friend, the man had said; when you're afraid, listen to the fear.

Carl was listening to the fear now, though he couldn't see anything concretely threatening in Ackerman's stance. There was just a look in his eyes; a look of violence. But Carl didn't throw up his hands. He didn't break and run. He was just being paranoid, he told himself.

Then the look faded from Ackerman's eyes, replaced by one of contempt. "Well, you're certainly living up to her description of you." Carl didn't even blush at that. He just stayed focused on Ackerman, the way a dancer focuses on a spot when twirling, to keep from keeling over. Ackerman pulled a checkbook from a table by the window. "What do you want? Money?"

Carl didn't answer.

"Come on. I know you're making it all up, but I don't want you causing trouble. How much do you want? I'm in a giving mood."

Carl weighed his answer. "Twenty thousand."

Ackerman laughed and threw the checkbook back in its drawer. "Get out of here."

"I know someone who saw everything that happened on that boat," Carl said, and he wasn't even lying.

Ackerman stared at him for a long while, then he took the checkbook out, scribbled on it, tore out the check, and handed it to Carl. It was for twenty thousand dollars, made out to cash. "Get the hell out of here."

Carl's hand was shaking as he took the check and walked slowly out of the room. He passed Mari but never focused on her. He was surprised he could make it to the door. His hand was cold with sweat when he turned the doorknob. Ackerman stopped him then, with a whisper.

"Don't come looking for more."

Carl nodded and was out the door in the bright sunshine,

blinding after the darkness of that room. He crossed the lawn and stumbled on the curb, feeling Ackerman's eyes on his back, clutching the check in his hand.

He rounded the corner, walking into the hissing sprinklers of a corner house, and the coldness of the water hit him with a shock. He dropped to his knees and let the fake rain fall on him as he played the conversation back in his mind.

He took a deep breath and struggled to his feet. He pulled open the car door and stared into the confused faces of Kit and Jesse.

"What's he like?" she asked anxiously.

Carl had forgotten that about her; she didn't tend to ask easy questions.

The first hard question she'd asked him was the first
thing she'd ever said to him. "Do you always eat your ham-
burgers in a circle like that?"

Ninth grade cafeteria at Stephen Foster High School.
Myriad smells filling the air: the garbage odor of state-
sponsored ground beef, the hospital disinfectant rising from
the floor, the locker-room scent of hundreds of boys and
girls just starting to smell of adulthood but too embarrassed
to use deodorant.

This was one of maybe a few hundred memories in
what Carl thought of as his "permanent file," the ones he
could recall at will to entertain himself when bored, or
that thrust themselves upon him in moments of vulnerabil-
ity. A playground beating at the hands of Lance Hoyt in
the sixth grade. Pacing in the alley behind a theater on
Santa Monica Boulevard and listening for the laughter of
the audience during the performance of his first professional play. The sight of his mother in that casket, her hair
done all wrong. Sitting on his father's lap in their station

wagon at Yellowstone, watching a bear peering through the window and trying not to be afraid. Getting his first job. Losing his first job. The aquarium-green glow of the dashboard lights off Jesse's breasts the first time she'd opened her shirt for him. Wallpapering his teenage bedroom with official rejection slips from *The New Yorker* and *Playboy* and *Alfred Hitchcock's Mystery Magazine*. The long night talking with Kit when they first decided to write together. The endless moments it took for the ambulance to arrive after his father's last coronary infarction. A tense bicycle trip to the 7-Eleven to buy a *Penthouse* magazine at fourteen years old. A tense car trip to CBS Television City to pitch a pilot idea to the network president at thirty years old.

These were among the most vivid scenes in the repertory theater of his memory, and what they all had in common was that somewhere they contained enough of a sting of embarrassment to keep them smarting and lively. His first meeting with Jesse was no different.

She walked up to his table and stood across from him, tray held in her hands, her long glowing hair parted razor-straight, her square-necked peasant blouse showing a fetching collarbone, her waist-hugging flared jeans tight around her beautiful buttocks (and here memory improves on ordinary perception, since he couldn't possibly have seen her behind from this perspective), her skin as white and smooth as vanilla ice cream. This was long before the days of Madonna and Courtney Love and the fashionably pale, wasted look. Tanned, gleaming Farrah Fawcett still ruled the average teen libido, and melanoma was a term reserved for medical journals. But Carl had been reared on some thumbed and dog-eared Grove reprints of Victorian pornography given him by an older cousin of uncertain sexuality, and those tales of ladies' maids and stable boys and imperious headmistresses lived in Carl's imagination, so that for him the creamy whiteness of Jesse's complexion seemed the ultimate of erotic perfection, full of the promise of languid nakedness he saw in certain unfashionable English paintings he admired, which he found out in later years were called pre-Raphaelite. As Kit was to say twenty years later, Jesse was very pre-Raphaelite.

Since he didn't think of himself as a young boy at the time, he didn't see her as a young girl in his memory now, but as a woman of his age looking at him skeptically through cool green eyes.

And himself? Up until a few years ago, he didn't see himself in this memory at all; he just saw the scene through his own eyes. Lately, though, the vision of himself had begun to intrude. Scrawny and wide-eyed. Hair uncut and ballooning out to form a helmet on his head, flipping out below his ears in the David Cassidy style of the day. Glasses thick and no doubt reflecting the fluorescent lights from the ceiling to make his eyes look white and blank. Short-sleeved madras shirt and unbelievably dorky loose-fitting chinos that all the hip J. Crew male models would wear in the nineties. But being ahead of one's time is no virtue in fashion. The lack of a pocket protector was a saving grace, though if he'd seen one, he'd probably have thought it a useful accessory. There he sat, alone at the table in that loneliest of times, the beginning of the freshman year, before friendships and cliques have been formed, when fear of rejection is the order of the day and the solitary and eccentric are easy prey, and yes, he was eating his hamburger in concentric circles, as was his habit. And she asked him why.

Well, it would take years of therapy to answer that one. Once he'd spent a whole "session" with Amanda discussing this very scene and the crucial impact it had on his life.

He'd tried to explain how sensible this eating habit was. "See, the burgers were tiny and the buns were all chewy and way too big, so there was a whole lot of chalky, gag-in-the-mouth bread around the outside with no burger in it. The idea was to eat that stuff first so you save the best bites for last."

But if those first bites were so bad, Amanda asked him, why eat them at all? Why not just tear off the excess bun and eat the part he enjoyed?

This had never occurred to Carl, and even at thirty-five it smacked to him of cheating. He tried to explain that going through the bad part was one of the things that made the good part good. The burger seemed richer and tastier if you'd earned it. Delayed gratification was the best gratification of all.

At fourteen, with Jesse standing before him, even if he'd had this explanation to hand he'd have had enough social sense to know that it didn't suit the moment. And it was no small moment. Standing across from him, tray still in hand, was this milk-white vision, blonde eyebrows arched in expectation over green eyes. Her question was a teasing challenge, of course, seasoned with mockery, but it was also an opportunity, for she was awaiting an answer. Give her the right one, and that tray might be set down and those flared jeans might touch the chair opposite him and he might be spared another lonely lunch period and gain so much more, something inexpressibly wonderful, the most valuable treasure known to teenage man—the attention of a beautiful woman.

The opportunity came so unexpectedly that his mind raced through subjects for a possible reply without conscious thought, finally landing on the ever-popular topic of cafeteria vermin. "I'm chasing a cockroach. That time around I almost got it." Not Robert Benchley perhaps, but it passed for wit in the ninth grade, and even now he approved of the rhythm.

A tense moment followed. She might roll her eyes and say "gross" and move on. Instead, she laughed. And her tray clinked down on the table. And she sat across from him. And what was more, what was gloriously more, she tried out a joke of her own. "I know. Mine got away. I'm thinking of asking for my money back." They both laughed, and in that moment his world changed forever in two ways. For the first time he learned the immense power of laughter. And for the first time, he fell in love.

And now, as his recollection built to its climax and he drove away from Martin Ackerman's neighborhood, Kit and Jesse sitting with him in tense silence, he found that he no longer saw himself in the memory, but that he was again looking through his own wide eyes, through those thick glasses, at the beloved face of Jesse and that it was the same face that was next to him in the passenger seat.

"So you're saying I married some fat guy who tried to kill me?" Eyebrows still arched over green eyes as she looked at Ackerman's check in her hands.

"All you're doing is delaying the inevitable," Kit said again.

"I didn't say he was fat," Carl said, ignoring Kit. "I said he was large. And I don't know what he tried to do."

"But that's what you think, isn't it? Jesus, is my taste in men really that bad?"

"You dated me, didn't you?"

"All you're doing is delaying the inevitable." This was Kit's favorite persuasion technique; saying the same thing over and over, till your only choices were to agree with him or kill him. He was still alive, so apparently it worked.

"All right, Kit. What's the inevitable?" Carl asked.

By now they'd settled into the brick courtyard of Old Town Pasadena, pretending they were hungry enough to eat a dinner of burgers outside Johnny Rockets, a fifties-retro diner. ("Jesus," Jesse had said on seeing the place, "fifties nostalgia has lasted three times longer than the fifties.") Kit took a swig from his anachronistic bottled water before responding, "Reporting this to the police."

Carl and Jesse looked at each other hesitantly and dipped fries into ketchup. "Report what?" Carl said.

Jesse jumped in. "Yeah, we don't really have any proof of anything."

"The authorities would just send her back to her husband," Carl said.

Kit nodded. "One thing at a time. I agree, there's nothing to report to the police. So why didn't we drop Jesse off at her house?"

"Because we don't know what kind of man we're dealing with. We don't know what he might have done to her." Carl sensed Jesse next to him, nodding in agreement, while Kit shook his head skeptically. The argument ping-ponged back and forth over the fries and bubbles of Coke, through the smoke of the cigarette Jesse lit from a new and, she had commented, horribly expensive pack of Marlboro Lights, which she extinguished angrily after the cries of outrage came from the tables around her. Kit's calm was frustratingly invulnerable, and Carl was forced to fall back on intangibles; the look of potential violence in Ackerman's eyes, the atmosphere of the room, finally coming up with what he felt was the clincher: "Why would he pay me off if he didn't have something to hide?"

"Honey, I've got so many things to hide, but I haven't tried to kill anybody."

"Jesus," Carl snapped, "this morning you were telling me she was a ghost. Why do you find this so hard to believe?"

"I guess it depends what you *want* to believe."

"What the fuck is that supposed to mean? Why would we *want* to believe this?"

Kit glanced from one to the other, then settled on Jesse. "You, because you're clutching at any excuse to delay the moment when you have to pick up the strands of this unknown life of yours." Back to Carl. "You, because playing hero is a hell of a lot more exciting than working on another script with me."

Carl was offended. "So that's what you think all of this is about? We're just using it as a diversion?"

"Exactly. Freud was wrong. The overwhelming human passion isn't sex, it's procrastination. The only reason we think about fucking so much is that it's the most effective way of putting off work."

"You know, you're not really involved in this," Carl pointed out.

"That's why I can see things so clearly. Now this has been an exciting morning for everybody. Really, a much more entertaining distraction than the usual ones, like having an affair or undergoing elective surgery or checking into a rehab clinic. But eventually it all comes back to real life. And real life for you, Carl, is going back to your house and working on our script. And real life for you, Jesse, is going back to your house and telling the people who love you that you're all right."

Before they could butt in, Kit was going on. "And maybe you're right. Maybe your husband did give you a long push off a short deck. Look at it from his point of view; that was when you were the Vegetable Queen, the 140-pound zucchini."

"For Christ's sake, Kit," Carl cut in, but Kit didn't give him time to express his distaste.

"You're right, it's awful. But you're well now," he said,

looking at Jesse with an out-of-place, kindly smile. "You're no longer something he might find in his grocer's produce section. You can talk now. You've recovered, minus a few crashed files in your hard drive and seventeen odd years. When you come back to him, you'll seem almost whole again. It'll be a miracle. It's cruel to keep that from him."

Kit let the thought hang for a moment, then pressed on. "And if you end up hating him this time around, or he keeps looking at you like Anthony Hopkins across the dining room table, well, you're free, straight, and twenty-one—walk out on him. Till then, try acting like a grown-up."

"But that's the problem!" Jesse was speaking up now, a bitter edge to her voice. "I'm not a grown-up. And I don't know who the hell Anthony Hopkins is. What am I, Kit? You're so smart, you tell me. Because I don't know if I'm a teenager or an adult. Or maybe I'm still the Vegetable Princess and this is just a daydream I'm having to pass the time. Forgive me, but I'm having a little trouble taking all this in!" She flung a french fry into her mouth, dropping a splotch of ketchup onto her dress.

Kit nodded. "So you need time to think?"

"If it's all right with you."

"To procrastinate."

"Fuck off. I suppose you do everything perfect in your fag life?"

Kit looked stung. "That's not a term people use much anymore."

"Oh, really? What do you call yourselves, 'Butt-fucking Americans'?"

Kit burst out laughing and turned to Carl. "She's delightful. I wish I'd known her when you did, Carl. I would have found my sexual orientation so much earlier."

Carl felt it was time to step in. "Kit, I know we need to get our work done. And we will. And I know you think we're letting our imaginations run away with us, but we'd both feel a lot better if we knew what really happened on that boat."

Kit leaned over to Jesse, smiling. "He's using his 'conciliator' voice. Doesn't it just make you want to kiss him?"

Carl kept on. "So if you could just find out, that would really put our minds at rest."

Kit seemed to be listening. "Uh-huh. And how do I do that?"

"Well, Martin said his brother was on the boat too."

"Right," Kit said, "and he must have corroborated Martin's story, or the authorities would never have believed it. So either he was in on the dastardly deed or, wonder of wonders, Martin was telling the truth."

"Kit, I'm flying blind, here," Jesse said. "Just try to find my folks, that's all *I* want. If I could go back to Mom and Dad, there wouldn't be any problem at all. Dad'll know what to do about all this . . ." Her voice trailed off, as if she began to doubt her words as soon as she spoke them; then she plunged on, as if afraid to entertain her own doubts. "Or if you could find my brother. Just somebody I know I can trust."

"Is that your full order, or would you like onion rings with that?" Kit asked.

"Kit, this is my life we're talking about," she was giving him her girlfriend look, "maybe I was really happy with Martin, but until I know . . ."

"Think about it, Kit," Carl piped up. "Can a relationship be healthy when only one party involved knows about it?"

That seemed to make Kit reflect. He looked back at them, discomfited. "I want each of you to answer me one question. Carl, if I try to find some of these people, will you start working on the script with me tomorrow?" Carl nodded. Kit went on, "Jesse, back in the seventies did you

at any time enjoy the music of the Swedish supergroup
Abba?"

"Not really."

"Then I will help you," Kit said.

The ketchup stain on her dress brought home to them that
Jesse had no other clothes, so Carl hesitantly offered to buy
her some things to wear. She agreed to it easily, as if it were
no big deal, and this bothered Carl a bit, until he reminded
himself that she was still thinking from her seventeen-year-
old perspective, where friends shared clothes and money
communally.

So he took her into J. Crew and went shopping with her,
all the time half hoping, half fearing that someone might
recognize her. He bought her two outfits; a white long-
sleeved polo shirt and silk trousers, and a square-necked
T-shirt (which displayed that still glorious collarbone) with
sky blue pants and a pair of white sandals. She watched
him hand over his Amex gold card in undisguised admiration. "You're such a grown-up," she said. And the silly
thing was, Carl felt a thrill of pride as she squeezed his
arm. Such a thrill he might have felt if she'd been there
with him at that landmark moment when he'd made his
first credit card purchase. Instead, he had felt . . . well, he
had no idea what he'd felt. He had no recollection of that
moment at all. He searched his mind, as he might use his
tongue to explore a cracked tooth, checking inexpertly
through the files of his memory. No, nothing there. He figured he must have gotten his first credit card in college. He
knew there must have been a first time he used it. Logic
told him that it must have been a fairly exciting moment, a
passage into adulthood. But the recollection seemed to
simply not be there.

Was that the way it was for her? He'd pictured her lack

of memory as a missing chunk in the pavement, a gaping hole over which she must constantly stumble. But this missing memory of his was nothing like that. Before he looked for it, he had never noticed its absence. Once he stopped thinking about it, he would stop noticing it. It would leave him with no sense of incompleteness. So was that why she could stand here on Colorado Boulevard at sunset and beam at the street musician playing "Can You Feel the Love Tonight?" on the steel drums and seem so simply happy?

Unless she thought about it, she could forget the fact that she'd forgotten anything. And that made Kit right, as, annoyingly, usual; it was this, as much as any fear of foul play, that was probably keeping her away from her husband and her home. As long as she was with Carl, she could pretend that she was the old Jesse, magically transported to the future. With large Martin, whatever kind of man he might be, she would always be the amnesia victim, mentally crippled and cut off from her life.

She wrapped her arm around Carl's, smiling the same smile she'd given him at the Greek Theater, during Dylan's *Blood on the Tracks* tour, when the tortured strains of "Tangled Up in Blue" had begun and they'd whooped and hollered in possessive excitement at hearing "their song."

"This place is so much *fun* now," she said, eyes wide, watching the people mill and windowshop. Seeing it through her eyes, Carl saw that it *was* fun. Here was one of the few places in the L.A. area where strolling and talking and jaywalking ruled the day and cars seemed an interference. Lapsing into an early, grumpy middle age, Carl had found the place too rowdy, too noisy, too full of goateed and black-garbed Gen Xers and baggy-pantsed post-Xers, too chaotic, and, well, too *lively* for him to feel comfortable. But with her there, with her youthful eyes to guide him, it all seemed vibrant and juicy.

She still held his arm, and now she leaned into him, and his nostrils were filled with the unmistakable fresh straw smell of her hair. Without even thinking, he put his arm around her.

The sensation was powerful. It sent the crowd and the noise rocketing away from him, leaving him aware only of his arm and the side of her body touching him. The full velvet softness of her body. The feeling of her warmth all down his flank. His fingers on her waist. The air awash with her scent. The easy intimacy of this pose thrilled him almost as much as their lovemaking of the night before.

And in the very instant that he made that comfortable gesture, the mood was spoiled and electrified by his awareness of it, and that arm that had fallen so naturally in place around her was now the occasion for furious internal debate over what he should do with it next. Hold her closer? Stroke lightly with his fingers? God, no. Let her go, then? But how? Too abruptly and it might seem like a rejection. A slight affectionate squeeze first? That might seem like groping. Well, *something*. Anything was better than letting the arm hang there like some dismembered limb, as he was doing now. And was her body tensing up now? Was she regretting letting him come this close to her? Was she expecting him to do something more? But what?

Thankfully, Kit saved the day by returning to them with a sack from Rizzoli's bookstore. They disentangled themselves quickly to greet him, and embarrassment or intimacy or whatever might have been brewing was spared on both sides. This didn't stop Carl from wondering, as they walked back to the parking structure, if she hadn't parted from him a bit more quickly than he'd parted from her, and from constructing many complex interpretations of what that might mean.

Meanwhile, Kit was showing Jesse his purchase: a new reprint of French erotic photos, circa 1890–1950, bondage and discipline emphasized. She didn't flinch. Though B & D was still an exotic perversion in the 1970s, not yet the almost cute home entertainment forum it had become by the '90s, no aspect of sex had ever been anything less than fascinating to Jesse. One thing did puzzle her. "I thought you didn't like girls."

"Oh, most gay men of refined tastes much prefer heterosexual pornography. In the homosexual variety you get the feeling that—how shall I put this?—everybody wants to be the girl."

"Really?"

"Oh, yes. Just settle back while Carl drives us home and I'll tell you the saga of Pee-Wee Herman."

As always with Carl and women, one step forward meant ten steps back. The shared intimacy of their sidewalk embrace seemed to leave them wary of each other as they watched Kit drive off from the house. Jesse even ran to Kit's car to detain him and whisper one further request, the nature of which was deliberately kept secret from Carl. But, unavoidably, they were left alone in the house. To do what?

Jesse sat on the sofa, grimacing over a cup of coffee, determined to make herself like the "grown-up drink." Carl joined her and, having no trouble reverting to his own acquired vice, set fire to his third cigarette of the day. She experimented with the remote until she found a Dodgers-Angels game on and stopped, staring in amazement. Nothing seemed to bring home to her the changes time had worked on the world so much as the notion of interleague play ("What does it do to the standings?" she wanted to know. "Do they use a designated hitter?") At least Vin Scully was still calling the game, his reedy voice plugging Farmer John's sausage and providing continuity across the decades.

They discussed the game. Jesse complained of the bruised ache in her rib cage and wondered where it came from. Carl ran out of stories about his job. The Dodgers lost. Come nightfall there was nothing for them to do but to go to bed. Their goodnight was strained when Carl tried a routine yuppie half-hug and cheek kiss, and Jesse, unfamiliar with the ritual, stiffened awkwardly as if she expected . . . more? Less? Carl was sick of guessing. Romantic attraction seemed to affect him with anti-ESP, leaving him even more clueless than usual.

Fully clothed, he fell onto the sofa to sleep, listening to Jesse climb into bed upstairs. I ought to be thankful nothing is happening between us, he told himself. Given the seriousness of her situation, it would only complicate things dangerously. Eyes wide, he stared up at the ceiling, exhausted but certain he'd be up half the night, reliving the events of the past night and day over and over.

Three minutes later he was sound asleep . . .

The school alarm rang loudly, jangling with an intensity he'd never heard before. The noise added to his discomfort, which was considerable, since he was sitting in the cafeteria stark naked and taking a surprise series of SATs with a rubber pencil.

Roxanne jumped on his chest and hissed, bringing him out of his dream. But the ringing continued. He sat up, cradling the cat in his lap, listening to the bell ring on and on. Damn. Somebody's security alarm had gone off. Damn. It was his.

He slid the cat off and stumbled over to the alarm pad by

the front door, wondering what the hell had set it off this time. Had the cat rattled the French doors? Had a strong wind forced open a window? Was there a crossed signal somewhere in the jungle of wiring under the house? It didn't take much to make the ancient system cry wolf.

Roxanne entwined herself between his legs, and he stumbled into the wall by the front door like a marathon runner hitting the finish line. Great, he thought, as he punched the code on the small keyboard, now I'm so awake I won't be able to get back to sleep all night. The ringing stopped, and he almost turned back to the sofa. But no, something was wrong here.

The little green light hadn't come on. There was a little green light that was supposed to come on next to the keyboard. He couldn't quite recall what the little green light meant, but he knew it was supposed to be there. And it wasn't.

He blinked, getting his mind working. Oh, yeah, he recalled, green light on means that all the doors and windows are closed and everything is fine. So green light off must mean something is open. Terrific, the wind must have blown a window open somewhere and now he was going to have to wander through the whole house to find it. He gave up all hope of sleep.

But wait, he thought, as he listened to the silence and felt his chest tighten involuntarily, there is no wind tonight. And wasn't there something else that might set off a burglar alarm?

"Jesse!"

He raced through the house, switching on lights as he went. No one had ever broken into the house before, and Carl had no plan of action other than to make as much commotion as possible and scare any intruders into flight.

"The cops are on their way!" he yelled, turning on the

stereo as he passed, letting Tommy Dorsey and Frank Sinatra blare "Fools Rush In" from every speaker in the place.

There it was. The kitchen door stood open, one of its panes shattered. And just beyond the kitchen was the stairway to the second floor.

"I'm coming up." He bounded up the stairs, taking them two at a time. Moving that fast, he didn't even see the man coming the other way.

Carl crashed into him at full speed, feeling the jar of the impact in every bone. His feet flew out from under him and he tumbled down the stairs, the intruder falling with him. His shoulder struck the edge of a tile step with a wrenching jolt. The man landed on top of him, knocking the breath out of both of them and twisting Carl's arm behind his back as they skidded down another step and slammed into the wall.

The stranger didn't even pause. He climbed over Carl and his elbow cracked Carl on the chin so that his neck snapped back and he tasted blood as he bit his tongue.

Instinctively, Carl reached up and grabbed a black shoe as it passed over his head. The man stumbled against the wall and dragged Carl down another step, bringing his head into contact with the tile floor. The dull thud on Carl's skull made everything go white for a second. The foot pulled free.

Carl's only thought was a furious need to stop that damned foot. He twisted over and snatched at it with his right hand, grabbing an ankle with a fierce grip. The foot kicked back at him, bouncing off his forehead. Carl's hand relaxed, and the ankle was loose. He felt a cool breeze float over him from the open front door.

Gone. The damned foot was gone.

"Jesus, Carl! Are you okay?"

He lifted his head to look up at Jesse on the landing, her eyes wide and full of concern.

"Yeah," he said, and then he could feel the pain. It came at him from all over his body: the wrenched shoulder, the bitten tongue, the twisted neck, the swelling lump on top of his head, the ragged gash over his right eye. He hadn't been in a fight since the Lance Hoyt incident in grade school, and he'd forgotten what this chorus of wounds could feel like.

"Should I get it?" Jesse asked inexplicably. Then Carl realized that somewhere under the echoing aches in his head the phone was ringing.

"Yeah. No. Wait." It would be the security company responding to the alarm. "Landvik," he said.

Jesse looked at him as if she thought he might be hallucinating.

"Landvik," he repeated. "It's the password. My mother's maiden name. Pick up the phone and say 'Landvik.' Tell them the alarm went off by accident. Tell them the cat set it off." The cat was curling around his head on the floor, purring to comfort him. "Hurry, or the police will be here."

She rushed off to the phone. Carl slowly sat up, grateful to discover no serious spinal injuries. Bracing himself against the wall, he struggled to his feet, noticing with alarm that his teeth no longer came together in quite the same even bite he was used to. Shuffling into the kitchen, he pulled out two bottles of painkillers. One brand for headaches, the other for muscle aches. He took four of each.

"Okay."

He turned to Jesse in the doorway. In his crumpled condition he hadn't noticed that she was wearing nothing but an oversized *Friends* T-shirt. The throbbing in his head got worse.

"Did you see who it was?" Carl asked her, lisping slightly through his ragged tongue and jangled teeth.

"No. I heard the alarm and just hunkered down. There was a shadow in the doorway. I thought it was you. Then you started making all that noise downstairs and it was gone."

"Did he see you?"

"I don't know. Was it my husband?" He could tell she still had to force herself to utter the H-word.

"I didn't get a look at him either."

She walked over to him, running her soft fingers lightly over the wound on his forehead. Carl winced in spite of himself, and she pulled away. "God, he really meant to hurt you."

"No, he was just trying to get away. He was probably as scared as I was." But no, Carl thought, as he eyed the kitchen door with its broken windowpane. Martin, or whoever it was, had heard the alarm go off as soon as he'd cracked that window. But he hadn't reacted as Carl would have—he hadn't run off or dived into a corner to hide. Instead he'd reached in and opened the door. He'd stepped into the house, alarm and all, and walked upstairs. There was no way he could have known it would take Carl as long as it did to figure out what was going on, no way for him to be sure someone wasn't waiting to leap out at him behind a corner. Had he simply not cared?

Carl pictured that damned black shoe and the way it had implacably moved forward, despite Carl's best efforts to stop it. Looking back, Carl realized he hadn't been beaten up at all; he had simply been plowed through. The intruder had been on his way out, as purposefully as he'd gone in, and nothing was going to stop him. There had been no panic or fear about the way the man had moved. No, he had entered the house with simple deliberation and left it the same way. The question was, had he achieved his purpose? Would he be back?

Jesse was gently daubing a wet washcloth on his bruised forehead, and he reached up and stopped her. "Throw some things in a bag. We're getting out of here. I don't think we're safe."

"Right." Immediately she turned and hurried off. Then she stopped in the doorway to ask, "Where are we going?"

Carl saw the look of simple trust in her eyes. My God, he thought, she thinks I know what I'm doing. For the first time that evening, he felt afraid.

8

"Man, he really made a mess out of you." Kit allowed a touch of concern to creep into his voice.

"You should see the other guy. I left a mean forehead print on the heel of his shoe." No need to let things get sentimental, Carl thought.

"I don't have to tell you how singularly unsuited you are for all this. I mean, you as a street brawler is really bad casting."

Carl sighed and looked down from the porch as the first hint of day illuminated the fenced-off reservoir below them with the inappropriately majestic name Silver Lake. He and Jesse had driven aimlessly through the dark streets for about forty-five minutes before he thought of coming here, where Kit had welcomed them drowsily but warmly. If a measure of friendship was being able to drop in on someone unannounced at 4:45 A.M. and have them brew you a fresh cup of coffee instead of slamming the door in your face, then Kit was a true friend.

"I didn't come here for more grief, Kit."

"Sorry, that's all I have to offer. Or so I've been told." He ambled back into the living room of his modest house, perched on a steep hill above Los Feliz. By now he could have afforded something much larger than this two-bedroom cliffhanger, but he kept the place out of sentimental attachment to his younger, footloose self.

Carl started to follow, but his eye was caught by the headlights of a car driving past the reservoir. Was it going to turn this way? He'd had the same thought on the drive here, staring down every pair of headlights on the road, afraid they might be pursuing him. No, this car, like all the others, turned away. Carl sighed. Living in Los Angeles all his life, he was used to worrying about random violence; worrying about violence focused his way was a new experience.

Jesse was in the middle of the living room, a tin of Band-Aids in her hand, petting the two barking corgies at her feet. "They wouldn't let me out," she said with a laugh, as the animals kept maneuvering their little bodies against her shins to block her way.

"Herding behavior," Kit explained. "It's instinctive. Jones! Dickens!" The dogs trotted over to Kit on their short legs and settled next to him on the couch. "I'm the alpha dog," Kit said pleasantly.

"I checked out some of the medical journals on the net," Kit went on. "I found some very fun stuff about your type of problem, Jesse. Seems there was an Italian man back in '92. He had a stroke and he forgot *everything*—his name, his wife, his kids. A *year* later, he was having some little surgery thing, and the procedure *reminded* him of an operation he'd had twenty-five years before, and everything started coming back. Just like that. Isn't that amazing?

"Another guy had a head injury, like you. Again, everything, *pfft*. One day he's playing *tennis,* and he makes a mistake, and he *remembers the mistake*. He'd made it before. And it all came back to him. His whole life. You can't make shit like this up."

But Jesse wasn't listening. She was settling Carl into an Eames chair by a window and carefully pasting a Band-Aid on the abrasion over his eye. Carl found her solicitous behavior toward his injuries touching, but a little unsettling. So many women Carl knew had grown to distrust feelings of maternal concern, having learned how skillful men are at taking advantage of them. Jesse had no such caution, and Carl swore to himself that he would never be the cause of her acquiring it.

He was about to reach up and take her hand with his, when Kit placed a telephone in it. He hadn't realized Kit had dialed until he heard it ringing on the other end.

"It's the police," said Kit. "Say hello."

Carl reached out and hit the cradle, cutting the connection. "What are you doing?"

"Well, don't you think it's time you two had professional help? And I mean that in every possible sense of the term."

The pounding in Carl's head was worse than ever, and the painkillers were doing nothing but souring in his stomach. "I'm not arguing with you, Kit. If that was Martin I met on the stairs, I'm not doing anything to send her back to him."

"You don't know who it was."

"This is the first time in thirty years anybody's broken into that house. I'm not prepared to call it a coincidence."

"Did you find my parents?" Jesse cut in, ending the bickering session before it got half started. Ending it and putting an odd expression on Kit's face.

"Not really . . ." he said. "I did find some stuff out, but I'm not sure I should tell you. You guys seem so easily agitated."

Even Jesse seemed to be losing patience with him. "Can't you see it's different now? *That* is not our imagination!" She pointed to Carl's bruised face and Kit hung his head for a moment.

"Okay, but I don't see how getting upset is going to help any." Still Kit relented. "The brother's name is Wesley Ackerman, works for your husband's company. Nepotism in action. Fancies himself an artist in his spare time. A photographer, if you call that art. I saw one of his pieces. Sub–Jerry Uelsmann multi-image crap. Oh," he added as an afterthought, glancing at Jesse, "rumor has it that you were having an affair with him."

Jesse sat upright. "What?"

"There, that's my point. Now you're agitated."

"Who said that?" Carl said, rising to her defense.

"Don't kill the messenger, people. I'm not saying it's true. Though when you tap into the secretarial gossip pool you come closer to truth than anywhere else on earth."

Kit had tracked down Martin's ex–personal assistant and told her he was writing an article on the firm for *Forbes.* ("All Americans are whores for interviews," was one of Kit's pet sayings.) After suffering through an hour of actually hearing about the chocolate business, he hit pay dirt, as planned, during the chitchat while he packed up his strategically scattered equipment.

"As an added bonus, the woman clearly dislikes your dear hubby and has something of a crush on artistic Wesley, so she was more than willing to engage in a little off-the-record character assassination. She even had one of Wesley's prints on her wall—a nude woman with an asparagus for a head, kneeling in a doorway surrounded by fleecy clouds. Unless I'm very much mistaken, the owner of that fine torso sits before us. I much prefer your real head."

But Jesse wasn't listening. Her face was flushed with

anger as she lashed out, "Sleeping with her husband's brother?!"

"I'm sure it isn't true," Carl said, trying to placate her. "And even if it is, I'm sure you had your reasons."

"For fucking my brother-in-law? Name a reason. I don't do that sort of thing. I don't cheat. I never cheated on you. Not even with Sid Norton, and he was a lot cuter than you."

"Sid Norton came on to you?" Carl asked, hurt.

"Everybody came on to me. When you went with your dad up to Big Bear last summer," she was too upset to correct her chronology, "all your so-called friends were nosing around me. But I wouldn't give them a second look, even though I was tempted a couple of times, because I was your girlfriend, and fidelity is something I absolutely believe in."

She collapsed onto the sofa and sank into its depths as if she wanted to bury herself in the cushions. "If this turns out to be true, I am going to be so disappointed in myself."

"Life's like that," Kit said. "How do you think Carl feels about turning into a lonely, prematurely middle-aged television hack who can't maintain a steady relationship?"

"Thank you," Carl said.

"Welcome," Kit said. "And me, I wanted to be Oscar Wilde and Truman Capote rolled into one and instead I end up as Paul Linde on a bad hair day. Time is a cruel dominatrix."

She smiled weakly, then pulled a pillow over her head and spoke through the layers of down. "You guys are writers. Make me up a new life."

Carl moved next to her and gently removed the pillow from her face. "Jesse, I know you. You are not a bad person. You don't know the choices you had to make and the reasons you made them. Who knows, maybe you're in love with . . ." But the name escaped him. He glanced back to Kit, flustered. "What's his name?"

"Martin?"

"No, the other one."

"Wesley."

"Maybe you're in love with Wesley. Maybe Martin deserved to be cheated on." He took her hand in his, deliberately forsaking any attempt at being cool. "Maybe it's all a lie. All I know is, you would never willingly hurt anyone or do anything cheap. I've known a lot of people in my life, and you're still one of the best." He gave an involuntary grimace at the clumsiness of the words and hoped she wouldn't laugh.

She did, but just a bit. And with the laugh a layer of tears floated over her blue-green eyes. She put her arms around him and said his name. People had been saying Carl's name to him for years now, but no one said it like she did.

Kit spoke up behind them. "I'd leave, if this wasn't my house. By the way, when are we going to start working on that script, partner?"

Carl settled next to her on the couch. The comforting hug seemed to have blended their personal buffer zones, so it didn't feel provocative to be this close to her. Instead, it felt comfortable, the way it had back in high school when they'd sat on another sofa, watching *I, Claudius* for weeks on end. Was she pulling him back in time just a little, as he was trying to pull her forward? Perhaps they'd meet at some middle ground. Say, 1987?

He took a deep breath. "You write the script. I'm not going in to work tomorrow. We have to talk to Wesley."

Kit shook his head. "We're a team. I don't write without you."

"You're always saying you're a better writer than I am."

"I know, but I need you there to prove it."

"Think about it, Kit," Carl went on, "this is getting more and more serious. If she really was having an affair with his brother, that gives Martin even more of a motive to try to kill her."

"Motive," Kit repeated mockingly. "The only people who have 'motives' are method actors and characters in *Murder She Wrote*." He sat on the coffee table opposite them. "I'm going to give you two reasons to drop this whole thing. One, you might be wrong. Two, you might be right. If you're wrong, you'll just make fools of yourselves and have a good time doing it. But if you're right . . . there could be actual danger. And don't take offense, but I wouldn't rely on Carl to defend you, Jesse. I mean, take a look at him."

Carl leaned forward and spoke with simple frankness. "Remember we always said if the Big Personal Moment ever came for either of us, the other one would cover for him?"

"Yes, but it was supposed to be *my* moment."

"You're right about me, Kit, I'm lousy with personal relationships. I don't have many friends. God help me, you may be it. I'm asking you, as a friend, to help me go do this."

Kit's head retracted, turtlelike, into his shoulders. "Okay, I'll write it. But anything that Dan and Mindy don't like, I'll say it's yours."

"Fair enough. Where can we find Wesley?"

Kit shook his head sadly. "He lives in Pasadena, but he's staying at your house up in Oakland."

Jesse didn't know she had a house in Oakland. Kit explained that it was the first house she'd bought with Martin. They'd kept it as a pied-à-terre.

"A what?" Jesse asked.

"Just a house up there . . ." He went on, after an uneasy pause: "You used to use it when you'd go up to visit your folks."

"My folks live in Oakland?" Jesse asked, and the wariness in Kit's eyes made Carl wish her voice didn't sound so hopeful.

"My source wasn't sure," Kit went on, haltingly. "She thought that your mother was living in a retirement community somewhere in San Rafael."

"What about Dad?"

Kit, who was never at a loss for words, couldn't seem to think of anything to say.

9

She didn't cry till they reached Ventura. Even then the weeping was more of anger than sorrow.

Her father had died two years ago. That was fifteen more years she'd had with him, Carl thought, as he watched her scrape tears off her cheek with the flat of her hand and spit them off her lip. Fifteen more years, and she couldn't remember any of them.

Carl thought of his own father in his last years, shrinking and fading to gray, finally disappearing into a ludicrous husk. Maybe it's just as well that you've forgotten, he thought. But it wouldn't be the right thing to say now. There was no right thing to say now. For once he had the courage to say nothing at all.

She stopped crying after a few minutes but sat in silence for an hour after that, a silence lasting so long that Carl feared she might have suffered a relapse to her mute condition. By the time they approached Santa Barbara, he couldn't take it any longer.

"I've been thinking," he said.

"Yes?" Her answer was fast, almost eager, as if she too had been feeling the pressure of the silence in the car.

"Even if we don't find your brother-in-law, or even if he won't tell us anything, there's another witness who saw what happened on that boat."

She saw where he was going and gave him an annoyed look. "Carl, who cares if I was there if I don't remember anything?"

"But maybe you *can* remember. Look, for all we know, you just started getting over your seizure, or whatever it was, the night before last. You've only been trying to remember for a couple of days. And you did have some kind of memory of that car accident in Glendale."

"I guess."

"So maybe there's a way you can remember, but we don't know what it is. If we could just find the right trigger. Maybe a therapist, or a hypnotist . . ."

She made a sour face. "I don't think so."

"Really, you read articles every day about hypnosis helping people recover repressed memories."

"They're not repressed. They're gone."

"We don't know that. Maybe everything we ever see is stored in our heads somewhere. We just have to find a way at it."

She squinted out the window. "Okay, I'll try it. Maybe I could see somebody tomorrow. Who do we call? Do you know anybody?"

Carl stopped short, surprised to be standing at the edge of this abyss to which he had stupidly led himself. "Yeah," he muttered, "I know somebody," and took the next exit to Montecito.

The voice was low and without inflection, the rhythm as soft and steady as a metronome.

"You let your face relax. It's easy to do this. To let the muscles of your jaw drop. To let your teeth part, just a little, as you relax. As you get that feeling, Jesse, of falling down into yourself. That cozy feeling you have, when you go to bed at night, of dropping away from your worries, from your body even, and into yourself. In your legs, all the way up through your thighs, you are feeling a wonderful sense of warmth, a soothing flow of peace and comfort."

Carl watched from across the room, Amanda's smooth tones filling him like smoke and having, as usual, the opposite effect of the one she intended. In this case, an erection, coupled with feelings of guilt and betrayal that were the very antithesis of relaxation. Having one old girlfriend of his use that maddeningly sexy, water-torture tone on another made the experience even more complex.

"That's good, you're doing fine, Jesse. Now, you can imagine a peaceful place." Carl watched Jesse's breath even out. "A special place. It can be a place that you've been to before. Or it can be a place in your imagination. You are calm there and at ease. You like being in this place. It's a safe place."

That was when Jesse lost it, covering her mouth to stifle her laughter, the way she did in Advanced Placement English, when Mr. Levy would read a line like " 'No,' he ejaculated!" from some Victorian novel. Her bad-girl-in-class laugh. It didn't make Carl's condition any easier.

"Is something wrong?" Amanda asked patiently.

"I can't do that," Jesse said, between sputters.

"Hypnosis isn't a matter of can or can't—"

"I don't mean that." Jesse's laughter had died to a tentative smile. "I mean, I can't think of a safe place."

Amanda threw Carl a glance, her dark eyes registering concern, apprehension, fascination. Were an analyst's eyes supposed to be that expressive? As Amanda collected herself to try again, Carl thought back over the wreckage of their relationship.

It is at the heart of modern romantic lore, enshrined in the great mythic works of our culture, from *I Love Lucy* and *The Honeymooners* all the way through *Roseanne,* that the happy couple is the arguing couple. That bickering equals passion. That it was only in dull (and quickly canceled) relationships that people actually got along.

In point of fact, Carl was here to testify that the things that might entertain the viewing audience in half-hour doses became simple agony twenty-four hours a day, seven days a week. Amanda taught him that.

Not that Amanda was cruel. Nor that there might not be someone out there who might find her constant questioning and examining and picking apart of every little gesture or word or thought positively charming. All Carl knew, after four long years, was that he was not that person.

They had met in the waning years of the Bush administration, when Carl was doing research for a failed pilot about a liberal psychiatrist with two children who moves in next to a widowed conservative judge who thinks he doesn't like kids. (*Both Sides Now,* it was called, "and if you feel like you saw it," Carl used to say, "that might be part of the problem.") Kit maintained that the show would have found its stride by season three, but since it was canceled after two episodes, that theory was never tested.

In the early days of development, when every show feels like it will run as long as *M*A*S*H* and win as many awards as *The Mary Tyler Moore Show,* Carl had taken it upon himself to do research with a real psychiatrist. (Kit was having an affair with a judge, so that front was covered.)

A friend had recommended Dr. Amanda Gold as the rough prototype for their lead character. Carl, in a fit of dra-

matic inspiration, had decided to see her undercover, posing
as a real patient, just to see what the experience was like. At
this point, he was one of the few television writers in the
country *not* in analysis. He became a convert to the process
once he met Amanda, and now he saw Dr. Mercer twice a
week. Merc was a muscular, curly-haired septuagenarian
with a Jack LaLanne smile, worlds away from the sight that
had greeted him when Amanda first let him into her Brent-
wood office.

Dr. Amanda Gold was simply, breathtakingly, beautiful.
Five foot four, with unfashionably long jet-black hair and
eyes so brown they were almost black, with dark circles of
worry under them, and under *them* a body so voluptuous
that she looked like a nightmare vamp from an Edvard
Munch painting. Carl, the Irish-Swede from Glendale, had
always been attracted to the olive-complected, suffering-
Slav type anyway, but he'd never seen a vision like this.
"A small, Jewish Sophia Loren," he used to call her in
their giddy, intimate moments. Then she'd ask to which
he was most attracted, the smallness, the Jewishness, or
the dubbed, overdeveloped Italian actressness? Before he
knew it, his mental erogenous zones would be laid open on
the table for analysis and his lust would dwindle under the
glare of her worklights.

But that uneasy future was invisible to him when he first
laid eyes on her and laid his body down on her couch (she
was a traditionalist) to launch into his rehearsed set of neu-
roses.

She saw through his charade in no time, of course, and
was quite indignant at his violation of her confessional. She
was, as Carl might have predicted, beautiful when she was
angry, and he was hooked on her from that moment on.

Their first night of lovemaking was wild beyond his
wildest imaginings. She was a voracious, teeth-grinding,

growling savage, and the sounds she made recalled the more visceral scenes in a David Attenborough nature special. She rode him so hard that he experienced equal parts pleasure and gratitude at not being injured, and when she was done, she fell off him and burst into great, wracking sobs, weeping on his shoulder as he held her tight and stroked her raven hair and asked her why she was crying.

"Because you stayed with me," she said, and all hope was gone for him then. She was brilliant, beautiful, intimidating and yet she was vulnerable and heartbroken and she needed someone. He was so in love by morning that the tooth prints on his shoulder kept him happy all day.

It had been over a year since their oh-so-civilized parting at Il Fornaio, and he hadn't spoken with her since.

Even as he took that Montecito exit with Jesse, he had been able to feel the oppressive weight of Amanda's stare, which always seemed to peer into his weaknesses, comprehending them all without understanding any of them. As he drove, he glanced at Jesse and tried to imagine what it was going to be like to bring these two characters from two such different parts of his life together. It seemed unlikely that they could inhabit the same room; rather like those disappointingly unconvincing special editions of DC Comics that brought Superman and Batman together.

"So how do you know this Dr. Gold?" Jesse had asked.

"She's just a friend."

"How long did you date her?"

"Why do you think I dated her?"

"You're a lousy liar, Carl. Either you dated her or you dated her sister."

"Okay. We dated for a while."

"Ooh, you're still lying. This is worse than I thought."

"Four years. We almost got married."

"Wow. What went wrong?"

"It just ended. You can't always say why. You know how it is when you break up with somebody."

"No, I don't."

And she didn't, Carl thought. How many thirty-four-year-old women could say that?

"Did you ever get married to anybody?" she asked, as if the possibility had just occurred to her.

"Nope."

"I wonder what my wedding was like. Do you think I had a big wedding?"

"Dunno."

"Mom wanted a big wedding. 'Member what our wedding was going to be like?"

He remembered. In a clearing in Topanga Canyon. She'd be in something simple with flowers in her hair. He wouldn't wear a tux. Sid Norton would play his guitar. Then they'd all hop in Lance Halverson's pickup and drive up the Pacific Coast Highway to camp out at Big Sur.

"Funny," she said, "that never happened, but I remember perfectly how it was going to be. So what went wrong with us, Carl?"

Carl braced himself. It was now or never. But the courage didn't come. "It wasn't any one thing. You went to Berkeley, I went to UCLA. We didn't think it would be a problem. We were wrong. We tried to see each other as often as we could, but we grew apart . . . things just faded away."

She stared at him, mystified. "How could we let that happen?" But she believed him. Which meant she was wrong—he wasn't such a bad liar after all.

"I don't know."

"Jeeze, I just realized how much I'm imposing on you. I

can't help it, I still think you're a part of my life. But for you, I'm just this old friend, turning up on your doorstep like a stray cat. You've got a whole 'nother life now."

He pulled up in front of Amanda's hacienda. "My life . . . could use a little imposing."

As they waited for Amanda to answer her doorbell, Jesse turned to him with a wonderfully ill-timed question. "Is she pretty?"

Carl tried to bob and weave. "Depends what you mean by pretty."

Amanda opened the door. She was in her workout tights, face glistening with sweat, her figure more taut and impressive than ever, and Carl wondered why old girlfriends never looked worse when you ran into them later. She inquired about Carl's bruised face, and he made up a weak excuse about a ski accident, not wanting to bother her just then with confusing details. She welcomed them into her house, apologized in a spectacularly unnecessary way for her appearance, and hurried off to change.

"That's what I mean by pretty," Jesse said.

"You have no right to be jealous. You're married to another man."

"That's not me," she said, wandering through the Santa Fe–style living room and handling a piece of expensive folk art as if it were the weird hunk of junk she took it to be. "That's grown-up 'Jessica'."

Carl snatched the brightly colored sculpture of the coyote from her before she snapped off a leg.

Amanda, in a fresh set of sweats and the terry cloth robe everyone was wearing on television this season, took them into the kitchen and poured them the inevitable cup of coffee. If she thought there was anything unusual about Jesse emptying five packets of Equal into her cup, she was too polite to mention it.

"Now, how can I help you?" She was giving Jesse a warm, understanding smile. Carl had forgotten that smile.

Jesse glanced over at Carl, and he could tell she was preparing herself. They had agreed to downplay the scope of her problem as much as possible, so that Amanda's professional ethics wouldn't be too sorely impinged on.

"Well, I was in a car accident a few months back. And I'm having a little trouble . . . remembering things."

"Hmm. As Carl should know"—a short look at him, the first sign of irritation she'd allowed herself—"I'm not a neurologist. But I do try to keep up with the literature. Are these memory problems retrograde or anterograde? That is to say, are you having trouble remembering things before the accident, or after the accident?"

"Both."

"Hmm. Now, when you say you have trouble remembering things after the accident, is this an ongoing problem? That is, when you get home tonight, will you have trouble remembering this conversation? Do people tell you that you have trouble retaining new information? Maybe Carl can help answer that."

"No," he said.

"No," Jesse agreed.

"Okay. So it's more like a blackout. One missing period of time, a few hours or a few days, and everything after that is normal?"

"More or less."

"And the retrograde amnesia, is it the same? A period of missing time and everything before that you can recall normally?"

"Yes," Jesse nodded, happily.

Amanda sipped her coffee. "This isn't unusual. And although I'm sure it's disconcerting, it might not even be that serious. If there'd been brain damage, say to your hippocampus or amygdala, that might have left you with serious memory deterioration. As it is, well, you have a chunk of missing time, perhaps due to a concussion, but your memory seems to be functioning normally. I wouldn't worry about it."

"But will I ever be able to remember any of that time?"

"Hmm. Possibly. Part of it. It happens. But usually not." She sipped her coffee, glancing over the rim at Jesse. "How much time are we talking about here? A few days? Weeks? Months?"

"Seventeen years."

For someone who professed to have little respect for comic timing, Amanda did a marvelously executed spit take.

Wiping the coffee off her robe, she grabbed Carl and pulled him into the hall.

"What the hell are you bringing her to me for? This is not my field! You have taken her to a neurologist, haven't you?"

"Of course I have."

"You haven't even taken her to a neurologist?" Okay, so he was a bad liar *most* of the time.

"*I* haven't taken her, but she's seen neurologists. Lots of them."

"What other symptoms did she have?"

"Well, she couldn't speak for a few months."

"Jesus! This is serious shit you're talking about. Look, I can see you care about her and I'm glad you've found somebody new—"

"She's not—"

"But I cannot treat her."

"I'm not asking you to treat me." Jesse had followed them out into the hall. "If you're going to talk about me, do it to my face."

Amanda turned to her, chastened. "I apologize. But this is not my area of expertise. I don't feel equipped—"

"I just want to try to see if I can remember one thing, one incident. Carl thought if you could hypnotize me—"

Amanda rolled her eyes. "It doesn't work that way."

"But you do hypnotize people?" Carl broke in.

"Sometimes. For stress. I don't do that past life regression shit."

"We're not talking past life," Carl said, "we're talking *current* life."

Amanda sighed. "All right, Carl, go brew some more coffee and I'll try to explain to you why this won't work."

As he stepped into the kitchen he heard Amanda ask Jesse, "How long have you known him?"

"Two years or twenty years. Depends how you look at it."

"I know the feeling."

Once she'd settled them into the kitchen she launched into her lecture. "First of all, you don't even know what you're talking about." How many of his conversations with Amanda had begun that way? "Memory doesn't work the way you think it does." She was perched on the kitchen counter now, cup of coffee steaming between her hands.

"Everyone thinks it's like some kind of video camera in the back of your head, taping everything you see and storing it for future reference. They picture something like the old card catalogs in libraries—if you could find the right Dewey Decimal number, you could just look up your memory for July 20, 1972, and there it would be, everything you had for lunch that day and the color of your mother's dress when she went off to work.

"But what you've got up there isn't anything like little eight-millimeter cassettes of your life. What's stored up there—and it isn't even in any one place, but scattered all through the structures of your brain—are impressions and senses and emotions of what you felt when certain things were happening. And even these are overlaid by the impressions you've had since then, about those same things and about other, connected things."

"Yes, I've seen *Rashomon,*" Carl said.

"But those characters were presumably liars or hypocrites, trying to paint themselves in the best light. What I'm saying is that the actual memories you keep in your head are not records of objective reality, whatever that is.

"Let's pick something. Tell me about the first time you two met."

Carl sighed. She knew the story already. "We met in high school. At the cafeteria."

Amanda's black eyebrows rose and she leaned back on the one arm. "Oh, this is *that* Jesse. This is getting more interesting."

Jesse broke in then. "No, we used to sit on the bus together. 'Cause you were friends with Sid and I knew Sid's brother Chris."

Carl frowned. "Sure, we used to do that, but that came later. The first time we met, you came up to me and asked about how I was eating my burger and I made you laugh."

"Well, maybe that was the first time we really sat down and *talked,* but before that we were always joking on the bus. You know, flirting like kids do. That was why I was so happy to see you in the cafeteria."

Happy to see him? Carl's frown deepened. "You were giving me shit. You were challenging me."

"Why would I challenge anybody? I was scared to death."

Carl shook his head, emphatically. "No, that was the first time I ever saw you. You were wearing that peasant blouse, with the little flowers around the collar."

"God, I wore that all the time. But I didn't get it till that Christmas. I remember, my mom hated it because it made me look like a hippie."

They stared at each other.

"All right," Amanda broke in, "there's no way of knowing who's right, and probably both of you are wrong about something. Though I'd bet that Carl's version has traveled farthest from the truth."

There's a surprise, thought Carl.

"I only say that because you've told the story so often. And every time we tell a story, we become more sure that we are remembering it accurately. In fact, however, every time we tell it, we change it just a little. We shape it. We tighten it and punch it up, just like it was a script. You even gave yours a little theme: The Day I Learned the Power of Jokes. And don't forget that you were telling the story to *me*. I was your retrieval cue, and your feelings toward me colored the whole scene. Turned it into a rebuke of my humorless nature. I wouldn't have laughed, you implied; I wouldn't have passed the test. I was the dark urban intellectual Jew held up against the laughing, Nordic, free spirit."

Jesse gave a nervous laugh.

"You think I'm full of shit," Amanda said coolly. "But that's how my memory of his telling that story is being colored by this retrieval setting and the irrational jealousy I'm feeling with you sitting there looking as beautiful as he always described you."

Jesse gave a half-smile, clearly not sure whether she'd just been complimented or not.

Amanda folded her legs up under the terry cloth robe. Now that she was mixing intellectual ideas with emotional discomfort, she was really hitting her stride.

"I'd venture to say that Carl's original memory of your first meeting isn't even in his head anymore. It's been written over too many times. That's one way we can forget things. Another way is when something just doesn't make enough of an impression on us to recall it. Maybe those meetings on the bus just didn't register to him the way the one in the cafeteria did.

"Another way to forget is, of course, damage to the brain, which is possibly what we're talking about in your case. Now it could be damage to the retrieval system or damage to the storage system. If it's retrieval damage, that means the memories are still in there, but you can't get at them. I suppose there's always hope that you could reach them somehow. But if it's damage to the *storage* system . . . well, what's gone is gone."

"But couldn't hypnosis—" Jesse tried to go on, but Amanda cut her off.

"Everybody thinks hypnosis is some kind of magic truth serum. Nobody's ever proved that memories reached through hypnosis are more accurate than others. They're just more vivid."

"Isn't that the same thing?" Carl asked.

"Not at all. There's a famous story of a Swiss psychologist. One of his earliest memories was of someone trying to kidnap him when he was two and his nanny bravely protecting him. When he grew up, he found out it never happened. His nanny made the whole story up. But he had heard the story so often he came to remember it, to make it a part of the fabric of his life."

Jesse stood up, frustrated. "But that's like saying we don't know anything. That everything we remember might just be made up."

"No, because in general, memory works the way we need it to. It gives a general idea of what's happened to us. It just doesn't work the way we think it does."

Amanda turned to Carl suddenly. "I faked that orgasm the first night we made love."

Carl stared, flabbergasted. "What?"

"There, now that's a moment you're going to remember. I said something wildly outlandish and humiliated you in front of your old girlfriend. Plus, you'll keep wondering whether what I said was true or not.

"Now when I said it, physical changes started taking place in your brain as it encoded the new information." She was really in full lecture mode now. "And not just in one part of your head. Different groups of neurons were encoding the experience in several distinct brain regions. The posterior regions of your cortex were taking in the self-satisfied look on my face. And also the texture of my robe and the color of this tile. The smell of this coffee, the sound of my voice, and that awful cowboy music somebody's playing next door. Another region preserved your feelings of outrage and betrayal. Somewhere else, those bits were cross-referenced with everything you know about me and about that night and about orgasms in general. And right now, still other regions of your brain, the convergence zones, are sending out codes to connect all those sensory fragments in all those different regions. They're forming something like a constellation in your brain. And that's a memory.

"Now you might keep that memory or you might discard it. It might fade through time or you might alter it. But if you keep it, and twenty years from now you find yourself making out with some unlucky woman who's wearing a terry cloth robe and the two of you are in a kitchen and she happens to brew a cup of Mocha Java, those cues may come together and those old sensory fragments might start firing again and reconnect to form that old constellation.

And then you may remember this moment and lose your erection and for that I apologize in advance." Amanda smiled, then continued.

"My point is," and Carl *was* wondering if she had one, "every memory is a little miracle of neurological engineering. We don't know much about how the process works, but we do know this: if the system is actually damaged, no amount of concentrating hard or looking at swinging watches is going to make it right."

She looked up at Jesse, and damned if there didn't seem to be a flicker of fellow feeling in those dark eyes. "I'm sorry," she said. "What were you trying to recall?"

"Whether my husband tried to kill me or not."

Amanda looked down into the depths of her Mocha Java. Then back up. "Maybe we'll try a little harder."

And so simple human concern overcame her vaunted professional ethics. Carl had forgotten that side of her, just as he'd forgotten the warmth of her smile. Of course it had been easier for him to survive the aftershocks of their breakup that way, to remember only the dark, brooding, unsympathetic side of her. Unfair, but easier.

All this Carl recalled as he watched Amanda's coral lips mouth the soothing words of hypnosis, falling into something of a trance himself. This time Jesse must have tried harder as well, because she had finally imagined her safe place, though she wouldn't tell them what it was.

Amanda's questions now were simple ones about Jesse's body and how it felt. The very boredom of the topic seemed to lower Jesse's defenses. In a calm, sleepy voice she described all the odd sensations her body was giving her. That dull ache in her left toe—she didn't remember injuring it. That stiffness in her right wrist—where did that come from? The heaviness in her waist and hips—that wasn't there yesterday.

Slowly, gracefully, Amanda brought her further and further into her body, until she'd left outside sensations behind and was close to that odd state Martin had described as her "seizure." It was hearing about that seizure that had finally persuaded Amanda that hypnosis might help Jesse after all.

Before that, she had been dead set against the procedure. She'd researched hypnotically induced memory recall and considered it a minefield of self-deception. "Sure you can come up with occasions where it's worked," she'd said. "There was that kidnapping up in Chowchilla where the bus driver was able to remember the kidnapper's license plate once they put him under.

"But just as often people come up with these bizarre stories of alien abductions and mass-baby-killing-devil-worshiping-sex cults. And no matter how outlandish the retrieved memory might seem, people come out of hypnosis sure that it's true. Because one thing hypnosis *does* do is increase the vividness of your visual imagery. And most people believe, like Carl, that a vivid memory must be a true one."

On top of all this, experiments had proved that it was possible for a hypnotist to implant a false memory. Under hypnosis a group of patients were given the idea that a loud noise had awakened them the night before. After the session, the patients were so sure of this new memory, that they still maintained it had happened, even after they were told about the experiment.

In the self-help seventies, some psychotherapists had even specialized in replacing people's unhappy memories with happy ones. Someone who was tormented for being too fat as a child, for example, might be given new memories of being a skinny kid. These "happy-face memories" were supposed to improve on reality. In short, Amanda could write a book on the reasons she'd never trust hypnotically retrieved memories.

But here she sat, bringing Jesse further and further into her "Vegetable Princess" days.

"How do you feel, Jesse?"

"Calm . . . far away . . ."

Amanda had explained that even though Jesse had been aphonic (Amanda's fancy word for mute) during her seizure, she'd be able to talk to them about it now, since they were conversing with her below the level of her conscious mind.

"Far away from what, Jesse?"

"From everything . . . from you . . . from the room . . ."

"Are you happy?"

". . . just . . . far away . . ."

"And how does your body feel?"

"There's a bruise on my side. It really aches."

"Do you know how you got it?"

"No, it's just there."

"Can you tell what's going on around you? Can you hear? Can you see?"

"Oh, yes."

"What do you see?"

"The ceiling . . . the room . . ." Her eyes were open and they moved slightly, but she didn't turn her head.

"Do you remember being in another room when you felt this way? Months ago. A different room?"

"Yes."

"What was that room like?"

". . . A room . . ."

"I want you to go back to that room. Can you go back to that room?"

"Okay . . ."

"Can you see it?"

"Yes."

"Whose house are you in?"

"I don't know. The man's house, I guess."

"What man?"

"The one who comes and looks at me."

"Can you tell me anything about the room?"

". . . A crack in the ceiling has the habit of sometimes looking like a rabbit."

"That's from *Madeleine,* isn't it? I like that book too. Can you hear anything?"

"Birds . . . voices . . . music . . ."

"What do the voices say?"

"My name . . . and other things . . . I don't pay attention . . ."

"What music do you hear?"

A pause, then she started singing in a small voice. " 'Once I laughed when I heard you saying that I'd be playing solitaire. Uneasy in my easy chair. It never entered my mind.' "

Amanda pulled Carl aside and asked in a whisper if she'd known that song in her teenage years. Carl shook his head; they'd listened to The Eagles, not Rodgers and Hart. But he told Amanda about Jesse playing it on the piano that morning and saying she'd never played the instrument before.

Amanda didn't seem surprised. "Procedural memory is a whole different animal. If only her temporal lobe structures were injured, it might not be affected."

"So you can do things you don't remember learning?"

"Well, do you remember learning to read?"

Carl looked back at Jesse, still singing softly, wondering if she were really back in that trancelike state of mind. "Is she remembering being in that room?"

"There's no way to verify it. Let's keep going."

The idea had come to Amanda when they told her all they knew of Jessica's accident and the temporal lobe seizure that had followed. If Jesse had been conscious

during that period, it might be possible to recall things
that she'd witnessed then using a concept called state-
dependent retrieval. The idea was simple, though it more
often applied to drug-induced forgetfulness; people who
have trouble remembering something that happened to
them when they were drunk or stoned, will sometimes be
able to remember it given the same dosage of alcohol or
pot.

To Carl it sounded like a joke—something out of a Chap-
lin film, or an episode of *Sgt. Bilko*. But Amanda wondered
if it might not be possible to use hypnosis to re-create the
state of mind she'd been in during her six-month seizure. If
they could create a match between the retrieval and encoding conditions, Amanda said, then Jesse might be able to
remember what happened on the boat.

She was just finishing her song as Amanda moved back
to her. " 'Once you warned me that if you scorned me, I'd
sing the maiden's prayer again. And wish that you were
there again. To get into my hair again. It never entered my
mind.' "

"That was very nice, Jesse. When did you learn that
song?"

". . . I just know it . . ."

"Tell me what you know about water?"

Jesse flinched. Carl, watching, flinched along with her.

"It's cold," Jesse said.

"Where is it cold?"

"Everywhere. All over."

"All over your body?"

"Inside, even." Her head was shifting slightly on the sofa
cushion now. Her voice, still sleepy, was losing its calm-
ness, becoming fretful and strained.

"Are you in water, Jesse?"

"Yes."

"Do you want to be in water, Jesse?"

"No. I want to get out."

"How did you get in the water, Jesse?"

But she didn't answer this time. Her head started shifting faster on the cushion, twisting like a worm on a hot sidewalk.

"Can you tell me, Jesse?"

Eyes screwed shut now, breath coming short and fast.

"Why are you in the water, Jesse?"

". . . because of the blood," she said.

10

Carl moved closer. Amanda held out a hand to stop him. "Tell me what you know about blood, Jesse."

"Don't want to."

"Is it your blood, Jesse?"

"Don't know."

"Where is the blood?"

"Everywhere. On the man's face. On me. On the deck."

"Deck?"

"On the boat."

"Are you on a boat, Jesse?"

"I was."

"Can you go back to being on the boat, Jesse? I want you to go back to being on the boat."

"Okay."

"You mentioned a man's face, Jesse. Can you see the man's face?"

"Yeah."

"Do you know him?"

". . . I've seen him. I don't know him."

"What is the man doing?"

"Fighting."

"With you?"

"No, with the other man. The big man."

"Do you know this man, Jesse?"

"I've seen him . . . I don't know him."

"Why are the men fighting?"

"I don't know. I wish they'd stop. He's looking at me."

Her breath was coming faster, her head tossing, her eyes opened wide.

"Who's looking at you?"

No answer.

"What is it, Jesse?" Amanda asked. "What do you see?"

Jesse screamed. He'd never heard a sound like that come out of her— high-pitched, tight, and full of terror. "Keep away! Keep away from me!"

Amanda took her hand now, and pressed her fingers to Jesse's sweating forehead. "All right, Jesse. Do you feel my hand? My hand is calming you down. You were afraid then, but you don't have to be afraid now. That was in the past. That was *then*. You're safe now. You came through all that fine and no one can hurt you here. Do you understand?"

Jesse nodded, weakly.

"Just thinking back," Amanda said, "not *being there,* but just remembering, can you tell me what you saw that frightened you?"

She screamed again, her whole body flexing in panic. "The blood is all over me! God! Don't touch me!"

"Who's touching you, Jesse?"

"The water is coming at me! Oh, God!"

"Who threw you in the water, Jesse?"

She was sobbing now, and twisting on the couch as if she

could feel the water dragging her down. Amanda was touching her forehead again, trying to soothe her.

"Jesse, now I want you to take two even breaths. Can you do that? I want you to fill your lungs."

Panting. Short, harsh breaths.

"Can you just take one easy breath?"

One rasping inhale.

"Good. Now, I want you to go back to your safe place."

A small whine. "It's not safe anymore."

"Yes, it is. Very quiet. Very safe."

Jesse breathed deep.

"Good. You're relaxed. Your body relaxes . . . easy breath . . . body relaxing . . . In a few moments, I'm going to wake you up. When you wake up, you'll remember everything you need to of this. Now you can see the numbers as I say them. Five, you're starting to wake up . . . four, you're almost waking up . . . three, almost awake . . . two . . ."

Carl counted right along, his shirt stuck to his chest with sweat.

"One, you're awake, Jesse," said Amanda.

Jesse's eyes fluttered open. Her skin was pale and her lips were dry. She tilted her head slightly to look at Amanda.

"Am I gonna remember all this?"

"Yes."

She smiled weakly. "I'm not sure I want to."

Amanda smiled back. "That's the problem most people have with memory."

Back in the kitchen, Jesse sucked coffee out of a mug like a pro while Carl sat next to her, both of them feeling drained. This was all becoming far too real.

Real, although Amanda was giving them a million reasons to doubt it. The moment it was over, Amanda had regretted the experiment, and her instructions now were simple: go to a doctor and then go to the police. True, hypnotically recovered memories were not admissible as evidence, but at least it would give them something to go on.

But would the police bother to go anywhere? Carl asked her. Or would they just assume that she was brain-damaged and remand her to the custody of her next of kin? Her husband.

"Carl, you don't even know if any of that really happened." Amanda's mantra.

"You saw the expression on her face. Could she react like that to something she'd just imagined?"

"You deal with actors every day. You know people are capable of anything."

They were out in the driveway by now, Carl helping Jesse, who still felt weak from her ordeal, up into the Jeep. As he walked back to the driver's side, Amanda took his arm with quiet urgency.

"I like her, Carl. Do the smart thing."

There wasn't any artifice in her voice; no presumption of superiority or wisdom in the sincere request.

"We'll think it over. We will."

Amanda released his arm with a sad smile. Carl climbed into the Jeep and backed out, watching her, surprisingly small in the driveway, watching them with concern. A good person, Carl thought. And if it made things more difficult and painful for him to remember that, so be it. A little difficulty was good for the soul.

It was late afternoon by the time Carl made it back to the main road. Neither of them spoke as the car rolled on. If Kit had been right before, if this had been a diversion, an adventure almost, now it felt oppressive and heavy. Ugly. Anything but an escape. Violence had been committed against her. Carl felt ludicrously unable to deal with this situation.

"Should we go to the police?" he asked finally.

"Hell, I don't know. Part of me thinks I must've made all this up. Things like this just don't happen to me. But then, who am I to say what happens to me?"

"So what do you think we should do?"

"I'm hungry," she said. "I think we should get something to eat."

So they went to a Denny's, and she felt completely at ease, because no one had even thought about redecorating it since 1975.

They pretended to debate the matter over their greasy cheeseburgers, but there was never really any doubt that they would press on north to Oakland. Neither of them could guess what they might learn up there, but anything would be better than these vague, shadowy images of danger she'd recalled.

Carl tried to cheer her up with a quick stop at a Music Plus on State Street, but the sight of all her favorite groups in the oldies section only served to depress her more. Still, a two-hundred-dollar charge on his credit card provided them with enough music for a respectable road trip—and for giving Jesse a crash course in seventeen years of pop, bridging the long gap from "You Light Up My Life" to "I Wanna Sex You Up."

As he drove, Carl glanced at her sorting through the pile of CDs on her lap: Michael Jackson, with and without the Jackson Five; Bruce Springsteen, with and without The E Street Band; George Michael, with and without Wham; Sting, with and without The Police; Annie Lennox, with and without The Eurythmics; Don Henley, with and without The Eagles. Carl had never noticed the trend before. Per-

haps that was what was wrong with the world these days—
no one stayed with their band anymore.

Jesse had The Beatles *Anthology* albums in her hands.
She'd cheered up a bit when she saw them, thrilled to find
out that at least *that* group had gotten back together again.
He didn't have the heart to tell her otherwise.

He used his car phone (and how impressed she was with
that ubiquitous gadget) and called information in Oakland
to see if her phone up there was still listed. The operator
connected him to the number, and he was surprised to hear
Jesse's voice on the answering machine.

"This is Jessica Ackerman. I'm not in right now. Leave a
message after the beep."

The mundane message left Carl thoroughly nonplussed.
There it was, the voice of Jesse's adult life, surviving,
ghostlike, on the phone lines. When the beep came, he
could barely summon up his voice.

"Hello, my name is Carl Rooney, and I'm trying to reach
Wesley Ackerman. I need to talk to you about, um, a personal matter regarding your sister-in-law Jesse. Jessica. I'll
be in town tomorrow. I'll call you then." Not a bad message, considering; one to pique his curiosity without giving
anything away.

They lapsed into silence as Carl drove on. His eyes
drifted to the rearview mirror. That Ford Taurus two car
lengths back. Had he seen it before, back outside Woodland
Hills? But then, hadn't he noticed a blue minivan like the
one in the passing lane just before he reached Encino?
There were too many cars, and too many of them looked
the same. How could he know if any of them were following him?

Their wedding-that-never-was was to have been the social
event of 1979. The year and the place were chosen during

one of their long, pot-hazed gabfests in Becky Holtzclaw's attic. After the wedding, the whole bunch of them would take a road trip up the Pacific Coast Highway. They would all get cabins near each other at Big Sur National Park (and no adult would dare to tell them they couldn't) and smoke pot and eat watermelon primed with vodka and laugh at the stars.

So when Carl's Jeep reached Big Sur several hours past sundown, and they checked into cabins at the Big Sur National Park (and no adult could tell them they couldn't), it had partly the feel of a second honeymoon; the sequel to a movie that had never been produced.

As always, the sequel was a disappointment compared to the original.

"Somehow I pictured something larger," she said, as she stepped into the cabin.

"Somehow I pictured something cleaner," he said, as he followed her in.

But coming in at nine in the evening, exhausted and unable to drive any further, they hadn't been offered much to choose from. Actually, they hadn't been offered anything other than a polite shake of the head and a No Vacancy sign. It was only on further questioning that Carl discovered there were a few empty cabins that had been closed semipermanently, victims of the National Park budget crisis. A sizable donation from Carl's wallet to the barely postadolescent ranger produced the keys to a cabin and an armful of bedding.

Jesse's mood had continued to darken as they drove north. He'd tried to cheer her in every way he could think of, from music, to jokes, to tales of all the good things that had transpired in the world since 1978. This last was, admittedly, a short topic, but even the news that we'd won the Cold War didn't seem to impress her. "How does James Bond find girls to fuck now?" was her only response.

Even as he lit a fire to warm the gloomy cabin, she said nothing, just looked around the room, examining it in the dancing light of the fire.

"What is that?" She was staring up at a thick white cobweb in a corner of the ceiling over the bed.

"It's an egg sac," said Carl, standing on the mattress for a closer look, "a spider's egg sac."

"Wonderful. Who's idea of a honeymoon spot was this?"

"I think Sid Norton's." He went on, hoping a playful show of jealousy might amuse her. "Maybe you should call him. He never went to Yale, by the way. He sells real estate in Pacoima."

"Stop telling me this shit. What difference does it make? I'm going for a walk." And she was out the door.

Carl reminded himself that she had every reason on earth to be moody, and any complaint he might make would be the height of selfishness. But selfish or no, he'd had his own secret agenda for this road trip. Of course, he'd wanted to help her, to find the answers to the questions that plagued her and to find out if her world was a safe place or not. But for himself there had been another hidden desire. He'd wanted to *talk*.

It depressed Carl to think how long it had been since he'd had a good, long, non–work related conversation with anyone. Apparently he'd said all he had to say to his few long-standing friends, and vice versa. Making new friends had become more and more of a chore as his thirties plowed on. The nature of his hometown didn't help—distance alone in L.A. made meeting someone for a cup of coffee a two-hour commitment. One might put up with that in the hope of eventually getting laid, but just to *talk* to someone? And how was a single thirty-five-year-old man supposed to meet new potential friends, anyway? At work, friendships were too often poisoned by jealousy and back-biting. And away from work? . . . They hadn't, as far as Carl knew, invented a "friend pickup joint" yet. Perhaps that would be the next big thing in L.A., once cigar lounges lost their cachet. A chain would surely open before the end of the century, probably run by the Starbucks people. For now, he was on his own.

So he was thrilled to have this new/old friend just fall into his lap—rather literally. He'd been locked in his quiet cell for too long; words were ready to pour out of him. Stupid words, perhaps. Dull pedestrian observations about the world and time and humanity they might be, but they were *his* dull pedestrian observations about the world and time and humanity. He wanted them to fly out of him and bounce off her and for her to fling her thoughts back at him and for the two of them to go off on foolish tangents and wild new courses, so that the flow of their conversation would be like an untamed, twisting river that no one could follow but them.

Instead, he was following her, silently, through the little paths between the cabins that twisted and turned in nonpatterns which would have been hard to follow in daylight. His pupils strained to dilate further and gather more of the dim starlight that filtered through the tall evergreens.

Where does she think she's going? he wondered, as the cabins dwindled and disappeared. They found themselves on a footbridge spanning a gurgling stream. She turned to him, her face a shadow in the dim light. "Where are we?" she asked.

"I don't know, I was following you."

It was hard to tell from her silhouette, but Carl thought he saw her smile. She stepped off the path and walked to a small pool where a thin waterfall splashed down. Here the stars shone brightly enough for him to watch her as she sat down on the banks of the stream, took off her shoes and socks, and plunged her feet into the water.

"I think I'll stay here for a while. It's kind of a relief to find a place where you're just as ignorant as I am. We're on equal footing here. Two people seeing something new."

Carl sat next to her, settling his butt into the wet moss. Why this would cheer her up he wasn't sure, but if it worked, more power to it.

"Take your shoes off," she said. "Put your feet in the water."

He hesitated. He'd just have to put his socks back on later. He hated putting socks on wet feet.

"Come on, do it."

He bared his feet. "Probably leeches in the water," he muttered as he dipped his feet in the cold, black water. "Jesus!"

"Fun?"

"No. It's muddy and slimy and freezing."

"I know, really uncomfortable, huh?"

"So why are we doing it?"

"I'm trying to build up some new memories." He was sure she was smiling now, her lips gray and luminous in the moonlight. "What do you think of this one so far?"

He leaned over and kissed her. She moved to him, wet hands encircling his neck. All at once, no disappointment, no dashed hopes. Only the soft adhesion of lips. Two bodies pulling close. Four feet slipping and sloshing in the cool muck.

She pulled him to her, and his hip turned on a rock, the sharp edge skidding on his flesh. Easy to ignore while he enjoyed the taste of cigarette on her tongue as it probed his mouth; an enticing, exotic flavor, like food seasoned with some long-forgotten spice. He reached for her breast, pivoting on his rock-impaled hip, forgiving the pain for the passion. As he turned toward her his knees sank into the cold mud, and he pressed his body against hers. She giggled and pulled him deeper into the water while he gasped and laughed.

A sneeze exploded from the silence of the woods. They were both suddenly still.

The water around Carl's waist was chilling, yet he instinctively lowered himself further in, craning his neck to peer into the silent woods around them.

"Hello?" Jesse called out.

Carl flinched. But no, she'd done the right thing. If all was innocent, a voice would answer back, and they'd both say Gesundheit and move on.

No answer came back.

"Is somebody there?" Jesse called again.

No answer.

They obviously couldn't just stay here half-concealed in frigid mud and water. Carl hauled himself out, pulling Jesse behind him. Shivering and dripping, they grabbed their shoes and climbed onto the footbridge. Wet and freezing, but alone.

Carl's shiver of relief was cut short when he saw a man down below at the turn in the path. As soon as Carl's eyes found him, the man darted into the woods by the stream.

Without speaking, Carl grabbed Jesse's hand and ran with her off the bridge. Down the slope and into the darkness of the evergreens. They raced over pine needles and moss. Their bare feet tripped on roots and dead stumps. His only thought was to put as much distance as he could between them and the creek.

Lights twinkled up ahead. The cabins were there. He raced on, gripping her hand in his, twisting and wrenching as branches whipped at his face. A godawful racket they were making, panting and crashing through the brush like a pair of rhinos. A blind dog could track them, Carl thought.

Suddenly they stumbled into a clearing behind a cabin. Carl grabbed Jesse and held her still, listening for the sound of anyone behind them. All was silence, except for the thunderous beating of Carl's heart.

Then Jesse gasped, and Carl turned to follow her gaze.

A man stood on the path about ten yards away from them. Carl thought his lungs would burst as he tried to quiet his breathing. Suddenly, a light flared near his face, and Carl relaxed. It was the ranger, lighting a hand-rolled ciga-rette with a Bic.

Wheezing laughter burst from both of them as Carl real-ized that they must have been running like escaped convicts from a poor overworked park ranger looking for a quiet place to smoke his joint.

"Your tax dollars at work," Carl whispered.

Still stifling laughter, they found their cabin. Carl unlocked the door, while Jesse wondered aloud if they should have bummed a drag from the ranger. Bad form, they both agreed.

They examined their wounds in the firelight, like soldiers returning from a campaign, giddy with relief; every new scratch they found seemed like a punch line to another joke. Face welts from whipping branches, bruises from rocks and stumps, feet crisscrossed with scratches and thorns—they were all the occasion for a new rash of giggles.

One cut on Jesse's heel was deeper than the others. Carl got a damp cloth from the bathroom and cleaned it gently, wiping the mud away. He noticed an old healed-over scar on the back of her ankle that he'd never seen before, but thought better of asking her how she got it.

"I wonder how I got that?" she asked, idly, tracing the crescent-shaped scar with her finger. He still didn't say anything, just kissed it once.

At that, their eyes met, and he remembered what they'd been doing before they were interrupted. From Jesse's expression, he could see that she remembered too. Well, there was no point denying that the mood had been broken. They were feeling friendly, relieved, and a little punchy. But not lustful.

"I guess we were starting to get a little carried away in the stream back there," Carl said.

She nodded. "But we're not now."

"No," he agreed, feeling his heart sink a little.

"So whatever we do now," she went on, "has to be a choice."

She was looking up at him, eyes wide and vulnerable. Waiting.

Slowly, he cupped his two hands around her face and kissed her softly, almost chastely.

"I choose," he said.

She took a breath and stepped away from him. Her eyes still on his, she crossed her arms at the bottom of her blouse and peeled it up over her head. A blur of cloth and her hair, still wet from the stream, fell in a mass around her shoulders and face. She unfastened her pants and let them fall to the floor around her feet. With a slight stumble she stepped out of them and brushed them aside.

Standing before him in the firelight, her porcelain skin gleaming pink, in just her bra and panties, there was no doubt what she was doing. She was offering herself to him for the first time. The first time, because Friday night in the greenhouse neither of them had known what they were doing. And back in '77, in his father's Volare, they hadn't known either. But here, tonight, they both knew. No excuses.

He stepped forward and took her in his arms.

If his wet clothes came off less gracefully than hers, there was still none of the clumsy groping of their previous encounters. Their movements were slow, easy arcs. They allowed each moment its own life, never rushing on to the next step before the last had been thoroughly experienced, tasted, touched, smelled, seen. No hurry. No need to prove a thing, or to rush ahead and seize unclaimed ground. There seemed to be no goal at all in their mutual wanderings over each others' bodies. It was a quiet stroll on a beach with nowhere to go and all the time in the world to get there. There seemed to be no hierarchy of touch between them now; every contact seemed equally electric, so that the brushing of his fingertips across her teeth was as fascinating as the feel of her tongue on his thigh.

They made their way to the bed, not stumbling or laughing, but actually holding hands, and watching each other in silent amazement. Amazement not because they were so damned beautiful, Carl thought to himself, aware that Brad Pitt never had love-handles like his, and that her body was not one of the silicone-enhanced, pneumatic Macy's-Thanksgiving-Day-Parade balloon bodies one saw while flipping past the Playboy channel on lonely nights. No, if either of them bounced as they moved, it was in all the wrong places, so their amazement wasn't based on lustful admiration. It was the humble amazement of gratitude. They were there. They had found each other.

He asked her if she wanted to make love, though the question sounded oddly after-the-fact, and she smiled and said yes, so he found his sopping wallet and pulled out a condom. She smiled and commented on his optimism in bringing that along. No, he said, he always had it with him. Then he told her about AIDS and she said it was the saddest thing she'd ever heard, but sadness didn't break their mood, since it wasn't based on frivolity this time. Still, he asked if she wanted to go on, and still she said yes.

So on they went, and he'd never felt the pulses of blood rushing through his body or the cleansing filling and emptying of his lungs with such perfect focus. Every nerve in his body, even the hairs on his head—even his fingernails, for Christ's sake, as they dug into the fabric of the pillowcase—seemed suffused in some warm liquid of pure, all-inclusive pleasure. For once his mind was not clouded with thoughts of timing and rhythm, of when to stop or when to rush forward. There was nothing to hold off from or hurry toward when every moment felt so equally perfect.

Then she made a sound, somewhere between a laugh and a scream. With another sound, this one in the vicinity of a gasp or a gag, she rolled over, toppling Carl onto the mattress in bewilderment—this was not a reaction he had ever induced before. The pillows tumbled onto his head, and when he plucked them off, she was pointing up at the ceiling, chortling and appalled all at once. "The spiders," she said.

He looked up at the egg sac in the corner above them and saw it disgorging, teaming, exploding with tiny spiders. Perhaps the warmth of the fire had hatched them, or perhaps it was simply their time, for the creatures were bursting forth like rain from a cloud, breaking their way free and dropping down . . . toward them.

With whooping laughs, covering their mouths to block newborn intruders, Carl and Jesse rolled from the bed to the floor and skittered over to the fireplace. There, checking each other's bodies like grooming chimpanzees, laughing and hugging one another, they watched as their honeymoon bed became a nursery for what seemed to be hundreds of black spiders that scampered through the sheets and blankets and pillows, exploring their new world.

They sat on the floor, and he cradled her back against his chest. She said it had all been so wonderful and wasn't it too bad about the interruption, but Carl said it was all right. "I'm not sure where we were, but if we'd spent any more time there, I would never have wanted to come back."

She turned and kissed him. "Can we go there again?" she asked.

"The first chance we get. But do we have to bring the spiders with us?"

With no hope of sleeping in that bed, they decided to put on fresh clothes and drive on.

The ranger caught them on the way out, surprised to see them leaving in the middle of the night. Carl explained that they had an early meeting tomorrow.

"Did your friend find you?" the ranger asked.

Carl and Jesse stared at him.

"Friend?" Carl asked.

"Yeah. Big guy. I met him on the hiking path a little while ago. He said you were expecting him."

All at once, Carl could feel every pain from every scratch on his body.

11

$\mathcal{A}$fter that, he very nearly did go to the police. They were being pursued, no question now, almost certainly by Martin or somebody sent by Martin. This somebody had had two chances to see Jesse; they had to assume he'd spotted her at least one of those times. They had to assume Martin knew she was alive. But did Martin know what condition she was in? Could Martin or his spy see that she was recovered from her seizure? Very probably. Could he tell she had no memory of what happened on the boat? Very probably not.

So Martin was out there, knowing he'd tried to kill her and thinking she knew it too. So she was a danger to him. So he was a danger to her.

So go to the police. Get protection.

But they kept going over and over it as they drove, drawing the whole scene in the air around them. At first the police would be concerned; then they'd learn about her neurological condition; Martin would act properly sympathetic; Carl would start coming off as a well-meaning but ignorant fellow who had acted irresponsibly by listening to the delusions of a brain-damaged woman ("And that's what I am," Jesse said, "there's no point in pretending I'm not"); Martin would get all noble and offer to take care of her. And once she was in his care? Carl would have no right to see her, because, however wrong it might seem, old high school boyfriends have no rights at all.

But a mother, Jesse said, a mother has lots of rights. If she was with her mother when she called the police; if it was her mother calling the lawyers and setting up the competency hearings; they couldn't ignore a person's mother. Even if it just delayed things, that would be enough. Enough time for detectives to investigate; enough time for her to prove that whatever was wrong with her, she wasn't incompetent. And she wasn't crazy. And she didn't want to live with that man.

So they agreed, though by now all the arguments were sounding more and more specious to Carl, that they would find her mother first. They would go to Jesse's house in Oakland. Quick in and quick out. Find Mom's address and then bolt to the retirement community, or whatever it was. Then Carl would call every lawyer he knew and every reporter he knew and a couple of friends he knew that worked on *Unsolved Mysteries*. They'd make sure that the story was so well known that even if Martin did end up getting custody of her, he couldn't just drop her off the side of a boat again without the whole world noticing.

A plan. A stupid plan, Carl admitted to himself, but it felt nice to have a plan.

1712 Rosemary Avenue was a sleepy Craftsman bungalow in one of the few enclaves of charm in Oakland that had survived the devastation of both the fires of '91 and the economic boom of the eighties.

Carl drove past it twice to make sure of the address, and

both times Jesse nodded in approval. "Now, that's more like it," she said. "I could see living there."

He parked the Jeep at the corner, thinking that made them less conspicuous, and then felt insanely conspicuous as he walked up the street with Jesse, in full view of the world.

They stepped onto the broad stone porch and Jesse peered through the diamond-shaped window in the big door, hands cupped around her face to cut the reflection. Carl rang the doorbell. No answer, other than the meowing of a cat from within.

"Wanna break open a window and look around?" she asked.

"Kit said Wesley was staying here. He might be asleep."

"Nope. I can see the mail piled up on the floor. Nobody's home."

"You still have those keys? The ones from the greenhouse?"

She found the keys in her pocket and one of them fit the door perfectly. She swung it open slowly, but neither of them walked in.

"I'm home," Jesse said.

Still they didn't move.

"Okay . . . ," she went on, "so we either go in and look around, or we wait for him to get here, or . . ."

"Or?" Carl asked.

This great unspoken "or" had remained unspoken in the long drive from Big Sur, but what they didn't say colored and energized everything between them. And it was simply "or we could forget the whole thing and run off together." Why fight to regain a life she didn't know and cared nothing about? Why not just start fresh and to hell with Martin? But as soon as the thought formed in his mind, Carl could feel dozens of objections swarming like antibodies to

destroy it. He had a life, a job, a house—how could he just
run away? And he couldn't just keep her in his house and
hope no one noticed. He couldn't introduce her at business
parties as his dead girlfriend.

She spoke, in tune with his thoughts. "I have to settle all
this first."

She stepped over the threshold, saying, "You know we're
going to find a body in here, that's what always happens,"
and shut the door behind them.

But there was no sign of mayhem in the living room. No
stuck record repeating ominously on the stereo. No sound
of running water washing the blood off Janet Leigh's man-
gled body in the shower. Everything seemed quite homey.

In fact, walking into this house, Carl understood why he
had felt so uncomfortable, so disappointed, in Martin Ackerman's house. Carl had gone to Martin's house expecting to
find where Jesse had lived. He'd looked for traces of her; the
scent of the girl he'd known. All he'd found was an interior-
decorated, see-how-much-money-I'm-making trophy. He
hadn't expected her to grow up to be that shallow.

But now he knew: that hadn't been her house. She'd
lived here. Here were the sun-filled windows, the honest
sloppiness, the colors, the flowers, the knickknacks, the
sense of fun, the gameboards hung on the walls in place of
art, the Cary Grant videos scattered on top of the TV, the
old vinyl records next to the old turntable, the homemade
cassette tapes on the bookshelf. The smell of Jesse.

Not that she'd had backgammon boards on her walls when
Carl had known her. Not that videotapes had even existed
back in the pre–home entertainment seventies. But these
things all seemed like things Jesse would have grown to love,
if she had grown older . . . which, of course, she had.

He looked through the self-labeled cassette tapes piled
haphazardly on the bookshelf next to the Maybeck fireplace

and saw that they fit the picture as well. Maybe it wasn't
Jesse's music from '78, but it was the music that followed
through on it. If she'd listened to Linda Ronstadt singing
"Don't Cry Now" and actually thought it was "cutting edge"
(or whatever the "cutting edge" term for "cutting edge" was
back then), it was right and proper that she should be listening to Mary-Chapin Carpenter now. Jackson Browne then,
John Gorka now. Loudon Wainwright then, Jonathan Rich-
man now. Emmylou Harris then, Emmylou Harris now.

But the biggest clue that this place was Jesse's home was
the simplest one: Carl felt at home here.

A scrawny calico cat leaped onto the broad wooden arm
of the Stickley easy chair next to Carl, who let loose a startled yelp. Jesse laughed, and the cat looked over at her. It
jumped to the floor, trotted to her, and entwined itself
between her legs, purring contentedly.

"I guess he was mine," she said, just slightly freaked out
by the strange animal's affection.

Carl knelt down to pet the cat. It hissed at him, baring its
teeth.

Jesse picked the cat up and cradled it in her arms,
scratching it under the chin. The purr was ecstatic. Jesse
took a turn around the room, taking in the heavy furniture
and the Arts and Crafts rug. "Man," Jesse's voice was low
now, like a child's in church. "I have the weirdest feeling of
déjà vu."

"Not exactly."

"What do you mean?"

"You *have* been here before."

Jesse shrugged in agreement.

"Do you see anything you really remember?"

She looked around expectantly, then frowned. "No . . . I
just feel uneasy."

Her gaze fell on a large framed photo over the mantel. In

washed-out shades of silver and white, a nude woman knelt in the palm of a giant hand. "Is that me?"

Carl looked closer at the sad eyes staring through the veil of hair toward the giant fingers cupping to close in on her. "Yep."

"Jesus, some kind of nice San Marino housewife I am, with my tits on display all over California."

"I'm beginning to think you were something of a non-conformist."

Jesse smiled, apparently happy at the thought. "Hey, my records!" She put the cat down, ran a hand over the records on the bookshelf, and pulled out Tom Waits's *The Heart of Saturday Night*. Her name was written across the top of the jacket in magic marker. Carl recognized the swirling signature she'd experimented with in her junior year.

She started to move on down the hall, and the cat jogged along with her. "Come on, Carl, I'm not wandering around here by myself."

"What are you afraid of?" he asked, joining her.

"Hell, I don't know. It's just creepy." Try as he might, Carl couldn't imagine how she must feel, walking through a place she didn't know, but that seemed to know her. Like a ghost auditioning for a place to haunt.

The small kitchen had a door to a backyard garden. The wall over the kitchen table was decorated with personal photographs. Childhood pictures of Jesse and Nicky and her parents. Christmases from long ago. And one wedding.

Jesse took the wedding photo off the wall and examined it before letting out a long sigh and handing it to Carl. "You want some coffee? I'm thinking I need some coffee."

Carl looked at the picture. Jesse's wedding. In answer to her earlier question, it hadn't been a big wedding. The church looked like a little wooden chapel from the Gold Rush days. Jesse's gown was an antique, all creamy satin and pearls. Martin, thinner but still bulky, beamed next to her in an ill-fitting rented tux; his hair was longer back then and grew in unmanageable curls that flew out from his head like solar flares. The grin that split his face from one huge sideburn to the other was of pure ecstasy. The best man stood at his side, a tall, angular, twenty-something kid who looked like he wanted to be anywhere but here. The ring bearer just *might* be Jesse's brother Nicky, grown older. The bridesmaid looked unfamiliar, but he couldn't mistake Jesse's parents off to the side, even if they were grayer and heavier than he remembered. That was the entire wedding party. Through a window in the corner of the chapel the hills of the wine country rolled off into the distance. Had they all driven in a bunch to some campsite after the ceremony?

"When do you think that was?" Jesse asked, as she opened the lid of the coffeemaker and peered in.

"I don't know, there's no date."

She pulled out the filter and looked at it, puzzled. Carl took over for her. She plucked the wedding picture from his hand and started pacing the room with it, trying to contain her nervous energy.

"So that's it. That's my big day, huh? Looks pretty neat. Wish I coulda been there. Do I look happy to you?" She held the picture up and Carl took it. How to describe the expression on her face?

"You look kind of wistful."

"Fuck wistful! I don't want to be *wistful* on my wedding day!" Without thinking, she swung open one of the cabinets and grabbed a plastic travel mug. "I want to be goddamn happy!"

Then a frightened look filled her eyes. The mug fell from her hand and bounced in the metal sink.

"What is it?" Carl turned to the door, expecting to see someone walking in.

"I knew where it was," she said, amazed. "I just reached for a coffee mug and I knew where it was."

"Did you remember?"

"I don't know, I wasn't thinking. I just knew."

"Are you sure you didn't just guess? I mean, it's a kitchen cabinet—"

"I knew."

"Okay, Jesse, look around you. Do you remember this house?"

She raised her head and looked, her expression a mixture of hope and fear. Her eyes scanned the room, searching for a clue, like a child looking at an *I Spy* puzzle book. She didn't stop till she had done the whole circuit and was looking out the window into the backyard. Then she spoke, very quiet. "Shit."

There was a key in the door and she turned it, stepping out into the backyard; the cat slipped out with her, never wanting her out of its sight.

Carl followed her into a little paradise. Tall adobe walls were thick with huge roses. Jasmine and wisteria tumbled over lattices near the back. In one corner sat a stone bench, encrusted with lichen. It was a peaceful, soul-nourishing place.

"Jesus," she said.

"What is it?"

"Remember when Amanda was hypnotizing me? I couldn't think of a safe place, so she told me to imagine one?"

"Yes?"

She turned to him and opened her arms just slightly, to encompass the garden. "This was my safe place."

Before Carl could respond, the front door slammed shut and they heard footsteps walking toward them through the house.

12

esse moved faster than Carl would have thought possible, bounding for the ivy-covered wall at the first sound from the house, not pausing for any of the confusing thoughts that raced through Carl's startled brain (Is it Martin? Did he find us? What if it's someone else? Are we going to be arrested? I've never been arrested. Wait, this is Jesse's house, why would we be arrested? Is it Martin?), so that she was already vaulting over the wall before Carl had even started to move. She was out of sight by the time he reached the wall and grabbed hold of the ivy. He felt the cat scrambling up his back and launching itself off his head and had only just started to pull himself up when he heard the voice behind him. "Excuse me?"

Carl turned, and the first thing he noticed was that the man in the kitchen door was not Martin Ackerman. The second thing he noticed was that the man was holding a gun.

"Do I know you?" the man with the gun said. He looked more annoyed than Carl would have liked.

Carl opened his mouth but his throat stayed shut.

"Do I know you?" the man asked again, sounding really peeved this time, as if he were talking to someone who'd taken his seat at a baseball game.

The odd thing was, Carl kept trying to figure out how to answer *that* question, rather than the more significant one: Was he about to get shot?

"No," Carl answered, not sure if he was supposed to lift his hands over his head or not; he felt critically ill-informed about the etiquette of situations like this.

"Did I invite you here?"

Carl started to wonder if these questions were rhetorical. But he answered, just to be on the safe side. "No."

"Then why are you here?" The man seemed more irritated than angry, as if Carl's breaking into this house was more offensive for its lack of civility than its illegality. (Carl imagined a version of that old etiquette cartoon in *Highlights* magazine: Gallant waits for an invitation. Goofus just walks right in and steals your stereo equipment.)

"I came to see you, Wesley." Taking a chance here, but Carl read somewhere that if you could get on a first-name basis with your captor, it made it harder for him to shoot you.

The gun was raised, threateningly. "We're not on a first-name basis, asshole."

Why did he have to believe everything he read? "Sorry. But I'm not a burglar, okay?"

"No?"

"Look at me, I'm wearing a Banana Republic henley shirt and J. Peterman tan chinos. These are Mephisto walking shoes at a hundred seventy dollars a pop. What burglar dresses like this?"

"I don't know. How do I know what a burglar dresses like? Sounds to me like you're trying to take advantage of the cultural stereotype of criminals as members of low-income minorities. That's not very admirable."

Great, Carl's first felony, and he had to get caught by a politically correct vigilante. "I'm just saying I didn't break in here. And what's it to you? This isn't even your house."

That made him think for a minute. "Whose house is it?"

"Jesse's."

"How do you know that?"

"I know her. I knew her."

"So it's okay to break into her house?"

"I didn't break into her house."

"Then how did you get in?"

Well, there was a problem. If he told Wesley about the key, he'd have to tell Wesley where he got it, and that would involve telling Wesley about Jesse. And so far, he hadn't felt inclined to trust Wesley.

"The door was unlocked." A weak lie, but the only one that came to him.

"No, it wasn't."

"It was." That's my story, and I'm sticking to it, Carl thought.

"I know I locked the door."

"Why would you lock the door? It's not your house."

"I'm the one asking the questions."

"Are you staying here?"

The man sighed. Carl thought he was gaining some kind of advantage, but he had no idea how to use it. "Off and on," Wesley said.

"Well, if there's a housesitter looking after the place, I can tell you they are notoriously unreliable. I once had one mail out a bunch of postcards from my house using a sheet of rare stamps I'd collected. You just can't trust them."

The man thought for a moment. "Emily was supposed to come by once a day to feed the cat."

"There you go." Blame Emily, whoever she is.

"Where is the cat?"

Now Carl looked guilty.

"Goddamn it, if you let that cat out . . . !" For the first time Wesley showed signs of real anger.

Carl raised his hands plaintively (not up but out). "Don't blame me. Emily's the one who left the door open."

"Shit." The man dropped the gun on the glass patio table, hurried inside, plucked up the kitchen phone, and dialed.

Carl looked at the discarded gun, episodes of a thousand crime shows filling his head, offering him two options. Either grab the gun and subdue his captor, or take advantage of his distraction and scale the wall to freedom.

The problem was, this house was where he wanted to be, and this man was someone he wanted to talk to. So Carl took unoffered Option Three instead. He went into the kitchen, poured himself a cup of coffee, and waited for Wesley to get off the phone.

He got a machine.

Carl could see the tell-tale slump, the transition from expectant speaker to hapless message-leaver.

"Hi, Emily, this is Wes. Call me." So it *was* Wesley, Carl noted. And he called himself Wes. That sounded a little better.

"Mind if I join you?" Wes asked. He grabbed a mug from the cabinet and poured himself a cup. "I see the coffee's already brewing. You sure made yourself at home. Used my favorite mug, too." The travel mug was still lying in the sink where Jesse had dropped it.

Carl sipped his coffee and took a look at this odd bird. Wesley Ackerman was improbably tall. His sandy blond hair was cut short and spiky in a way that might have been trying to evoke Sting but succeeded only in evoking Stan Laurel. There was a bit of the skinny comedian in the sad eyes, too, behind the round designer frames. Around his mouth there was a hint of a smile that Carl hadn't noticed when the gun was distracting him; the look of a deadpan comic who was funny only as long as he refused to admit he was joking. Carl started to wonder if there was a joke here he wasn't getting.

"It isn't your favorite mug," Carl said, testing him. "It was Jesse's."

Wes's eyes seemed to betray nothing, except that eyes were never that still without effort. "You're Carl Rooney."

Carl felt a surge of apprehension. Was this the man Martin had sent after them? "How'd you know?"

"I heard your message on the machine."

"You *are* living here, then?"

"Sometimes. I hate to see the place empty, and Martin, that's her husband, he doesn't seem to know what to do with it."

"Funny that you left her greeting on the answering machine."

Wes's shrug was sad and tired. "It's a lot to explain. For a long time she was sick and she couldn't speak, so I liked to be able to call and hear her voice. Then after she died, well . . . erasing it seemed so final." He picked up the wedding photo from the counter and hung it back in its place on the wall. He sat at the table next to Carl and smiled his half smile again. "I remember your name. Jessica told me about you."

Carl felt himself blush; Wes, seeming to sense his discomfort, quickly added, "Don't feel bad. We *all* let her down. I think she got used to it after awhile. Not that she brought it out in people but . . . well, do you believe in predestination?"

"I never really thought about it," said Carl, who had often thought about it.

"I'm not talking about fate or anything. My brother's always accusing me of being too spiritual, but that's not what I mean. I just mean . . . you are who you are, right? So Jessica's the kind of woman who'd fall in love with guys like us and think we're special people who can do anything and she'll try to help us and . . . well, we're bound to disappoint her. Because we're not special. I'm the kind of fool who walks into his house and sees a burglar and the only thing he can find to defend himself with is a toy gun. And you're the kind of fool who sees it and thinks it's a real one."

Carl looked out through the patio doors at the plastic gun on the glass table. "Well, fuck me," Carl said, "I guess I was too scared to notice."

Wes laughed. Then Carl laughed too and he realized that, very much against his will, he was starting to like this guy.

"I want to talk about Jesse," Carl said.

Wes nodded and stepped back out onto the patio. Carl followed him, glancing at the garden wall where Jesse had disappeared. Where had she gone? Was she still waiting on the other side? Had she hightailed it back to the car? Had the next-door neighbors nabbed her for trespassing?

Wes was standing by the rosebushes that crowded the back of the house. Flowers bloomed wildly in huge, human head–sized blossoms, with wicked black thorns like the ones that defended Sleeping Beauty's castle. "These were her babies," Wes was saying. "She'd spend hours on them. Nurturing, fertilizing, making sure they had sun. Then she'd cut them back. She was vicious at that. Really, you'd have thought she killed the poor things. But they always came back for her, just like this.

"That's her bedroom window." He pointed to a basement window, peering out through the roses at ground level. "Very unusual for a house like this to have a full basement.

She used to stand nude on her desk, looking out the window there, trying to spot the aphids, she used to say, when they didn't know she was looking." He cupped one of the massive blossoms in his hand. "Best crop she ever had. She'd have loved it." His voice trailed off and for the first time, he looked sad.

He shook it off with a smile, and again Carl thought of Stan Laurel. But some sort of Alternate Universe, Bizarro, tragic Stan Laurel. A Stan Laurel whose Ollie had betrayed him—left him to drink and dissolution. Stan Laurel by way of Eugene O'Neill. "So, what did you have to say?" Wes asked.

Carl looked at the window and pictured Jesse there, nude. How did Wes know about that? Did it mean he really was her lover? Or was it just something she'd told him about? But nude aphid spotting? It was hard not to like that. "Well, there's so much . . ." How deeply should he plunge? He remembered his hesitation at Martin's house and the information it had garnered him. "I haven't seen her for years," he lied.

"Yeah, I know."

"You said she mentioned me."

"Sure. You always go through that, don't you? 'What's your favorite movie? What's your favorite song? Was your first lover a jerk?' "

"What did she say?"

"Let's see. *Annie Hall,* I think, or maybe *His Girl Friday.* 'It Never Entered My Mind,' definitely, the Ella Fitzgerald version. And no, she didn't call you a jerk."

Carl's eyebrows lifted.

"You're surprised?" Wes asked.

"A little," Carl laughed.

"Well, there was that too," Wes laughed as well, "but she had good things to say about you, mostly. I think if you'd given her a call sometime, she would've gotten a kick out of it."

Carl didn't answer right away. Why had he never made that call? Because he could never find the words to make it right? Well, now, of course, there was no need. "I always meant to."

"Well . . . we all mean to do things."

And then there was one of those silences Carl hated. It took a special kind of man to let conversation dry up in just this way. Women, he imagined, might hug and cry at a moment like this. Other kinds of men, Slavs and Italians, you know, the ethnic types, might be able to cry and drink and sing old songs in minor keys. Rednecks might punch each other a few times and then go hunt something. But his type of man, *Homo suburbius,* could only sit awkwardly and look for a way to change the subject.

Fortunately, Carl had one easily to hand. "Anyway, when I heard what happened . . . and what was in the papers was so sketchy . . . you were there, weren't you?" So he'd gotten to the point after all, if only to end an embarrassing moment.

Wes nodded.

"So . . ." Take that plunge, boy, Carl told himself. "Did it happen like they said in the paper?"

"Did what happen?"

"The boating accident."

Wes took another sip from his beer. "Oh, it was no accident," he said, and his smile was as brief as a heartbeat.

Carl froze in place. What had he just heard? He was thinking of what to say next when, from out of nowhere, the cat plummeted from the sky and landed on his shoulder, sinking its claws in for traction.

Carl yelped in pain as the cat skidded down his back to the ground. Carl yelped, but he didn't make that weird choking sound. He looked at Wes and heard it again—a gurgling, strangled gasp. Why was he making that sound, and why was he staring at Carl in that wide-eyed, terror-stricken way? Had the cat ripped open Carl's throat without him knowing?

Then Carl saw that Wes wasn't looking at him. He was looking past him to the top of the garden wall, where Jesse was sitting, staring at them.

"Hi," she said.

And Wesley made that noise one more time before he fell on the ground.

13

Carl looked down at the lump of Wesley on the flagstones. "Looks like he's seen a ghost." It was a phrase people threw around without thinking. Carl would never use it the same way again.

Jesse still sat on the wall, looking like an appalled Humpty Dumpty. "I thought you guys went inside."

"We did," Carl said unhelpfully.

She dropped down into the garden and crossed to Wes, moving slowly, afraid to get too close, like someone examining a dead animal on the road. "Is he okay?"

How was he supposed to know? Carl bent down to lift Wes's limp body. With Jesse's reluctant help they half dragged, half carried him into the kitchen and dropped him into a chair. His tall body folded like a carpenter's ruler onto the table.

"Is he dead?" Jesse whispered.

Carl felt his wrist for a pulse, but either Wes didn't have one, or Carl didn't know where to feel. He laid a hand on the unconscious man's back and felt it swell. "He's breathing." Then, "Do you recognize him?"

Jesse made a face. "No. It's hopeless. I'm never going to remember anything."

Carl asked her what she'd thought she was doing, climbing over the garden wall and running off on him like that.

"I thought you were right behind me," she said. "But when I hit the ground on the other side, there was nobody with me but the cat.

"I waited for you. I tried to listen through the wall. I could hear your voice, and it didn't sound like anything was wrong, but how could I know? I didn't know what to do. Climb back over the wall? And what? Save you, I guess. That would have been the brave thing to do. But just the thought of seeing Wes there, in 'my house,' "—Carl could hear the quotation marks she was putting around the words—"it made my skin crawl.

"I was afraid, I guess. Then I couldn't hear your voice anymore and I really got scared. It was the first time I'd been alone since this *thing* happened to me. Really alone. Cut off. And the only person who knows about me isn't there anymore . . . I panicked. I climbed back over and . . ."

Carl embraced her, happy to forgive her her moment of cowardice if she'd do the same for him. She hugged him quickly, then pushed away.

"Let's get out of here," she said.

Carl looked back at Wes, still sprawled on the table. "We can't just leave him here after he's seen you. He'll think he's gone crazy."

"That's a plan." But she must have agreed because she stayed in the room, searching through pieces of paper by the phone.

"What are you doing?"

"I must have an address book. Something that says where Mom is."

Carl suggested she check her bedroom and told her it was downstairs. Jesse looked a little surprised. "How do you know that?"

Carl nodded toward Wes. "He told me."

Jesse considered for a moment. "You don't think he was really my boyfriend, do you?"

Carl tried to break it to her easy. "Kind of sounded like it, hon."

She turned her head to get a better look at his profile on the table. "Definitely not. Definitely not my type."

And she was off down the stairs.

Carl bent over to recheck Wes for signs of life. Should he wake him or leave him alone? There used to be an old wive's tale, didn't there, about not waking fainting victims? Or was that sleepwalkers? He recalled that liquor was supposed to help, so he dug around till he found a bottle of tequila and downed a shot. Much better, he thought.

"Carl?"

He ran down the stairs and found her standing by a wall in her bedroom. The room was simple and stylish. A pine four-poster bed, piled high with down comforters and thick pillows. A desk under the window, a wicker chest at the foot of the bed. But she was ignoring all this and looking at a wall. A wall covered with photographs. Photographs of Jesse, or parts of Jesse. A foot here. A hand there. Jesse's nude torso suspended above the Pyramids. Jesse's stomach opening up into the lobes of an oak leaf. Jesse's eyes, reproduced ad nauseam, as stars over a night view of Burbank. Black and white images, lovingly rendered but bizarrely dissected; the effect was of a romantic edition of Gray's *Anatomy*.

"Is this me?" she asked.

What could Carl say? He knew all those parts of her so well, not just from Friday night, but from places deep in his memory and his heart. And the man who took them, Carl thought, knew those parts just as well.

Jesse stared at the pictures and rubbed the aching spot on her ribs.

"Did you hurt yourself again?" Carl asked.

She moved her hand away, annoyed. "No." She moved to the desk now (her desk, Carl reminded himself) and flipped through the Rolodex. She plucked out a card and sprinted for the stairs. He followed her so that he almost collided into her back when she stopped at the kitchen door.

Wesley was gone.

They moved into the room slowly, peering around the corner into the living room.

But his voice came from out on the patio.

"I'm sorry. God, Jessica, I'm so sorry." He was staring at Jesse, and though his eyes were blue, they looked dark and sorrowful in the sunshine.

They stood still as he approached her. "It's all right," Jesse said, though Carl could see she was far from sure that it was.

Wes stopped. "God, you *did* talk. You're looking right at me. I never thought I'd hear your voice again. I never thought . . ." He reached out and took both her hands in his. Carl could see her stiffen, trying not to flinch. But Wes didn't seem to notice. "I love you."

Then she *did* flinch, and Wes couldn't help but see it.

Tequilas all around as they sat at the kitchen table. Carl was a drink ahead of the rest, but he didn't mind.

"You don't remember me at all?" Wes asked for the fourth time.

"It's not just you," she said, as if trying to cushion the blow. "I don't remember any of this. I don't even know the cat." The cat (Wes had said his name was Patches) was purring on her lap.

"It's like a miracle," he muttered to himself. "Where have you been?"

"I don't know."

"Were you just wandering all this time?"

"I don't know." Carl could hear the impatience she was trying to disguise in her voice.

"Don't be mad," Wes said. "This is a lot to get used to." So he can read her moods too, Carl thought. He knows her well.

Wes shook his head, as if hoping to juggle the pieces in place. "It's funny to see you smoking."

She stubbed out her cigarette on a saucer. "I don't remember quitting either."

"It's like some kind of fairy tale. You come back to me. You're healed, you're alive. But you don't know who the hell I am." Then a thought struck him, and he turned to Carl. "You said you found her *Friday* night. What have you been doing with her? Why didn't you call somebody right away?"

Jesse spoke up quickly. "We didn't know who to call. He didn't know where I lived."

Carl was surprised to hear Jesse being that cautious, but he didn't see any need to correct her.

When Wes spoke next he looked at Jesse, ignoring Carl completely. "Look, there's an awful lot I have to fill you in on." He pulled his chair closer to her. "And I'd really like to talk to you alone."

Jesse held the cat up in her arms, as if to block his way, a shocked laugh on her lips. "No, no. Look, I don't know what you're going to tell me, but if . . . if you're going to say there was something going on between us, well, I don't know, I just don't know. And even if it's true, I don't know. I'm not, you gotta understand, I'm *not that person.* Not yet. I don't think I ever will be. Besides . . . Carl and I are kind of together now."

Wes looked stunned. He wheeled on Carl in a burst of anger. "What the hell are you doing? If you've been taking advantage of her condition—"

"I have not!" Carl said indignantly, all the time thinking that he had, he had, what else could he call it?

"Boys!" Jesse was on her feet now and the cat was running for a place to hide. "There isn't time for this shit! We have more important things to worry about."

Wes looked down at the floor like a scolded schoolboy. And Carl only saw this out of the corner of his eye because he was looking at the floor too.

"Funny," Wes said, "you never used to swear."

"Oh, I cleaned up my act. Dad must have been happy." She lit another cigarette and sat back down. "Now let's get down to it. Tell me how I died."

Wes started with the aftermath of the car accident, going into detail in his description of her seizure. All those symptoms Carl had heard about from Martin. Carl wanted to stop him, to tell him he didn't have to go through it all again, but the look of fascination in Jesse's eyes kept him silent. She needs to hear this, Carl thought.

"Sometimes I'd talk to you and think, my God, you're fine, you're taking it all in, everything I'm saying. But nothing would ever come *out*. And I never knew if you were conscious of everything around you, just unable to respond, or if you didn't even know I was there. Were you? Do you remember any of that?"

"No," Jesse said, with a new empathy in her tone.

"And it should have been *me* taking care of you. Instead, you had to depend on *him*. On Martin. A man with no imagination. No faith. He just believed whatever the doctors told him. So they filled you up with drugs and stuck you in their damn tubes to make little colored maps of your brain. They treated you like an *object,* a *test dummy,* Christ's sake, without anybody thinking how scared you must be.

"I knew they'd never reach you that way. They just tortured you and drained Martin of every cent you two made with his stupid chocolate. I told him just to let you rest, but he wouldn't listen to me . . ."

She poured him another tequila. Discomfort was vying with compassion all over her face, and Carl guessed this was the only gesture she felt safe making. "So, uh, stupid question, but . . ." She was stammering, like someone asking a doctor to tell them the worst. "There was . . . something between us?"

Wes just looked at her. "You wouldn't think somebody could forget that. Yes. We were in love."

She looked at him now, as if she was trying to see something, the way you look at an actor someone tells you is attractive but you just don't see it. "And did we . . . were we . . ."

"Were we lovers? We fought it for a long time. But yes, we made love. Once. One beautiful time."

She kept her poker face until he said "beautiful." Then she had to glance away.

"And we were going to do the right thing," Wes went on. "We decided that day. You were going to go home to Martin and confess. You were going to divorce him and start over with me."

"But I didn't?"

He blinked twice. "You had a car accident on the way home."

That reached her. A momentary flinch and then she tried to recover. "Wow. That's rough." Carl could read the discomfort all over her. It was as if a stranger were unloading all his personal tragedies on her lap and she didn't know how to respond. But he wasn't a stranger, and the tragedy was hers.

He agreed that it was rough.

"You blame yourself, don't you?" she asked.

"Why not? I keep thinking you must have been distracted, rehearsing what you were going to say to Martin. If you'd been thinking clearly when that car stopped in front of you . . ."

Jesse's expression softened as she saw the pain in his eyes. "I'm sorry."

"Why should you be?"

"I don't know. I feel like I've put you through something . . . and I shouldn't have."

Wes smiled weakly. He likes her pity, Carl thought. At least it's something she's feeling for him.

"Do you want to hear about the car wreck?"

"Why not?"

"It happened on the Colorado Street Bridge."

Jesse looked a little surprised. "I figured they would have torn that down by now."

"They were going to. You were one of the leading figures in the fight to save it. Contributed a lot of money to the cause. It was quite a victory . . . You used to drive over it whenever you had an excuse. You loved the curve of the span—those glowing glass street lamps. You'd always ignore the practical routes across the arroyo. From my house to your house. You'd always take your bridge.

"If you'd been on the freeway that day, when that car stopped in front of you, maybe things would have been different. Maybe you'd have had room to maneuver, a shoulder to swerve on to. But no. You were on your two-lane architectural white elephant, and that's how it repaid your loyalty. By destroying your mind.

"I've been taking pictures of it lately. I manipulate them in the darkroom, making little improvements. 'The Colorado Street Bridge on Fire.' 'The Colorado Street Bridge after the Big Earthquake.' 'The Colorado Street Bridge Being Blown up by Terrorists.' " His quick smile again, and then a tiny laugh.

She shivered a little and tried to bring him back to the story. "Did Martin know what was going on between us?"

"He found out. At the worst possible time, of course. Right after the car accident. There was . . . evidence. A letter you'd written. Sort of a draft of what you were going to say to him . . .

"Of course, that ruined things between us. We'd never been close as brothers, but we'd at least trusted each other. That ended that. The worst thing was that anything I said about you, any advice I tried to give about your treatment, was all poisoned. I was lucky he even let me see you. Thank God he did, though. I was the only one who didn't *scare* you. You were *happier* with me than with Martin and his doctors. I loved you and you knew that."

Jesse looked away. Carl thought, She may have known it then, but she doesn't know it now.

"What about the boat?" Carl asked. "What happened?"

"The boat," Wes repeated. He sipped the amber liquid as if to brace himself and went on. "Well, the trip was my brilliant idea. The boat was the first thing you bought with the money from his shops. Your first 'rich person' luxury. You called it the *Cacao;* kind of a chocolate in-joke. Martin didn't sail, but you taught him, and he was good at it. I never learned. I get sick.

"But you loved it so much, I thought it might still mean

something to you. Just the feeling of being on the water. I
thought that might reach you in some deep place . . ."

He drew himself up with a breath and went on. "You
kept the boat moored in Ventura, so we went out toward the
Channel Islands. Beautiful day, not a cloud in sight, good
breeze.

"And you sat there, face red from the wind, spray in your
hair. Happy? I don't know. Martin said I was fooling myself
to even use words like that with you. But, anyway, you'd
always *been* happy in this place, so maybe some part of you
might have recognized it as a happy thing.

"The wind came up just as we were about to head in. The
Santa Ana winds whip down the flatlands through Oxnard
and tear out into the harbor. The islands catch them like a
funnel and focus them, so it's like a wind tunnel out there.
All the weather in the Southwest gets sucked through that
spot, like the drain in a bathtub.

"Choppy water. Black clouds. Hot, stinging winds. We
couldn't make any headway. We had to tack—is that the
right term?—out around Anacapa, trying to find a way in.

"I'm a piss-poor sailor, and I didn't even know enough to
vomit out of the wind, but Martin kept telling me to do
things and he kept doing things. Hours never passed so
slowly in my life. It was way after dark, and we were still
heading out to sea."

"How was Jesse?" Carl asked.

"Well, you know, rough water never bothered you." Wes
smiled at her, answering Carl's question, but talking only to
her. "You just sat there, serene, in your element." Carl
blinked back emotion, remembering that he'd also thought
of water as her element.

"Finally we made it outside the islands so we were able
to rest for a minute. I mean, the sea was still choppy as hell,
but at least I wasn't dry-heaving my lungs out and it didn't

feel quite as much like the boat was going to flip over at the next swell. So we had a moment to think . . . and that's what did us in. Isn't it always?"

A small, bitter smile, and then Wes stopped talking. Carl and Jesse waited, as if they were both afraid to nudge him on. Finally, he sighed and resumed his story.

"Martin . . . he'd never really talked about what had happened between us. Made a great show of putting it behind him, of forgiving and forgetting. As if it was some momentary weakness on our part and we must just pretend it never happened.

"But for me . . . well, it wasn't over. You'd chosen me. It didn't matter what condition you were in, we were still soul mates. So I still looked after you. It was just natural, just simply right that I would go to you on the boat and wrap the blanket tighter around you and wipe the spray from your face. But I guess there was something in my touch . . . something Martin saw. Some easy affection that touched a nerve.

"He lashed out at me. Everything came out. Things he'd been holding in for months, for years. For a lifetime. Bitter, ugly, cutting things.

"He had every right, of course, but I still fought back. Defending you. Blaming him. Saying things I could never take back. Both of us standing on that rocking deck, throwing poison at each other, like that would help somehow.

"And he hit me. He doesn't look like a violent man, but he's always had that side to him." Carl recalled the look of violence in Martin's eyes and the instinctive fear he'd felt when it was directed at him.

"Not that he's a street fighter or anything," Wes went on. "Just that sometimes the anger gets too much for him, and it's the only way he can let it out. Clumsy, awkward punches. No skill, but he's so damned big, he doesn't need it. That huge ham fist of his hit me in the face, with all his weight behind it. My neck snapped back, and there was this stinging pain in my nose."

His eyes were closed now; he might as well have been alone and reliving it all in his memory. How many times has he done just that? Carl wondered. "I lost my footing and fell against you. There was blood pouring out of my nose and my lip. I knocked you against the rail. The boat rocked the other way and I fell back, down onto the deck, blood and vomit and tears just flowing out of me, like everything inside my body was trying to get out. To go someplace else."

"I don't know how long I lay there. It couldn't have been long. Not minutes. Just seconds, I think. But I don't really know. All I know is, when I looked up . . ."—he opened his eyes and stared at her—"you were gone."

"Gone?" she asked.

"What happened?" Carl demanded.

Wes set his drink on the coffee table. "What Martin told me happened. When I fell against her, I knocked her into the sea. Into the waves." He looked at her again, as if he'd forgotten she was there. "So it was my fault again."

"You couldn't save her? Didn't you look for her?" Carl asked.

Wes squirmed in his chair. "You couldn't see anything in that water. It was so dark and choppy. I tried to radio for help, but I didn't know how to work it. I went to ask Martin and . . . I realized he was taking us away. Leaving you.

"I asked him what the hell he was doing, but he didn't say anything, didn't even look at me. I tried to stop him, but he shoved me away. I went back to the radio, but he came up behind me and ripped the wires out. He said it was better this way, didn't I see that? He was protecting me. And it was better for Jessica too. To have an end to it all.

"And he kept taking us away. Well, what the hell could *I* do? I couldn't jump in. I couldn't swim in that water. I couldn't stab him or strangle him or throw him overboard or any of the million other things I wanted to do because it wouldn't have done any good. I couldn't sail the damn boat.

"So I just sat on the deck and watched him, hour after hour, going God knows where. I think he wanted to sail off the edge of the world.

"We hit a rock sometime in the middle of the night. We *should* have drowned, I'm sure that was the idea, but something happens when the water starts coming at you. Something animal takes over and you want to survive. We got into the inflatable dinghy and Martin sent up a flare.

"No one should have found us, but, of course, *that's* when good luck starts kicking in. When you don't want it anymore. The Coast Guard picked us up. And they searched for her, but they weren't searching in the right place, were they? They thought she'd gone in where the boat sank, so they were miles and hours away from the right place."

"Why didn't you tell them that?"

He came to his feet. "What difference would it have made? It was too late for her. Why ruin my brother's life too? I just kept my mouth shut and let him tell his story. He still had hope that there was life at the other end of all this. Well, his hope was the only positive thing I could see in the world right then, so I let him have it."

Wes leaned against the wall and looked at Jesse, drained and exhausted.

Carl leaned forward. "There was another boat out there on the water, wasn't there?"

"I saw a light on the horizon. But it was too far away."

"I don't think it was, Wes," Jesse said.

Wes turned to look at her. "Somebody saved you," he said.

"I guess."

He didn't say anything, but what was on his mind was obvious to all of them. The somebody hadn't been him. "I'm so sorry," was all he said.

"Don't be," she said. There was compassion in her voice, but no affection. If Carl could hear the lack of it, how must that cut at Wesley? "You shouldn't blame yourself."

He looked at her, helpless, hopeless. "I never thought I'd have to explain all this to you. It's like Judgment Day."

Carl spoke up. "I understand why you didn't say anything then, Wes." Wes looked at him idly, as if he couldn't care less what Carl understood. "But it's different now. She's here. So it will make a difference now. You *can* accomplish something. You can protect her."

"How?"

"You can tell the truth."

"What truth?"

"That Martin threw me off the boat," Jesse said.

Wes swallowed, and Carl could hear the click as he ground his jaw. Then a remarkable thing happened. Carl saw the man's face relax completely, the tight, aged-paper skin seemed to loosen and fill out, the lines around the eyes smoothed themselves, years seemed to fly from him with one breath, and there was Stan Laurel at peace.

"Is that what happened?" he said.

"You know it is."

Slowly, he nodded. "Yes. I guess I always knew. But I thought it was just something I was telling myself. So I didn't have to believe it was my fault."

"No," she said. "Martin just made you think it was your fault. So you'd protect *him*."

He smiled his sad grin. "That sounds right." Wes sat forward, as if he was about to go into action. But the move never finished. He just stopped, perched on the edge of his seat. "God, I just had a scary thought. Suppose you'd gone to see Martin first instead of me? God knows what he would have done."

An awkward pause followed that. Carl filled him in on the visit to San Marino, the break-in at Carl's house, and their subsequent suspicions that Martin was following them.

"That's not good," Wes said. "That's not good at all."

"Do you think he'd follow us?" Jesse asked.

"He's a very thorough man, my brother. If he really did what you say he did, he wouldn't want to leave things unfinished." Wes looked at the two of them through the clouds of smoke from their freshly lit cigarettes. "I wish I smoked."

"So what do we do?" Carl asked.

"First we go see Mom," Jesse said.

The two men were nonplussed by this sudden, childlike demand.

"No," Wes said. "If Martin is looking for you, that's the first place he'll go. Besides, she won't be any help. She's not well."

Jesse blanched at this. "What's wrong with her?"

"Just . . . she's old."

"He's right," Carl said. "We should think this through before we start doing anything."

"You can think all you want. I want to let my mother know I'm alive."

"Wait, wait," Wes said. "We have to be careful. We can't reveal you until we're ready. I mean, whatever we believe, I still didn't see Martin do anything. And you . . . you have to *remember.*"

"All right," Jesse said, suddenly agreeable. "But let's fig-ure it out fast. Are you guys hungry? I'm going to make some lunch."

She got up and started to bustle about the kitchen. Wes offered to help her, but she brushed him off, irritated, and told him to go into the living room and put on some music, saying it was too damned quiet in here. He went, obediently.

"You don't usually give in this easy," Carl said.

"I'm not giving in, I'm making lunch. Go keep an eye on that guy," she said, nodding toward the living room.

"You don't like him, do you?"

She pondered this. "Maybe it's just that I don't like him nearly as much as he thinks I should."

Carl went in to join Wes, who was slipping a cassette into the stereo. "Making sandwiches," Wes said. "She isn't usually so domestic."

Carl shrugged. "She's younger now."

Howling blues blared from the speakers.

"I like that," Jesse called from the kitchen. "Who is it?"

"Marcia Ball, one of your favorites."

"Good for me," she said.

But then the music went all garbled and sour—the cassette was eaten by the machine. Wes pulled it out; black tape trailed from it like jellyfish tentacles. "Disemboweled another one," he said. "Good music always dies young."

He crossed to the turntable (a real old turntable, with a needle and everything) and put on an old black vinyl Eagles record. He moved the arm in position and dropped it—there was that so familiar yet forgotten explosion, the "pow" of the needle hitting the vinyl. Then the traveling noises, the hisses and pops and crackles as the needle made its way to the first groove. So much music, and the record hadn't even started yet.

Jesse walked into the room and set a couple of beers on the coffee table. "How come I don't have one of those CB things?"

Wes looked amused; it was the first time her loss of memory had struck him as funny. "Compact discs? You don't believe in them. They don't get scratches. You can't affect them, you used to say. They don't change when you listen to them. There's no relationship there."

"Boy, I sound pretty pretentious," she said, heading back into the kitchen.

"Oh, I agreed with you," he called after her. "I remember when my first girlfriend left me, back in high school, and I just listened to that Beatles song "For No One." I just listened to it over and over again. Played it to death, as they say. But you really could do that. That song deteriorated, it wasted away, the grooves wore right down. It didn't just communicate Paul McCartney's pain, it felt my pain. It got so you had to put a quarter on the arm just to make it play. If I were to put it on for you now, you could still hear the heartache. But the CD? You just hear four guys in a recording studio somewhere." He paused for a moment. "I guess that *does* sound pretentious, doesn't it? . . . Doesn't it?"

But there was no answer from the kitchen, and Carl suddenly realized why Jesse had been so agreeable.

He went to the kitchen, and of course there was no one there. The cat was looking out the back door window, missing her already.

Carl sprinted out onto the porch and he just had time to call himself an idiot before he saw his Jeep drive past the house and disappear down the road.

14

Carl slammed the door and called himself an idiot again, just in case he'd missed it the first time.

"Where is she?" Wes asked, with real fear in his voice.

"Where do you think? She went to see her mother."

Wes used one of the words he said Jesse didn't use, and Carl told him to find his car keys. They were going after her.

Unfortunately, Wes was no better at keeping track of his keys than Carl was, and it took them several precious minutes to spot them on the kitchen counter. They were sprinting to the door when Carl heard footsteps on the porch. She changed her mind, he thought. She's not so stubborn after all, he thought.

He thought that until he saw the shape of the silhouette in the diamond-paned window in the front door. That wasn't Jesse. That was a big man. A Martin-sized man.

Carl changed his stride just enough to throw himself against the wall next to the door so the silhouette couldn't see him.

The bell rang deafeningly loud next to Carl's ear. Wes grabbed his arm and pulled him into the kitchen.

"Wes?" the man on the porch said. Carl had no doubt now. He'd recognize Martin's phlegmy voice anywhere.

"What's he doing here?" Carl whispered as they fled into the kitchen.

"I don't know. Did he follow you?"

"I don't know. I don't think so."

"Well, I'll keep him here." Wes handed Carl the keys to a Ford Explorer. "You get Jessica and bring her back."

"Where am I going?"

"St. Paul's in San Rafael."

"What if Martin's still here when we get back? How will I know if it's safe?"

"I'll give you a signal."

Wes was gone, hurrying to the front door, before he told Carl what the signal might be.

Hell with it. Carl moved to the door, but it was locked. He reached for the key. It wasn't there. Looking through the window, he saw it lying outside on the flagstones. Cute, he thought. She was trying to slow him up.

He stood there, listening to the voices in the living room.

"What are you doing here?" That was Wes.

"I should be asking *you* that." That was Martin. "You've gotta stop hiding up here."

"She said I could use this place whenever I wanted."

"Oh, Christ, let's drop this. We have to talk."

Carl very much wanted to hear them talk, but unfortunately they were walking his way.

He darted down the stairs just as he glimpsed Martin, white shirt dark with sweat, stalking into the kitchen. Moving as quietly as he could, Carl crept down into Jesse's room.

Here the voices were too muffled for any effective eavesdropping, but the aphid-spotting window was waiting for him, right above her desk. Easy enough to slip out and be gone.

He moved some stuff off the desk to make room for the climb; her phone, her Rolodex, an IBM ThinkPad. He stopped, looking at the computer for a moment, listening to the rumble of voices, still safely above him. Going through personal computers was a new bad habit; a social vice, rather like going through the host's medicine cabinet at a party. One found out so many interesting things.

He turned the computer on and found WordPerfect 5.1 on the opening menu: a friendly old word processing program for beginners. The documents had names like MOMLET, TAXES, BOBFORM—and, about halfway down the list, JOURNAL. He opened that one and a screen full of single-spaced writing appeared.

FEBRUARY 16, 1994. Well, here we go again. Another in a long series of journals I never seem to keep. Maybe this new toy will help me.

Carl's heart beat faster. How long did she keep this journal going? He hit GO TO PAGE 200 and read from the top of the screen:

situation with Wesley continues to break my heart. Jesus, I'm actually afraid to even be writing about it here. What if Martin found out? What would he do?

"Son of a bitch!"

He jerked away from the screen. That had been Wes's voice. He heard a chair scrape across the floor above; garbled voices raised in anger.

Carl opened a drawer, pulled out a disc, slipped it into the A drive, and copied the file.

"Don't walk away from me!" That was Martin now, furious. And there were footsteps on the stairs.

The machine whirred on.

"If you have something to tell me, tell me!" Martin's voice was closer now; halfway down the stairs.

Don't tell him, Carl prayed to himself, don't tell him. The machine went quiet. Carl popped out the disc, leaped onto the desk, and slipped out the window into a maze of rose thorns.

He dragged himself through them, praying, as they stabbed his fingers, that a large hand wouldn't grab the cuff of his pants before he could get away.

Clear from the bush, he rolled onto the flagstones, then sprinted to the wall and vaulted over it, just as Jesse had done. He raced through the neighbor's yard and around to the driveway, where the Explorer was waiting.

He started the car and backed out, praying that Martin couldn't hear it from the basement. He was doing a lot of praying lately, and it seemed to be working. So far, so good. Except that he had no idea where San Rafael was.

Gas station attendants don't give directions much anymore, and they sure as hell don't know where the local retirement communities are located. Still, Carl found one who was at least willing to slip him the phone book through the metal drawer in his bulletproof glass cage, and with that Carl was able to find St. Paul's Hospital and Sanitarium. Amazing things, phone books.

Carl's idea of nursing homes was not a pretty one. Too many *60 Minutes* exposés on elderly abuse and homicidal male nurses had colored his thinking, as had one visit with his father to a dingy, overgrown trailer park in La Jolla. But St. Paul's was nothing like that. Green rolling hills with little New England cottages sprinkled on them, it looked like the college campus of Carl's dreams. It made him want to grow old fast, so he could move in.

He was greeted in the main building (a Cape Cod far from Cape Cod) by a receptionist who looked like she was having a very puzzling day.

"Jessica Ackerman? Yes, she *is* here, but . . ."

"Yes?"

"Well, apparently there was some confusion, though I don't quite see . . . I mean, I've spoken to her husband several times over the past few months and . . . well, we were of the understanding that . . . that is to say . . ."

"That Mrs. Ackerman was dead?"

"Yes," the receptionist said with a few rapid blinks of her gray eyes. "It's in our records."

"Then you'll have to change them."

"Oh, yes, but . . ."

"I mean, you *did* see her today."

"Yes."

"And it *was* her."

"Yes."

"So she's not."

"Not?"

"Dead."

"No. Not, but . . ."

"So there must have been some mix-up," Carl said, smiling all the while.

"Yes. A mix-up. But how?"

"You know," he shrugged. "These things happen."

As if they ever did.

Mrs. Holland's cottage was one of the very nicest, on top of the hill with the most pastoral view.

The puzzled receptionist left him there and hurried off. Carl hadn't wanted to be announced, and she'd shown no desire to see Jesse again.

Carl stepped into the cottage and found a bland room decorated like a Holiday Inn. No one there. He crossed through the parlor to the patio.

There, sitting at a little glass table, was Jesse's mother. Or rather, a shrunken, balding, bleached version of Jesse's mother. Still, she seemed herself. Friendlier, actually, than Carl remembered. She smiled at him happily. "Oh! I have company!"

Carl smiled back, but before he could answer, Jesse stepped in from the bathroom. The corners of her eyes were red from crying.

Mrs. Holland looked happier than before. "Jesse! Why didn't you tell me you were coming?!"

Jesse sighed. "I've been here, Mom."

"You could still call. Is this a friend of yours?" She nodded to Carl, still smiling.

"It's Carl Rooney, Mom. Don't you remember him?"

Jesse's mother stared at him in polite confusion. "Rooney . . . Didn't your son used to date my Jesse?"

Carl felt a weight growing in his heart. Alzheimer's. Even his father had been spared that.

"Yes," he said. Mrs. Holland poured them all some cold tea, and they drank it.

Afterward, he drove Jesse back to Oakland in his Jeep. Let Wesley pick up the Explorer on his own time; Carl didn't think Jesse wanted to be alone.

"I know it was stupid to go," she said. "I know it gave me away. I know they've probably already called Martin and told him I was there. But I had to see my mother. That's more important than all this other shit, don't you see that?"

Carl said he saw that.

By the time they'd reached the Richmond–San Rafael Bridge, she'd told him the whole story.

•   •   •

The bureaucratic confusion her appearance at St. Paul's occasioned might have been amusing in another context. It had taken them quite some time to believe their eyes rather than their paperwork and let Jesse see her mother.

They hadn't told Jesse what was wrong with her mother. Of course, they thought she'd know. But when she'd asked if they'd told Mrs. Holland her daughter was dead, the lady at reception had just shrugged and said they'd *told* her, as if that didn't make any difference. That's when Jesse started to guess.

Her mother's cottage was clean and comfortable but with no trace of her own personality, and Jesse wondered how she could have dumped her mother here, away from her family, alone? Again she wondered what kind of woman she'd become.

Her mother was out on the patio, sitting at that little table sipping tea from a coffee mug. This couldn't be her, Jesse thought, couldn't be Mom. Hair gray and sparse on a shiny pink scalp; eyes wide and staring, set into deep, black circles; hands frail and laced with ropey veins. Mom was small, yes, but not this small. Circles might appear under her eyes after a sleepless night, but never these scooped-out, pimply grooves. And her hands—Jesse remembered the strength of those hands as they kneaded bread, as they hauled her baby brother everywhere for the first year of his life, as they steered the family station wagon on summer vacations to the Grand Canyon and all points east. These hands were having trouble holding that mug steady. And would Mom ever drink tea out of a coffee mug, anyway?

If this reminded her of anyone, Jesse said, it was of her grandmother, on those frightening family visits to Chicago. Jesse remembered, at four or five years old, dreading those trips to that cold, alien, urban place. Dreading the thought of being in the same room with the old woman, so cold and pale, so angry and unpleasant, so accusatory. Dreading her mother's efforts to care for Nana and the always vicious rebuffs they engendered. Dreading the long, tense dinners, with Mom trying to make conversation and Nana swearing, using words little five-year-old Jesse had never heard, words that seventeen-year-old Jesse would become quite proficient with, words that (according to Wes) thirty-four-year-old Jessica would reject—words that made her mother stammer and fall silent. Dreading those silences, with nothing breaking them but Nana's grotesque slurping as she gummed and spit and slobbered her food in a way that little Jesse found riveting and repulsive at the same time. Dreading Nana's inevitable shrieking outburst about how no one took care of her and no one visited her and why didn't *Louise* ever come by, *Louise* didn't love her, *Louise* was an ungrateful little cunt, and her mother trying to calm her, saying, "I'm Louise, I'm here, it's me, I love you, Mommy," and Nana never hearing, never knowing, never caring. Dreading most of all the drives home, with Mom crying, the only times Jesse remembered her mother crying, saying how horrible it was to have someone you love turn into someone completely different.

Now here was her mother, slobbering, just a little, as she sipped her tea. Jesse sat down next to her and just looked at her. As she looked, her eyes became slightly accustomed to the changes; she saw her mother's face beneath them, and she breathed a little easier.

Her mother looked up and saw her. In a gesture Jesse remembered across seventeen years of breakfast tables, her mother adjusted the collar of her housecoat and patted her hair. "Jesse," she said, "nobody told me you were coming."

Jesse started to cry.

Her mother asked if she was all right—if she'd been eating enough. Jesse told her she'd put on about fifteen pounds and then her mother asked if she'd been eating too much. Jesse laughed at that. She seemed no crazier than the average mother.

Her mother poured watery tea from the pot into another mug and apologized for the lack of proper teacups. Jesse said that was all right and her mother smiled back and said the mugs keep the heat in better anyway.

How totally practical, Jesse thought, admiring her mother's common sense and relieved to see that things weren't as bad as she'd feared. Now, looking around the cottage, it all looked quite cozy and homey. Maybe her mother liked it here.

"Nice place," Jesse said.

Her mother looked around, curious. "Yes," she agreed, then looked to Jesse, "do you like it here?"

Jesse hesitated. "It seems nice."

"Well, I'm sure you'll make something nice out of it. Though I don't know why you insist on moving out when you have a perfectly nice room at home."

Jesse felt her throat go a little dry. "Mom, I'm not living here. You are."

Her mother looked up, surprised at that, but not too surprised. She laughed, kind of embarrassed, and said, "Is that right? I get confused sometimes. That's what your father says, anyway, although half the time I think it's him."

Jesse searched for something to say. "How's Nicky, Mama?"

"Oh, he has a cold. Had to keep him home from school. And Dr. John wouldn't give him anything 'cause he said it was viral, but I always say, 'Give the boy something. He *likes* to take medicine.' That's one thing about your brother, never a problem swallowing a pill. Not like you, who'd spit up everything."

"What did Dad say?"

Her gray lips vibrated in a sarcastic snort. "You know your father. 'Nobody ever died of a cold,' he says. But the child's so *uncomfortable*. I hate to see that."

Jesse reached out to touch her mother's hand on the mug. They'd never been given to physical displays of affection in her family, so her mother looked up in surprise.

"Is something wrong?" her mother asked.

"Dad passed away, Mom."

She looked away from Jesse's face, thinking, as if this news sounded vaguely familiar. Then she nodded. "I know, dear, it's so sad." She sipped her tea, very neatly, then looked back at Jesse. "But he should be home soon."

Jesse knocked her cup over, spilling the tepid tea. Her mother sopped it up with a paper napkin. "You and liquids. Always a disaster waiting to happen."

Jesse went to get a towel. It took a good deal of searching to find a dishrag in the ill-stocked kitchen. By the time she made it back, her mother had blotted up the spill with the soggy, shredded napkin. Jesse sat down and poured herself some more tea.

Her mother looked up at her and once again adjusted her hair and collar. "Jesse, nobody told me you were coming."

Jesse smiled, nervously, "I wanted to surprise you."

"Have you been eating?"

"We just said all this, Mom. Don't you remember, we've been talking."

Once again the nervous laugh. But now Jesse could see the terror it was hiding. "Oh, that's right. Getting old, I guess. That's what your father says. Did he say when he'd be back?"

And yet she knew who the president was, when Jesse asked her. "That Bubba person. Clinton, the draft dodger. What's this country coming to?" Clinton, Jesse gathered, had evaded the draft like everybody else who could during the Vietnam War. But according to her mother, Vietnam was still going on. How, Jesse asked, could Clinton dodge the draft if he was president? "Well, that's why he wanted to be president, I guess," her mother reasoned, "for the deferment." But what about Nixon, Jesse asked. Wasn't he president during Vietnam? There couldn't be *two* presidents. Her mother agreed that it *was* odd, but "somehow it just worked out that way."

Jesse went to brew a fresh pot of tea and when she came back her mother looked up at her, once again, in pleasant surprise and arranged herself. "I didn't know you were coming, honey, I'm not even dressed."

Jesse remembered a science fiction story by Pierre Boulle she'd read once. A man found a magic stopwatch. When he pressed the right button, he could go back and live the last minute over again. Well, of course, he was a bad man and somehow he used this watch to rob banks and take advantage of women, always escaping in his magic minute. But in the end, God knew how, he was thrown out of an airplane. And by the time he'd pulled the watch out of his pocket more than a minute had passed. So all he could do was relive a minute of falling, over and over again, never making it back to the plane, never having the courage to end it and let himself hit the ground.

And Jesse thought, Well, there's Mom. Trapped in her magic minute. Always waiting for Dad to come back; for someone to tell her where she is and why she is here.

Jesse set the pot down on the table a little too hard, and a bit of tea sloshed out. "You and liquids," her mother sighed.

Hurrying around the table, Jesse knelt next to her mother and embraced her. Her mother sat upright, surprised and uncomfortable. "Are you all right, dear?" Jesse felt a claw-like hand press itself against her forehead, checking for a fever.

"I got married, Mommy."

Her mother sighed. "That's right. Of course. I wish I could have been there."

"You were there, Mom. I saw you in a picture. But I don't remember it, Mom. And I don't remember Dad dying, or Nicky growing up, or anything."

Suddenly, her mother seized her tightly and held her. "Oh, dear," the old woman said, and it wasn't a polite expression of affection or an embarrassed cover-up of emotion. It was something true and honest from deep within her that said, My God, you too?

The women held each other tight. But after a moment her mother relaxed her hold and began stroking Jesse's hair, and murmuring, "It'll be all right, dear," and Jesse knew that she'd already forgotten what they were talking about. But Jesse went on, letting her mother hold her and touch her hair, thinking, We're both the man with the watch, we're both falling out of that airplane. The only difference is I'm going to hit bottom, and she never will.

They drove on in silence for a while, Jesse with tears streaming down her face, racked from reliving the scene, Carl not knowing what to say, looking around the car for a Kleenex or a napkin or something. She ended up wiping her eyes on the tail of her shirt.

On the AM radio a girl was singing about going down on someone in a theater, but Jesse didn't even comment. She must have been getting used to that sort of thing by now.

She lit a cigarette. As she watched the glowing ember at the tip of the third one, she started toting up a list. "All right. Let's see what we've found out about me. Jessica doesn't smoke. I smoke. Jessica doesn't swear. I swear. Jessica listens to the blues. I think the blues sounds like a bunch of sick dogs. Jessica cheats on her husband and dumps her mother in a sanitarium. I don't think I like Jessica very much."

She blew a cloud of smoke and turned to Carl with sudden resolve. "Let's not go back. I mean it. I don't want Jessica Ackerman's life. I don't like anything about it. My husband wants me dead. Let's leave it that way. Let's go and start over somewhere new. You and me."

"All right." Carl couldn't believe what he was saying. No, he thought, he could believe it; what he couldn't believe was how easy it was. How easy it was to give up this life he'd built. Why not? "Success" had brought him money, yes, but also loneliness and disappointment. Kit had been wrong to call this a distraction. What it was was an escape. And he was going to take it.

They were driving up the hill to the Oakland house, and Carl had an irritating thought. "But we have to tell Wes."

"No, I don't want to."

"It's only fair. We can't just leave him like this. You meant so much to him. And he—"

"He didn't mean anything to me. Not to *me*. All that stuff, it didn't happen to *me*. Why pretend it's a part of my life when I don't even remember it?"

"Look, it'll be quick. We're almost there."

"What if Martin's still there? It isn't safe."

"He said he'd give me a signal."

As they turned the corner, they could see her house. And the black smoke billowing from the roof and the licks of flame darting from the basement windows.

It was a hell of a signal.

15

Brakes screamed as Carl's Jeep fishtailed to a stop in front of the burning house. The phone was in his hand before he even thought about picking it up. He'd just dialed 911 when Jesse hollered, "He's still in there."

No time for thought. Carl handed her the phone, told her to stay in the car, and leaped out, running all the way to the porch before her next sentence really registered. "The poor thing's so scared!" Odd turn of phrase, he thought, until he saw the yowling cat in the living room window.

Well, sometimes it was better not to stop and think. He grabbed a stone from the walkway. He wasn't sure how the flames inside might react to the sudden rush of air from a broken window. Would they come rushing out, incinerating him and the cat?

Only one way to find out. He threw the stone and saw the cat leap back from the window, hissing in outrage. Picking through the shattered glass, he opened the casement window and peered in.

Smoke but no fire. The cat was arching his back by the

sofa. Memories of news bulletins about some poor idiot who died in the Malibu fires going back to get his dog went through Carl's mind as he glanced back at the Jeep, then climbed through the window. Maybe that poor sap hadn't been an idiot after all. Maybe he was trying to impress a girl. Or was there a difference?

Calling "Here, kitty, here, kitty, kitty," and holding his breath at the same time, Carl walked hunched over, trying to get close enough to pounce. But he moved too soon, and the cat dashed off toward the kitchen.

Moving after it, he felt the rush of heat from the kitchen. Every instinct told him it was now or never; if the damned cat went in there, he'd just wish it luck in the rest of its lives. He dived forward, fully extended, and grabbed the cat's back with his outstretched hands as he belly-flopped onto the floor. He pulled his hands in, dragging the unwilling animal back from the brink of the inferno.

Terrified, the cat screeched and howled, ripping at his arms as he hauled it into his chest, trying to keep the squirming body still. His eyes were shut as he lay there, wrestling with the frenzied mass of fur and fangs and claws. A new blast of heat shocked him and he opened his eyes.

He could see into the kitchen now. But it wasn't a kitchen anymore. It was the inside of a wood stove. A world of flame. The heat dried all the moisture from his eyes. The air was too hot to breathe. Heat seemed to penetrate the skin of his face, to flay it away. At least he hoped it only *seemed* to.

And the noise was startling. Appalling. It had never occurred to Carl how *loud* a fire would be. The roaring and popping and cracking of all those things in there being consumed and transformed was deafening. But one sound cut through them all.

"Jesse?"

Wes's voice. From within the flames.

"Is that you?"

A crash then. Things being knocked over and exploding with billows of smoke.

Carl was on his knees now, still crushing the wriggling cat to his chest. There was Wes, struggling to make it through the kitchen, his path blocked by the flames. Even through the warped air, Carl could see that his face was bruised and beaten, his eye swollen, his nose and lips covered with blood. Wes stood still, just staring at him as if he couldn't believe all this.

Run to him, Carl thought. Drop the cat and run to him, slam him through the glass doors and out into the backyard. Out into the cool air and no fire.

Carl opened his mouth to yell that he was coming and felt his tongue and throat parch as the heat flooded in. Before he was able to make a sound, the ceiling fell on him.

A sudden cascade of weight and heat, of plaster and smoke, of dust and flames rained down on him.

And the cat got away.

Most hospitals don't call them ERs anymore. They call them EDs, Emergency Departments. That's just one of the things that damned TV show got wrong, Carl thought. No doubt it was mistakes like that that kept the program from being a hit, he told himself with a wheezy, smoky laugh.

The ED in Oakland was an efficient place. The doctors and interns or whatever they were bustled about in a professional panic, giving their patient all the benefits of their expert skill.

Carl could hear this quite clearly as he lay in a corner, forgotten on a gurney. He didn't know who that lucky patient was, but Carl guessed he was the same guy who always pushed his grocery cart up just as a cashier was opening a new line. Some bastards have all the luck, Carl thought, as he heard them call out for more plasma.

He lay there for some minutes, listening to the improbable medical jargon and the moaning and tears of fellow neglected patients before he had the courage to lift his head and look down at himself.

The first good news was that he could lift his head. Second, he wasn't swathed in bandages and covered with skin grafts. Actually, he looked pretty much like himself, in his own clothes, dirty but unburned.

He tried to focus on the pain that had awakened him. To locate it more precisely. There. His right arm. It was wrapped in gauze, and the sleeve of his henley had been cut off at the shoulder. Damn, he thought, idiotically, and aware of the idiocy, I really liked that shirt.

The pain was enormous. Hot, cold, and nauseating. He thought back nostalgically to the relative comfort of his fall down the stairs Saturday night. Good God, was that only two days ago? It was, if today was still Monday. If he hadn't been in a coma for months, forgotten here in the corner.

He slid his legs off the gurney, pleasantly surprised that they still supported his weight. He wanted to find the exit, so he located a nurse and told her he was looking for a patient named Rob Petrie, confident that if she thought he was a civilian looking for help she'd do nothing more than usher him out. He allowed himself to be ushered.

Jesse was at a vending machine in the waiting room, watching it spit her dollar bill back at her. Some of his pain even vanished when he saw the look of happiness and concern on her face as she spotted him. Some of it.

When he was through wincing from her affectionate hug, he asked, "Did he get out?"

"Yes," Jesse said gratefully, "but he climbed up a tree and I couldn't catch him."

Carl blinked, confused, until he realized she was still talking about the damned cat. Did she even know Wes had been in the house?

She went on, telling him that the fire truck had pulled up right after he'd climbed through the window; they'd dragged him from the flames, rolled him into the ambulance, and brought him here. She didn't mention anyone else being saved.

So she didn't know, Carl thought. Well, this was hardly the time to tell her. He took her arm and started leading her to the exit.

"Where are we going?" she asked.

"Away," he said. "I thought we decided."

"What about your arm?"

"I'll buy some Advil at the pharmacy on the way out."

But in the end he thought better of it and bought some Tylenol and Excedrin too.

The drive to Lake Arrowhead took the rest of that day and night and much of the next day. For the first hours they drove in tense silence, Carl subdued by pain and a growing sense of guilt at not having told Jesse about Wes's fate.

But as Oakland receded into the distance, relief started to set in. What if the worst was over? they asked each other. If they vanished efficiently enough, would that be the end of it? If Martin wanted her gone, wouldn't he be satisfied if she obligingly disappeared? Of course, they'd be letting Martin off the hook, and they debated the morality of that. It was a big question, and neither of them were used to big questions. Let them find a safe place, they told each other; a place to regroup and think. Then they might be ready to tackle it.

Carl and Kit jointly owned a little cabin in Arrowhead up in the San Bernardino Mountains, ninety minutes southeast of L.A. They'd gone up there together to work on unsold pilots and unfinished screenplays; they'd gone up there separately to work on unhappy romances. It was the only resting place Carl could think of.

As they drove on, relief and pleasure at Jesse's presence overcame his pain and guilt, and they began to *talk*. Indeed, this journey became everything Carl could have wished for in his lonely fantasies of conversation; a nonstop, free-form discussion of morality and life and time and the world. The car was filled with their words and thoughts and laughter as they drove on, so that he hardly noticed the sun setting and rising around them, hardly felt the circulating pain in his arm.

It was Tuesday afternoon by the time they made it to the little mountain town. Jesse had driven the last leg to let Carl rest, but he hadn't slept, he'd just leaned his head back and watched her steer. God, she was beautiful when she steered.

They stopped at a little supermarket with a Tyrolean theme, staying close to each other as they filled the cart. Like George Bush, she was amazed by the laser bar code reader at the register. Unlike George Bush, no one seemed to think less of her for it.

They were so tired by the time they made it to the little cabin off the mountain road they were barely able to unload the groceries before falling into bed, not even bothering to undress or draw the curtain to block the bright sunlight. Carl marveled, as he snuggled spoonlike against her back, that only last Friday his life had been its normal, deadly self. Now, in one week's time, he had a new life. A new purpose. A new hope.

As he pressed his body against Jesse's, he felt content for

once, and it was a feeling so unfamiliar to him that he decided to savor it. A warm feeling in the belly; a comfortable set to the bones and joints, despite all their aches and pains. A totally illogical feeling, considering all the unanswered questions and tension of the past days. Of course, as soon as he thought of the questions and the tension, the warmth in his belly cooled, and his joints started to cramp and his wounds to flare up, and contentment ebbed away from him, to be replaced by his usual state of low-grade worry. Well, let it go; trying to grab onto it would only make it fly more quickly.

He shifted his good arm under Jesse, moving carefully so as not to disturb her sleep. He noticed with a nonsensical rush of affection that she was snoring. She snores now, he thought; isn't that cute? And he wondered when, if ever, he'd come to find that soft, rumbling sound annoying.

Moving to embrace her, he forgot about the burn on his right arm. He hissed in pain when he touched her. She sat up, concerned, and banged his arm again.

"What's wrong?"

"Nothing," he lied weakly, his eyes tearing up.

She leaned back on her elbow, looking down at him sympathetically. "Look at you," she said, brushing the lump on his forehead with her fingertips. "You're a wreck since I met you."

He tried to laugh it off with a mock tough-guy stance. "Wreck me, baby."

She didn't laugh, though. She ran her fingers, featherlight, along the scratches the cat had left on his unburned arm, making the scabs itch in a pleasant way.

Then she kissed him, warmly and tenderly. Her tongue brushed his lips and caressed his teeth, replacing the aftertaste of fire with the flavor of tobacco. Her hands gingerly found the safe places to touch him. He embraced her, and the pain that followed was ignored or swept along by new currents of pleasure.

He couldn't support himself with his arms, so she climbed on top of him, straddling him in her chinos, the afternoon sun making the red highlights in her hair gleam like copper. Looking up at her, he noticed that the past days had been hard on her, too. Scratches on her face from their run through the woods; lines of worry around her mouth; bags under her eyes from lack of sleep. They made her look more beautiful than ever.

She was unbuttoning her blouse, and he was just reaching up to help her, when the doorbell rang. Bending forward, her breath hot in his ear, she whispered, "Ignore it."

He nuzzled her neck, agreeing wholeheartedly. But then, damn it, he looked out the window and saw who it was and knew that he couldn't.

16

$\mathcal{W}$es was more singed than burned. He stood in the doorway, his eyes and lip swollen, his eyebrows gone, his short hair charred. Despite the passing of a day and a change of clothing, his whole body gave off the smell of a bad perm.

"What happened to you?" Jesse asked, as Carl led him to the kitchenette and she pulled a Mexican beer out of the fridge.

He suckled the tall neck gratefully before answering, "I tried to reach you." He was looking at Carl with apologetic eyes. "The fire was just too much. I had to break out through the back. Thank God they found you."

Jesse looked at him, puzzled. "You were there?"

Wes looked at Carl, puzzled. "You didn't tell her?"

Well, why didn't I? Carl asked himself. Now he had to look guiltily around the room and make excuses for himself. "I was waiting for the right time."

They let that slide, though he could see from Jesse's expression she wasn't satisfied. Why had he left her in the dark? And why did he feel guilty, when he hadn't done anything wrong? Was it because he'd secretly been glad at the thought that Wes was out of their lives? Don't be ridiculous, he told himself. He had no reason to be jealous of Wes. Jesse didn't seem in the least bit attracted to him. But she had been once, hadn't she? She'd made love to him once. Was that enough for Carl to want to see a man dead? No, Carl told himself, no way near.

During this internal reverie, Carl lost track of Wes's story, but he gathered that Wes had gone to the hospital to look for them.

"You'd already left, so I didn't know what to do. I took the shuttle back to L.A. and went to your house. A friend of yours was there feeding your cat."

"Kit?" Jesse asked.

"Yeah. I asked him where you might go, and he told me about this place."

Good old Kit, Carl thought sarcastically. But he'd done the right thing, hadn't he? Of course he had.

"How did the fire start?" Carl asked, trying to make himself part of the conversation again.

"Martin," Wes said with a sigh. "I confronted him. I know I shouldn't have, but I couldn't help it. Oh, don't worry, I didn't tell him you were alive, Jesse. He doesn't know that. Yet."

"But he saw us," Jesse said. "At Big Sur, he must have."

Wes shook his head. "He was following Carl. He wanted to find out how much he knew. He saw someone was with him, but . . . well, it would never occur to him that it would be you. You being there is such a complete impossibility."

"So we're safe," Carl said, resisting the urge to thank him very much and pack him out the door.

"For now," was Wes's only answer. "But he followed you to the house." For once Wes was actually talking to Carl.

"He knows you talked to me. I told him you were the man on the other boat, just to see how he'd react." Thanks so much, Carl thought.

"When I saw his expression . . . well, he looked caught, that was how he looked. So I knew then, I knew you were right. He was hiding something. So I accused him of trying to kill you."

What an incredibly stupid thing to do, Carl thought as he watched Wes talking to Jesse.

"That was when he lost it. He started pulling your photographs off the wall, shattering the glass, ripping them to pieces. I lost it, too. I jumped on him. He just brushed me off. Started hitting me. He hit me for a long time." Wes shrugged. "I guess I must have passed out. When I woke up the room was full of smoke. He'd started a bonfire of our pictures on the bed." His eyes were full of bitter regret. "Our" pictures, he said. They must be very important to him, Carl thought.

"That was when I heard Carl banging around upstairs. At first I thought it was you." Wes glanced over at Jesse. "I don't know why. I made it upstairs and I saw him . . ."

"Did he mean to kill you?" Jesse asked. Carl stirred uncomfortably at the look of concern on her face. Well, why shouldn't she be concerned for the poor sap? Carl thought. He's been beaten and burned. And all for her sake. The only thing abnormal about this scene was Carl's jealousy.

"I think so," was Wes's answer.

They sat in silence for a time.

"You *have* to remember," Wes said finally. "You have to remember what happened on the boat."

"I can't, Wes, it's hopeless." It was the first time Carl had heard her say his name and he tried to suppress the queasiness the sound produced.

"Have you really tried?"

She looked at him, exasperated. Carl liked that better. "Of course, what do you think?"

"I don't think you have. I think you've been afraid to. I don't think you've wanted to remember."

Instead of getting angrier, she sagged a little. "I can't say I'm exactly eager to relive all this crap . . ."

"It wasn't all bad, Jessica," he said, and the tender nostalgia in his voice made her look at him with real affection.

"I didn't mean that."

Wes sat back in the flimsy metal chair, blinking rapidly. "It's still"—his voice broke a little—"it's hard to believe you can't remember."

"Maybe I will eventually. I came back this far. I'm supposed to be dead, after all." She laughed for a moment, but stopped when she saw Wes wince. Odd to think that her "death" bothered him so much more than her. "I'm sorry. I just, I can't imagine what you must be feeling. I mean, I guess we cared for each other and we—we—we had something but I . . . I can't even imagine it, I'm sorry . . ."

Wes lifted his hand, smiling tightly. "It's all right. It took fifteen years for you to fall in love with me before, I can't expect it to happen overnight this time." He laughed, trying to make a joke of it, but the hint of hope in his voice was heartbreaking.

Jesse tried to think of something to say. "How . . . how did we meet?"

"Oh. It was at Martin's coffee shop. The first one. You were a cashier."

"Nice to know I could hold down a job."

"Actually, you shortchanged me. But I didn't mind. I thought you were beautiful. I wanted to buy you a coffee, but you worked late, and I was on my way to the airport . . . Next time I came out you were already dating Martin."

Jesse shook her head, mystified. "What did I see in him?"

Wes thought it over. "I was surprised myself. He'd never been very good with women, and I certainly never expected him to end up with someone as . . . well, with someone like you. But I think you were attracted to his drive. You weren't that interested in the business itself, I don't think, but you loved his passion for it. Maybe you were a little adrift in your life just then and you needed a focus.

"It was almost *violent* the way you two went at that business. You dropped out of school and you *lived* and *breathed* that place. Sometimes I think it was successful because of your sheer force of will. You always hated coffee, so you talked him into concentrating on the cocoa and the chocolate. You were the one who came up with the whole Maya gimmick. You read up on the history and archaeology, you took cooking classes and found these old, forgotten ethnic recipes. Remember this was years before the political correctness thing and the whole 'green' market, and there you were with all the essentials: Indians, the environment, helping Third World countries. By the time you were done you made people feel like buying a cup of cocoa or a candy bar was more virtuous than joining the Peace Corps."

"Did I mean it? Was I for real?"

"Oh, yes. I think that's why you never became a partner. You didn't want to have to look too closely at the fine print."

"I didn't want to dirty my hands?"

"You weren't in it for the money anyway. The first five or six years, building it all up, that was fun for you. It was an adventure. After things were going smoothly, you pretty much lost interest. By the time Martin sold out, you didn't care anymore. That wasn't what you wanted anyway."

"What did I want?"

"We always talked about opening a gallery."

She thought for a moment, then nodded, frowning. "To show your photographs. And before that I wanted to help Carl with his plays. Then I made candy with Martin. You said I was 'kind of adrift' back then. When have I *not* been adrift? Sounds like I just latch on to anybody who passes by and . . . adopt *their* dreams. What kind of person does that?"

Carl spoke up. "Look, I think we'd all come out pretty badly if we just judged the broad sweep of our lives like that."

"Maybe that's the only way to judge a life," Jesse said. "The rest of you can't do it because you get lost in the details. I don't have that distraction. I can see myself for what I am." Her face was set in a stern expression, and for the first time Carl thought she looked older than her years.

Wes was looking at his hands and frowning. "I'm not doing this well. I don't want to say anything to make you think badly of yourself. That's not what I think. That's not what anybody thought." He ran a hand over his short, singed hair. "It's just, it's a lot to ask, to recap somebody's life for them."

Carl suddenly remembered the computer disc in his pocket—Jesse's journal of the last few years. But he had no computer here read it with; he always brought his laptop up when they worked. For now they'd have to rely on Wes's version of events, and Carl was still jealous enough to keep the disc's existence to himself.

"So how did you and I"—Jesse found it hard to ask the question—"happen?"

"Okay." Wes nodded quickly, several times. "Okay. All right. I, uh, well, after college I wanted to be a professional photographer, but, uh"—Wes smiled one of his lightning-quick smiles—"the industry blacklisted me just because I had no talent, which is very un-American, don't you think?"

Carl recognized his own kind of joke. We must be her type, Carl realized. He could almost see Jesse's ad in the personals: "Attractive woman looking for insecure, self-deprecating underachiever with good sense of humor and a love of oral sex."

"Those weird pictures of me in my bedroom," Jesse said, not particularly tactfully, "you took those?"

"Yes. You asked me to take them. You always loved my work. You told me I had a real eye and, I don't know why, but I believed you. You didn't know a thing about photography; bought an Ansel Adams calendar once, that was about it. But I believed you, because *you* seemed so sure. So I started taking pictures of you . . ."

She sat back, a little less friendly. "And that was how it started, huh?"

"Not right away," he said quickly, as if trying to correct a bad impression. "I mean, we knew each other for years. You were my sister-in-law, for Christ's sake. This wasn't easy for us."

She nodded, lips pursed, and folded her arms across her chest.

"It started . . . well, it started *starting* about a year and a half ago. I was up in Oakland on business a lot, and you'd come up to visit your mother. We spent a lot of time together. We thought it would be fun to make some pictures."

"Of me naked? That *sounds* like fun." She tried to smile

at that, but it was a tense, unfriendly smile. Carl could see that, now that he was changing from victim to lover, her old discomfort with him was returning.

"We figured we were friends. It never occurred to us anything could *happen* . . . But you were unhappy with Martin, of course, and I'm unhappy on principle, so I suppose it was inevitable that we'd end up being unhappy together. Still, for the longest time it was just about the pictures. It was so exciting for both of us to be *making* something. Creating. You were always pushing me to do more with the images. To have a vision and follow it. God, we'd fight about it and end up laughing . . . The pictures all look kind of silly to me now." He turned to Carl. "What did you think? Silly or art?"

Carl cleared his throat. "I never learned to tell the difference."

Wes laughed. "I'm not sure you're supposed to. At least that's what you used to say, Jessica. You really grew into a remarkable person, you should know that."

Jesse shrugged, noncommittally. She's blocking all this out now, Carl thought. She can't afford to let any of it in.

Wes must have been able to sense the wall she was putting up; he moved to her, as if to reassure her. "I don't want you to think that we just jumped into bed together, just casually. We fought it. Sometimes I think if we hadn't, if we'd just pounced on each other right away, it would have been better for everyone. The tension wouldn't have kept building. We would have just *done* the damned thing and felt ashamed of ourselves and gone on with our lives. But we didn't."

She shrugged again. "Great, so at least we had the decency to feel bad before we started fucking."

"It was nothing like that!" His voice was harsh, making both of them jump with surprise. Quickly, he composed himself. "We fell in love. We couldn't help ourselves. And we made love *one time*. One beautiful time."

That phrase again. Jesse raised her hands in surrender. "Okay, time out. Too much, too much."

Wes stopped, stricken. He must have known he'd gone too far, but he couldn't seem to stop himself. "If I could just talk to you. If you could just come back to my house—we spent so much time there, I know you'd remember it. If I could just be with you alone, Jessica—"

"Nobody calls me 'Jessica!' " She seemed surprised by her own anger and tried to explain. "I mean, that's what my mother calls me when she's mad." She laughed a little, trying to soften her outburst. "I'm sorry, but you keep acting like there's something still between us, and you gotta understand, there's just . . . there's not." She gestured to her head. "It's not there anymore."

Carl tried to restrain a sense of satisfaction. He should have given Wes more credit.

"Sorry," Wes said, suddenly intellectual and distant. "Understood. Let's try another tack. What's the most recent thing you remember?"

Jesse waved a hand, uninterested. "Just . . . stuff from high school."

"But what exactly?" Wes went on. "I mean, do you remember Carl dumping you?"

So it was to be war, Carl thought. Too bad he didn't realize it before the death blow was struck.

17

$\mathcal{J}$esse spoke to Wes, but she was looking at Carl. "No, I don't remember that." It wasn't a nice look.

"Okay," Wes went on, still all clinical innocence, "that dates it pretty exactly at 1978." Then he "noticed" her look, which hadn't gotten any nicer. "He did tell you about that, didn't he?"

"Oh, yes, in detail," Jesse said. " 'Drifted apart,' isn't that how you put it?"

Carl squirmed, impaled. "Yeah, well, you know . . ."

Wes still hadn't gotten over his surprise. "I can't believe you didn't tell her about that, Carl. Especially if you're trying to start the relationship up again." The guy just wouldn't shut up. "Did you think she wouldn't find out?"

Yeah, if you hadn't opened your big mouth, Carl wanted to say, but didn't, because, despite its sterling reputation, the truth never got you anything but trouble.

"There hasn't really been a lot of time," Carl said.

"You had time to lie, though, didn't you?" Jesse just wouldn't stop looking at him.

"Look, I chickened out, okay? But it's a complicated story and I needed to find the right time to tell it."

"Now's good," Jesse said.

Wes broke in, helpful as ever. "Give him a break, Jessica. You forgave him for this a long time ago."

"Good, now I get to do that all over again. Let's hear it."

Carl couldn't figure out how to begin. If only she could just suddenly know; no matter how she might react it would be better than having to live through telling it.

"What happened?" she went on. "Did you start slipping it to Becky Holtzclaw, is that it?"

"No," Carl said, wishing it was.

"Be fair, Jessica." More help from Wes. "He was just a kid. He got kind of freaked out when you told him you were pregnant."

So now she knew, Carl thought. Oh, joy.

They did everything in cars.

Talked in cars. Partied in cars. Listened to music in cars. Fought in cars. Made love in cars.

And, remember, this was in the days before the bucket seat was standard. Back then, the front seat of a car was a roomy sofa—a teenager's living room. No seat belts automatically embraced you as you started the car. You were free to move as you wished.

And they wished. Sitting sideways, facing each other, discussing politics and the world and how the Republicans could never come back now that Carter had been elected. Reclining in each other's arms, flesh touching where clothing had been opened, watching the stars through the windshield. She, sitting in the middle of the bench seat, pressing herself against him, arm around his neck, hand in his lap or on his chest, breathing into his ear, never letting him go.

Are bucket seats worth the price we've paid? Get rid of

them all, Carl often thought, the harnesses and the air bags and the flashing warnings and all the clutter that wraps us up like an overprotective mother who never lets her child take enough chances to learn to live. Bring back the bench seat and the push-button car radio, the rock-hard dashboard and the impaling hood ornaments. Bring back that night when "Rhiannon" played on the car stereo and he let it all slip away.

They hadn't been embracing then. Carl had sat in the Volare with his back against the door, his knees drawn up on the seat between them. Jesse sucked on a Marlboro, her door half-open to let out the smoke. The car didn't beep to tell them the door was open. Cars didn't talk back to you in those days.

"I have some money . . ." he said. "Enough to . . . I can help."

Carl didn't know the right words to use. He wanted desperately to do the right thing, and these days he was pretty sure "the right thing" meant offering to pay for the abortion.

"How?" she asked, exhaling smoke dramatically.

"I can take you to a clinic," he said. "I'll pay," he added quickly, hating the way it sounded. As if he were offering to pick up the check for a pizza.

She looked over at him from across the long length of the front seat. "So you want to get rid of it?" she asked.

This took him totally by surprise. It was one of the phrases that stayed with him for the rest of his life. One that floated up to his consciousness, jerking him awake as he drifted off to sleep in many beds over many years.

"What else can we do?"

She shrugged. Lost. Alone. Why couldn't he reach her? There was a gulf between them now, and he couldn't be sure that anything he might say wouldn't make it wider.

"What do you want to do?" he asked her.

She didn't answer.

"I mean, do you want to have it?" He knew she was Catholic, but he never thought she was *Catholic*.

"I already have it. I've already got it, Carl. The question is, what do we do . . . with it."

"Well . . . um . . ." There were four goals in his mind. To get her to stop talking foolishly. To get her to agree to an abortion. To not lose her. To find the magic words that would make things what they were before.

"Don't you think we're a little young to think about getting married?" he asked.

"Weren't we thinking about it?"

"Well, sure, but in the long run. And I'll marry you right now, if you want. I will. But we were talking later. Weren't we? And you're the one who said we should see other people, so we find out who's wrong for us." He played that last line like a trump card.

"And you still want to do that?"

"I never wanted to do that. You were the one. Stop acting like this is all my fault. I am not deserting you."

"If I decided to have the baby, what would you do?"

"Oh, man, do you think this is fair?" None of it was fair. They were always so careful about wearing protection, and this *one time* the condom breaks. He'd pulled out when he felt it tear, but it was too late. There was the rubber hanging off his shrinking cock like a split sausage skin. And from that one bit of bad timing, all this.

"No, it's not fair," she said.

"No, really, do you think it's fair—"

"No."

He couldn't believe this was Jesse he was talking to. She was the radical, firebrand feminist of the school. He remembered her rage when Amy Petteway started going through the cafeteria, passing out pamphlets with pictures of aborted fetuses. The screaming match they'd had by the lunch line: Amy declaiming about promiscuity and the sanctity of life, Jesse passionately standing up for a woman's right to control her own body. He'd never loved her more.

"I'm not saying it's fair." She was looking straight at him for the first time that night. "And I'm not saying it's right. All I'm saying is, if I let you off the hook now, if I decide to have the baby but if I never ask a thing from you, if I promise never to even call you again, would you still say you'd marry me or would you let out a big sigh of relief and get on with your life?"

He looked right back at her. And he didn't say a word.

She put out her cigarette, opened the car door, and walked away. He didn't call her and, like she promised, she never called him.

She watched him as he finished his story. Still smoking. Still Marlboro Lights. Same brand, same expression.

"So what happened? What did I do?"

"I don't know." And that was what damned him in his own eyes more than anything else.

But Wes was there with the answer. "You had an abortion. It was nothing you were ashamed of. Nothing you were proud of. These things happen. If anything about it stayed with you . . . I guess it was your disappointment with Carl. You used to say that was when you learned to expect less from people. But you forgave him. I mean, you understood. He was very young."

That's right, Wes, Carl thought to himself. Keep defending me. I'm not quite six feet under yet.

Jesse was running her tongue along the inside of her cheek; her coldest expression. "When were you going to tell me all, Carl?"

"Never." Great, *now* start being honest. "I didn't want you to know about it. The way I handled all that . . . it's the only real regret of my life. It's like I was tested and I failed. Anything I could have done, fighting with you, marrying you, dragging you to the clinic, anything would have been better than walking off like that. I was a coward. I wish to God it had never happened. So when you forgot it, well, I thought maybe I could pretend it hadn't."

She just stared at him. It wouldn't wash, he knew, not with her and not with himself. You couldn't use cowardice to erase cowardice.

"Okay." Wes again. "I'm sorry. I shouldn't have brought this up. This wasn't the time. Let's just stay focused on the situation at hand. I still think, if you come back to my house, there are letters you've written me, pictures. I'm sure they'll help you remember—"

Jesse wasn't listening; her eyes were still fixed on Carl. "And you never called? Never even tried to find out what happened? How I was doing?"

How could he explain? At first he'd been pissed with her for thinking the worst of him and stomping out of the car so dramatically, so he'd refused to be the first one to call. And every minute, every day that his phone didn't ring, little breaths of relief escaped from him. As she had predicted they would. Then it was too late to call. She must have done whatever she was going to do. How could he face her then?

"Look, I can't defend myself," he told her. "I don't even want to."

"And last Friday, that was the first time you saw me since then? The first time you even talked to me?"

"Yes." God, this was sheer torture. When a nightmare got this bad, he usually woke up.

"And that's what you do? You don't beg me to forgive you? You don't tell me you're sorry? You just take me out to the shed and fuck me?"

"What?!" A chair scraped across the floor and Wes was on his feet, his fists clenched at his sides. Carl flinched from the naked aggression in both their eyes.

"Fine, hit me! You'll be doing me a favor!"

But they didn't hit him. Wes took a breath and relaxed. Carl knew Wes was smart enough to understand he'd already done more damage than any blow could.

"I think you'd better go," Wes said, through clenched teeth.

"What?" Even after all this, Carl couldn't believe that.

Wes looked annoyed. "Just for a little while. There's a McDonald's in town. Get us something to eat." He looked over at Jesse. "We need to talk."

Carl was slack-jawed, unable to comprehend that the word "we" could ever mean Jesse and Wes. He turned to Jesse, knowing that Wes was overplaying his hand. "Jesse?" he asked.

"I'll have a McChicken Sandwich," Jesse said, coldly.

Great. On top of everything else she had to order something they don't make anymore.

18

$\mathcal{W}$hat he needed was a diner. Something out of Edward Hopper, preferably, but he'd have settled for the one from the old Linda Lavin sitcom *Alice*. He needed a blowsy, old, gum-chewing waitress or a hangdog, seen-it-all-and-then-some short-order cook to tell his troubles to and to give back folksy advice. Instead, he got a pimply teenager in a paper hat who asked him if he wanted a Mayor McCheese souvenir plate. Not the same thing at all.

He sighed over his fries and soda and commiserated with himself. Being completely in the wrong was something he wasn't used to, which was good, he supposed, but left him poorly equipped to deal with this situation. Okay, he'd done a bad thing way back then, no question. And he'd done wrong again when he lied to her about it. Point conceded. The defense rests. The defense curls up into a ball and begs for mercy, in fact.

All that didn't stop him from feeling angry and misunderstood. What was he supposed to do with those feelings? Wallow in self-pity? Become petulant and lash out? Join

Jesse and Wes and gang up on himself? Drive to the Pleasure Chest on Santa Monica and pick up some whips to
lash himself with?

He couldn't focus his anger on Jesse; that was patently
ridiculous. She had every right to be pissed at him, though a
part of him instinctively felt she was being unfair. But no, if
anything had played unfair in this, it was Fate, which had
chosen to test him at the young age of eighteen. He'd do
better now, he felt sure. Almost sure.

Anger at Wes? Now he was a much more attractive tar-
get. True, he'd spoken nothing but the truth. Still, Carl
couldn't help but impugn his motives. He'd been trying to
drive a wedge between Carl and Jesse, and he'd succeeded,
at least momentarily. And his mealy-mouthed apologies and
defenses of Carl had seemed a particularly sleazy tactic.
This wasn't a man to be trusted, Carl told himself.

Or was that just jealousy speaking?

Carl took a long time over his Big Mac, watching the sun
go down through windows plastered with Disney memora-
bilia, savoring each rancid onion morsel and knowing he'd
be savoring them for days to come.

Well, regrets he could do nothing about. The only question he could really grapple with was this: what was Jesse
feeling? How deep was this breech Wes had created? Would
she be over it by the time he got back, a little grumpy but
forgiving? Would she take longer to thaw, making him suf-
fer, making him perform some unknown labor to earn forgiveness? Or would she be pissed forever? Had the scales
fallen from her eyes as far as Carl was concerned? Did this
failure of his go so contrary to her idea of him that she
couldn't love him anymore? That extreme seemed unlikely.
But then, so did immediate forgiveness. But even if the
middle scenario was true, he had no idea what he could do
to redeem himself in her eyes.

So what was he going to do now? Stay here? Keep away from her and avoid the issue? He'd tried that for the past seventeen years and it had followed him every step of the way.

These unpleasant thoughts were intruded on by the wailing of a small child at the next table. She was heartbroken because the toy in her Happy Meal was the same toy she'd gotten in her last Happy Meal, making it into what Carl would call a Miserable Meal for everyone in the restaurant. The girl's father was trying to placate her by saying that they'd come back, again and again, until she got the toy she wanted. Carl burped back some Special Sauce and thought, Now that's commitment.

Then he realized. That *was* commitment. Coming back again and again. It was the best anyone could do. If he came back to Jesse now, if he kept coming back, she'd have to realize eventually, later or much later, that he hadn't really deserted her back then. Because here he was. And here he always would be.

He got their sandwiches and left the restaurant with a light heart. He pulled out of the parking lot, onto the twisting mountain road, singing along with Trisha Yearwood on the radio, not minding that some asshole with his lights on high beam was tailgating him, knowing full well that Jesse would still be pissed at him when he got there, that she might be pissed at him for the rest of the century, but happy all the same, because he knew he'd wear her down in the end. Because he loved her. She couldn't not see that. Even if she didn't laugh tonight when he walked in and handed her a Happy Meal.

The headlights now blinded him in the rearview mirror. Some local redneck trying to show the city jerk in the fancy sports utility vehicle who really owned the road. Well, let him have it, Carl thought, looking for a place to pull over.

But the lights were so bright, he could hardly see the road ahead. Didn't that asshole realize how dangerous this was? It was hard to believe he could drive so close to Carl's rear bumper without—

Slam! The Jeep shuddered and swerved from the impact. Shit.

He floored it, speeding ahead and straining his eyes to see the twisting blacktop. On the left, sloping trees crowded the one-lane road. On his right was nothing but a dead drop down the mountainside. Now the other car was speeding up right along with him, its headlights brighter than ever, the sound of its engine impossibly close.

He jerked the rearview mirror down to rid himself of that fucking light, but it kept flooding in through the back window. He just had time to see the hairpin curve in front of him before the next impact. But he didn't have time to turn.

Carl's neck snapped and cracked as the other car smashed into the Jeep, propelling it forward toward the cliff. Another smash. The grinding roar of torn metal and the explosive blast of the air bag in his face.

He couldn't breathe—from the impact, and because of the straitjacket grip of his shoulder harness. He opened his mouth and sucked air in, struggling to remember the process, comforted by the knowledge that if he were dead he wouldn't be bothering.

The air bag was limp now, a flaccid sack hanging obscenely from the wheel. And he was still on the road. The crumpled front end of the car was kissing the crumpled guardrail in front of it. And in front of that was nothing but air and bright stars and a drop down the mountainside. Guardrails, Carl thought. What a fabulous invention. He was going to devote the rest of his life to the praise and promotion of guardrails.

And it was dark, he realized. He tilted the rearview mirror back in position; nothing but empty road behind him. The maniac and his headlights had gone. What kind of redneck asshole would do something like that? He could have been killed . . .

Carl froze, a sick feeling gripping his stomach. Martin. Why hadn't he realized? Martin had found them.

Jesse. He had to get to her now. He cursed the slowness of his brain and turned the key to start the engine up again, but all he heard was the tortured grinding of broken machinery. He yanked at the wheel in frustration.

Light. He glanced up at the mirror. Someone was coming. Thank God. He'd be able to flag them down and get help.

But before he could even open the door, he saw that the lights were coming way too fast, and they were way too bright.

He had a second to brace himself before it hit. There was no air bag this time to protect his face as it cracked into the steering wheel. The guardrail failed him too, ripping apart like the ribbon on a finish line as the Jeep sailed off the road, off the side of the mountain, and into the dark night air.

19

*I*ncredibly, the radio still worked. Carl hung like a bat, suspended in his bucket seat, and listened to Reba McEntire's version of "The Night the Lights Went out in Georgia." Easily one of his least favorite songs. Now he was going to die listening to it and probably have it stuck in his head throughout his entire stay in purgatory. Just his luck.

He had no idea if the car had fallen for seconds or minutes before it hit. He had no idea if it had rolled over once or twice before it came to rest like this, upside down, lodged against the trunk of a pine tree. He had no idea how long it would stay balanced here before it continued its descent. He just wished that fucking song would end.

There. Now Charlie Rich was singing "You Don't Know Me." Much better. There was a song you could really die to.

The sound of his own laugh scared Carl back to reality. What the hell was he doing making bad-song jokes at a time like this? Was he faint from loss of blood? Had he had a concussion? Did he have no sense of occasion?

There he went again. Carl tried to concentrate on the

pain and on the danger of the situation, to stop his mind from floating off again in his own personal form of hysteria. He couldn't let shock, or whatever it was, lull him into a complacent haze until the car dropped off the mountain with him in it.

Carefully, he reached to his hip and pushed the red button to release the seat belt. With a click, the pressure on his chest was gone and he oozed into a crumpled heap on the ceiling of the Jeep. He lay still for a long moment, waiting for the shifting of his weight to cause the car to slip forward.

All still. He reached to the power window switch and rolled the window down (or was it "up"?), breathing in the cool night air. Now or never. Here goes. This is it. A few dozen more slogans of determination and he made his move.

The idea was to do it all in one quick roll, to pivot himself out the window like Jackie Chan, disturbing the Jeep's balance as little as possible.

Instead, it took minutes of clutching and crawling and scrabbling and grabbing and pulling before he dragged himself out onto the cool dirt and rolled away, putting as much distance between himself and the car as he could.

If it had been a movie, the Jeep would have exploded in flames at that moment, or at least plummeted on down the hillside. Instead, it rested there on its back like a forlorn beetle. He stared at the wreck and thought, My God, that's why I told people I bought this thing. Because it was sturdy enough to withstand an accident. So the old trooper had done its job. He was sorry to see it go.

He gulped in deep lungfuls of night air and checked his mind to see if he was thinking rationally. An impossible task, he told himself, since my mind is doing the checking. He decided to assume he was sane until somebody told him different.

Climbing up the steep slope of the mountainside, Carl remembered his last car accident, a sideswiping collision that had totaled his BMW, spinning it like a top around the intersection of Laurel Canyon and Ventura. That time he had sat frozen in place, afraid to move lest he might aggravate any latent whiplash. Now he was rock-climbing his way to the road, not taking a second to reflect on the shooting pain in his shoulders or to wonder why he only seemed to be seeing out of his left eye. Caution seemed to belong to a long-forgotten part of his life. That was all to the good. Caution wouldn't serve him now. If he'd survived, he knew the reason. To get to Jesse.

He made it to the road, climbing over an unbroken guardrail, wondering how far he'd traveled from the scene of the accident. But why call it an accident? Call it an assault. Call it an assassination.

The idea now was to flag down the first car he saw, but when a pair of headlights came into view, he instinctively ducked behind the guardrail, hiding himself as a Chevy Nova drove on by. Hardly a death car, a Chevy Nova. But then, he'd never seen what kind of car it was that attacked him. All he'd seen were those damned headlights.

Fortunately, the next vehicle that came by was a one-headlighted motorcycle, so Carl felt safe enough to step out and wave it to a stop. A good choice, probably, since bearded, potbellied Hell's Angels don't find the sight of a beaten, bleeding man with one eye swollen shut sufficiently unusual to cause them to ask prying questions.

The cabin was locked when Carl got there, and no one answered his knocking. He broke the window and reached in to unlock the door before he remembered that he still had his key. He started to wonder just how crazy he was getting.

There was no one in the house. No sign, no trace of Jesse

or Wes at all. Even Jesse's bag was gone from the bedroom. If he'd had to, he couldn't prove she'd ever been there.

He stood in the middle of the living room, vibrating from the tension of having nothing to do. An Ambrose Bierce scenario, in which none of this ever happened, flitted through his brain; he'd just imagined it all in the moment of the car wreck.

Fuck that. He turned on the TV for a cold dose of reality. Good God, he thought, as the set glowed to life, it was his show. He recognized the odd sitcom patois of joke-setup-joke and remembered that he and Kit had written this episode. A million years ago he'd sweated blood to make those hoary plot twists seem light and natural, to make those jokes sing. It was like having a glimpse of a previous life. He couldn't imagine doing any such thing.

He switched the set off and noticed a note pad on top of it. The page was blank, but on the torn edge at the top there were still fragments of handwriting from a sheet that had been ripped off. He could recognize the upper loops of a capital *C* and a lowercase *l,* and between them, the curved tip of an *r;* just the way Jesse wrote his name.

Carl snatched up the pad, recalling scenes from a dozen forties mysteries. He found a book of matches in the kitchen and held the flame up to the tilted page, just like William Powell had done with Myrna Loy at his side. But William Powell had been able to make out more than lines and scratches, and he certainly hadn't set fire to the paper. Carl dropped it into the sink before it singed his fingers.

It didn't matter. He'd read enough before the fire consumed it. He'd made out five letters: *Marti.*

Martin had found them.

Of all the things Carl had been ill-equipped to do, this had to be the most ill: crouching under a bush, waiting to assault the next person he saw, with no idea of what might happen next. But hysteria had carried him this far and he saw no reason for it to let him down now.

Once he'd seen that fragment of Martin's name on the paper, he had rejected all his long-cherished notions of polite, civilized behavior, and he was surprised how much good that had done him. Renting a car from the Lake Arrowhead Avis before working hours would have been impossible for the civilized Carl, who would have smiled and nodded and apologized for inconveniencing anyone and might, perhaps, if pushed to the limit, have resorted to a sarcastic witticism that would have gone right over the agent's head. But the rude, snarling, uncivilized Carl, the Carl who didn't care that this stranger might not like him, that Carl got exactly what he wanted. Which was a Ford Taurus and a full tank of gas. That Carl drove like a bat out of hell, broke dozens of traffic laws going down the mountain into Pasadena, and made the trip in record time; and no cop stopped him, because the grace of desperation sat on his shoulder.

So here he was, in this bush outside Martin Ackerman's front door in the cool hours of early morning, with no plan other than to wait for that door to be opened by someone, anyone. Someone going to get the paper or the mail or anything at all. Then he would plow into someone, pile-drive him into the house, and find Martin. Or find out where Martin was. And what he'd done with Jesse.

Carl's muscles ached from crouching, but otherwise he felt surprisingly little pain. Perhaps he was getting used to it, perhaps his pain receptors were overloaded, or perhaps he simply didn't have the time to hurt. The swelling in his right eye had even gone down enough for him to be able to see through it. A little.

He fell forward in surprise as a jet of water shot out at

him from the ground. The lawn sprinklers. He lay there in dirt fast turning to mud, feeling foolish and undignified. He banished those thoughts. If he started caring what he looked like, he'd start drifting back to the old Carl. And this was no job for him.

The front door opened.

Carl moved as soon as a human shape appeared. He launched himself from the shrubbery, right into the man's chest. A soft, flabby chest. Carl drove himself into it, feeling the man fall back, surprised to realize that it was Martin himself, in T-shirt and shorts.

The big man caught himself before he could fall and tried to hold his ground. The expression on his face told Carl that he must look gratifyingly terrible.

He had never thrown a punch in his life, but Carl put all his strength into this one, crashing his fist against Martin's jaw and sending him sprawling back onto the floor of the front hall. Not even glancing behind him for witnesses, Carl stepped in and slammed the door, moving to Martin, ready to do something to him, anything, to make him tell where she was.

Then, out of the corner of his eye, he saw something on the stairs. He didn't recognize it at first, because it just shouldn't have been there.

But it was there. And it brought up a question that puzzled Carl so much, he had to remind himself to speak.

"Where is she?" The edge was gone from his voice, damn it. It sounded more like a question than a demand.

Martin looked up at him, confused and hurt. Not the right expressions at all. "What?" he asked. Dear God, was that a hopeful tone? This scene was starting out all wrong.

"Where's Jesse?"

Martin came slowly to his feet, his eyes reddening and blinking, his lips tugging down at the edges in odd little spasms, his voice breaking as he spoke. "They called me from the nursing home . . . they said she was there . . ."

"Don't stall me, damn it, where is she?"

Before Carl's eyes, Martin melted, liquid flowing from his eyes and nose as he sagged and let loose a huge, ragged sob. "Oh, God, is she really alive?!"

Martin pitched forward and Carl found himself holding the big man, or trying to, as he wept and slid slowly down Carl's body, pulling him down until they were both sitting in a heap on the tile. Carl found himself instinctively patting the big man's shuddering back, thinking, This isn't right, this wasn't the plan at all.

Jesse's calico cat was still watching them from the stairs. After a few moments it came over and started purring, wrapping its slinky form around the huddled men on the floor, and Carl found himself asking that puzzling question again. What kind of man burns down somebody's house and then saves her cat?

20

Carl knew Martin wasn't acting.

He'd spent twelve hours a day for the past seven years with good actors and bad actors, and he'd never seen a performance of shock and relief that even approached this in commitment and honesty and total lack of vanity. The man had collapsed into such a quivering, blubbering wreck that it was embarrassing to even look at him.

But that didn't mean Carl believed him. He couldn't afford to believe him. Believing him would be unwise and unsafe. Believing him would be too fucking confusing. So Carl searched every inch of the house and yard, looking for signs of her, signs of concealed rooms or hidden prisoners, signs of freshly turned earth or new brick construction, signs of gore on hardware or suspiciously clogged woodchippers. But there was nothing.

Martin hadn't moved from the sofa where Carl had dropped him when he began his search. He looked up as Carl walked in. He had never been unconscious, Carl noted.

He hadn't fainted, the way Wes had when Jesse had appeared over the wall. He'd simply imploded.

"Is it true?" Martin asked.

"Don't fuck with me. You know it's true! You saw her in my house."

He looked up at Carl like an abused basset hound. "I don't even know where you live."

Carl petted the calico and it took a swipe at him with a claw. "You saw her in the woods. You followed us up to Oakland. Don't deny it, I saw you there."

"I . . . I went up to talk to my brother. About you, yeah. I was worried about what you said."

"Is that why you set fire to her house? Is that why you tried to kill your brother?"

Martin shut his eyes and fell back against the sofa. "Oh shit, you're just a crazy man."

Carl wouldn't let himself be confused. "I heard you fighting. I *know* it happened."

Martin opened his eyes, head sagging forward. "Okay. We got into a fight, I . . . he makes me so mad some-times . . . he . . . he gets these ideas and you can't shake him out of it . . . so I got a little rough with him . . . you gotta do that sometimes, it's the only way to get through to him . . . but I left and he was fine. Then I got a call at the hotel. About the fire. And I thought, Shit, Wes, what did you do?"

"Right, blame him." Carl couldn't believe the nerve. "I saw him in the house, Martin. He barely made it out alive."

"But he *is* all right?" Martin looked relieved. "Thank God. I've been trying to reach him." Then the relief died in his eyes. "Why the hell should I believe you? You're as crazy as he is."

He stumbled to the bar and poured himself a Dewar's. So this is the kind of man who drinks it, Carl thought. "When I got there, they said they'd pulled somebody out of the fire. I figured it was Wes, but when I got to the hospital he'd run off. Then I got that message from the nursing home. I thought they must be crazy."

"Everybody's crazy but you, huh?"

Martin ignored him and petted the calico. "I found Patches wandering around what was left of the house. Jesse really loved this cat."

Carl sat down. "You call her 'Jesse'?"

Martin shrugged. "Sometimes. She used to like it. She used to like me." He shot back the Scotch and looked even sicker than before. "If she's really alive, why didn't you bring her here?"

"She's afraid of you."

Martin looked at him, shocked. "What?"

"You're a violent man, Martin."

He sputtered, offended. "I never . . . I have a temper, all right, but I never . . . Who's telling you these things?"

"Jesse."

Martin set the glass down with a sharp clink. "Get the fuck out of my house."

"That's right, she can talk now, Martin. She can tell everyone what you did to her."

Martin moved amazingly fast for his size, his bulk flashing around the sofa, his fist flying in a blur. Carl had time to throw up his hands to block the blow, but all that meant was that it was his own hand that smashed into his swollen eye rather than Martin's.

Carl fell, pure dead weight, the stored-up pain from his injuries flaring out from his wounded eye and dropping him, incapacitated, to the carpet. Colored lights and fractals filled his eyes—pain so strong he could *hear* it, like the vibrating throb of a bass player in a rock concert.

In time it quieted to simple agony and Carl was able to

see the world around him again. Which was mostly the huge figure of Martin staring at him, dumbly. He'd probably never seen a light blow fell a man so completely. Carl realized, gratefully, that the completeness of his collapse had saved him from further blows.

"You okay?" Martin asked.

"You fucked me up pretty bad when you wrecked my car."

Martin shook his head sympathetically. "You really are completely insane, aren't you? Did you escape from a home or something?"

Carl pushed himself up on one elbow, realizing that in an odd way his weakened condition was giving him the upper hand here. "Yeah. Tell everybody I'm a nut case. But I'm not the only one who saw her. You can't get rid of all of us."

Martin gave a soft, phlegmy sigh. "Is there someone I can call? Is somebody supposed to be taking care of you?"

"Damn it, stop!" Anger made the pain in Carl's head blossom all over again, but he went on. "Don't you see? I know what happened! It's no use to lie! But we don't care. Neither of us care. Just let her go. That's all she wants. All she wants is to be away from you! Can't you see that?"

Martin looked at him with dull comprehension. "I've known that for a long time. I never beat her, no matter what you imagine. I just bored her. I was dull. And for somebody like Jesse, that's a kind of abuse right there. But what could I do about it? A dull man can't stop being dull any more than a genius can stop being smart. All I could do was watch her love me a little bit less every day."

"Is that why you threw her off the boat?"

This seemed to barely register on Martin. He was playing the "Carl's just a raving crazy man" act to perfection. "Please."

"We have proof, Martin," Carl lied. "There's no good pretending."

"You can't have proof. It didn't happen!" He was getting angry again. Carl recoiled at the thought of more pain, but knew he had to keep pushing.

"You tried to kill her, Martin!"

"Why?! Why would I do that?"

"You wanted her out of your life."

"That's bullshit."

"You were jealous."

"Of who?" Incredulous, furious. Carl knew he'd be pummeled in seconds.

"Of your brother!"

But the blows didn't come. Instead the anger evaporated. "Of Wesley?!" Martin started to laugh. A rolling, bitter laugh. "She didn't even like him."

Carl's head swam. It was too much, it was all too much. It was such an easy lie to make, saying she didn't even like the man she loved, the man she was leaving her husband for. Easy and flattering to Martin. It was the sort of lie a guilty Martin would be sure to tell, to protect himself and to protect his ego.

Except for one thing. Jesse didn't like Wes. It was that simple. Carl had seen it all along. He'd assumed it had been discomfort at meeting an old lover she didn't remember. But now Martin had put a label on the feeling, and Carl saw that the label fit. She just didn't like the guy.

So? Did that mean everything Martin was saying was true? If so, then what? Carl's head swam as he tried to make sense of all these conflicting versions of Jesse's life and near-death. Only one person had ever known the real truth, and she was missing. And even if he found her, she wouldn't remember.

Carl struggled to get to his feet, but as he pushed off with his hand, it slipped on something and he fell back to the floor, groaning like an old man. He grasped the object his hand had slipped on. A thin plastic square. A computer disc. It must have fallen from his pocket when he collapsed. Jesse's journal. A memory of another kind.

"Do you have a computer?" Carl asked. Just the kind of non sequitur a crazy man would come up with.

21

Carl took the Colorado Street Bridge into Wes's neighborhood in Pasadena. The blond masonry, the delicate yet ornate arches, the way the structure curved, gently, to catch the far hill like an incoming wave, made it one of the most beautiful bridges in the world, featured in countless prints, paintings, postcards, and picture books. John Barrymore had leapt to freedom from this bridge, escaping from his police-inspector-brother Lionel, in the old picture *Arsine Lupine*—but in the film the bridge had been in France and had, presumably, spanned water. In real life, a leap from the bridge onto the hard scrubby earth of the Arroyo Seco beneath had quite a different outcome, giving the span its other name, Suicide Bridge.

Somewhere along here, Carl couldn't spot just where, Jesse had lost half her life.

The arroyo below had changed less than any other place in L.A. since Jesse's day. Huge trees and large funky houses were still sprinkled along the edge of the twisting road that overlooked the deep chasm of the dry riverbed.

Wes's house, on the west side of the arroyo, was an elegant Craftsman just under the rainbow arch of the bridge. Their friend Lyn Bushnell's house had been just like this, Carl remembered, and Jesse had always envied her for living in such a romantic spot, so different from Glendull and environs.

He parked his rented car across the street and two houses down from Wes's. He stared at the house in the rearview mirror. Wes's Ford Explorer was in the driveway, and the front bumper was smashed in.

He took a deep breath. The chances of her being there were slim; the chances against her answering the door when he knocked on it were astronomical. Climbing out of the car, running across the street, ignoring the objections of his abused body, he made it to the door like a character in a war movie, racing to take the pillbox on Hill 23. There, he was at the door now. If he'd been spotted, things would be happening in the house now. God knew what. So knock, he told himself; don't give them time to think. More important, don't give yourself time to think.

He knocked, wincing from where he'd split his knuckle on Martin's jaw.

No answer.

No answer forever, he thought, his heart sinking. He'd never see Jesse again and he'd never learn the truth about any of this until they laid him in his grave and St. Peter filled in the details.

Jesse opened the door.

"Carl, thank God!"

She hugged him tight. Carl felt her happiness, and all his worry and apprehension flooded away. She was here. She was safe. She was happy to see him.

Pulling him into the house, she looked out down the

street, like a spy admitting someone to a safe house. Making sure he hadn't been followed.

"Are you alone?" she asked.

"Yes," he said.

Carl looked around the house. It was very different from Martin's, more like Jesse's house in Oakland. Warm, dark, and humorously cluttered. Odd collections of pottery and old clocks lined the walls. And more pictures of Jesse.

"We have to go," Carl said.

"I know," she replied, "he's packing."

Packing. Carl was sick of this feeling of always being two steps behind everyone he was talking to.

"How did you get away?" Jesse asked, all anxious concern. Carl had two thoughts of equal importance fighting for space in his head—he didn't know what she was talking about; thank God, she wasn't mad at him anymore.

"Well . . ." Carl hesitated. "How much do you know?"

"Just what Wes told me. I was so *mad* at you, you stupid. What were you trying to do?"

Good question. "Just, you know, what I had to."

"It was because of the way I acted back at the cabin, wasn't it? I'm so sorry. You don't have to try to make up for something that happened a million years ago. You've done enough."

"No, it wasn't that . . ." These were all good things, things he wanted to hear. But he couldn't hear them now.

"I felt sick leaving you," she went on. "I wrote you a note, but Wes said it was stupid to leave it, in case Martin saw it. I've got it here somewhere."

She started looking through the clutter of the living room and Carl grabbed her arm. "Is Wesley here?"

"Yeah." She turned to holler over her shoulder. "Wes!"

"No!" She turned to him, surprised. "I need to tell you

something," he said. "When I went out to McDonald's last night, Wes followed me."

"I know. I sent him." The look of surprise on his face made her go on. "Well, you'd been gone so long, and I'd been such a bitch. I kept trying to call you in the car, but you weren't there. He offered to go find you. That's when he saw Martin following you."

"He told you that?"

"Why shouldn't he? So he called your car phone and you told him your plan."

"My plan?"

"You had to be an asshole hero and try to lead him away. But where have you been? Why didn't you meet us back here, like you said? I thought I lost you."

She embraced him again, holding him tight, like she never wanted to let him go. Let this moment last forever, thought Carl.

He heard a door shut behind them and turned to see Wes, a pair of suitcases in his hands.

A moment of dead silence. Carl remembered an old technique he'd learned from improv sessions in acting class; when in doubt, take over the scene.

"Are those the only ones you could find?" Carl asked, striding forward, full of purpose.

"What?" asked Wes, his face slack in amazement.

Jesse was more helpful. "There's a duffel bag in the hall."

"Great." Carl took the bags from Wes and set them on the coffee table. "That's not enough, but it'll have to do. We're going to have to take your car," he said to Wes. "Mine's out of commission."

"God, what happened?" Jesse asked.

"It's a long story." He smiled at Wes, a tough-guy-who's-seen-it-all smile, he hoped. "Let's just say that brother of yours is a hard man to lose. I led him all over Southern California before I lost him."

"Really?" Wes said. He was dumbfounded, and Carl could hardly blame him. But he couldn't ask for explanations, not with Jesse right there.

"Do you have the route planned out?" Carl asked him, hoping he could get someone to tell him where they were going.

"Well . . ." Wes stammered.

Jesse was at his side, a map unfolded, pointing to a route marked with a yellow highlighter. She traced it with her finger down to the Mexican border. "We're taking small roads the whole way."

"Good thinking," said Carl, all business.

"Well, it was your idea," she said, amused.

Carl glanced at Wes. "Was it?"

"That's what Wes said."

"Wes is too modest."

Wes had to say something. Carl saw frustration and confusion breaking out all over him as he tried to figure out why Carl was playing along with his lies. "Martin . . . where did you leave him?"

"Out in the desert. I drove him off the side of the road. He's okay, but I did a number on his car. I think it bought us some time." Carl glanced over at one of the clocks—an antique with a cast metal statue of Franklin Roosevelt at the wheel of the ship of state. Ten after six, it read. That couldn't be right; it was nowhere near that late. Looking closer, he saw that the clock was stopped; the second hand was dead still. He glanced around at the other clocks. They were all stopped, he saw now. All at around that same time. Weird, but he couldn't stop and ask extraneous questions; he'd break his momentum and hand the floor to someone else. He seized a suitcase and barged on down the hall, moving toward one of the bedrooms.

Tossing the suitcase onto the bed, he started throwing open Wes's dresser drawers. "We can't carry much, but who knows when we'll get to do any shopping." He was chucking Wes's clothing into the suitcase, willy-nilly. Jesse and Wes were in the doorway now, but they were stopped still. He looked up, and saw the walls.

Pictures of Jesse covered the walls of Wes's bedroom. They were not the weird, dislocated abstracts of the Oakland house. These were simpler, more beautiful, more loving. Black-and-white shots of Jesse, posed very simply, but very erotically. And they stretched from floor to ceiling, filling every available inch of space, turning the room into one huge collage. It was chilling in its devotion.

Jesse—the real, living-color Jesse who stood in the doorway—was blushing red. In the excitement of flight she seemed to have forgotten about this side of her relationship with Wes.

Carl stared at one picture closely. The white of the image was blinding, like a cloud fading into smoke. Jesse was nude and spread-eagled against a wall—the wall in the living room of this house, Carl saw, recognizing the Roosevelt clock from the mantel. The only bit of color in the image was a purple bruise on her side.

"Do you want to take any of these pictures with you?" Carl asked, trying to come up with something unexpected.

Wes stuttered. "No. Yes, but . . . I can't."

"I just realized," Carl said, full of concern, "all those pictures in the Oakland house. Did you have the negatives?"

"No."

"Then they're gone. I'm sorry."

Carl went back to packing. Jesse started to back out of the room, looking too embarrassed to stay. Ask another question, he told himself. Keep her here. Keep the initiative. He saw another clock on the night table. Small, brass, octagonal. Stopped at 6:07.

"What's with the clocks?"

"It doesn't matter," Wes muttered.

"They don't work," Carl said obtusely.

"Yes . . . it's a story. There isn't time."

Carl made a show of looking at his watch. "Oh, there's time. Martin can't have made it back from the desert yet."

"Martin isn't . . ." Wes caught himself, glancing over at Jesse. He couldn't say it, not with her there.

Wes sat on the edge of the bed and patted the mattress at his side, still looking at Jesse. She sat on a chair in the corner.

"The idea was to stop them all at once," Wes explained, speaking only to her. He thinks he can win her over with this story, Carl realized, knowing it was a risk letting him talk. "But I couldn't quite do it. You know, it takes time to get from one clock to the other, and with some of them it was actually a little tricky to figure out how to make them stop. If you look around the house, you can see how long it took me. The one out there on the mantel—the FDR one—that was the one I started with. Stopped it right at six. Then that Deco one by the bed at 6:21, that was the last one. So that's how long it took, twenty-one minutes."

He turned to her with an expectant smile.

"Do you want to help me start them again?"

Jesse didn't answer right away. "Why did you stop them?" she asked finally.

He had the Deco clock in his hands. "When I came back from the boat trip, I just couldn't accept what had happened. What I'd let happen. I couldn't believe you were dead. I knew they were still searching, so I thought, 'Maybe there'll be a miracle, maybe they'll find her.' So I went around and stopped all the clocks right then. I said I'd let *you* start them, if I ever found you. If you ever got better."

He handed the clock over to her. She didn't take it.

"Is something wrong?"

"It's just . . . it's a little too—'too,' isn't it? Kind of theatrical?"

He looked hurt. "You like theatrical things. I thought you'd appreciate the gesture."

The discomfort on Jesse's face was palpable. But she was a caring woman, and she must have been able to see how much this meant to him, because she reached out to turn the crank on the back of the clock. Then she pulled back.

"No, I . . . I don't think I should do it. You should do it."

He set the clock down and stared at the floor. Jesse looked stricken. She moved closer to him, about to reach out and touch him. Suddenly, his head jerked up and, involuntarily, she backed off.

He looked at her, amazed. "You can't be *afraid* of me . . . Oh, Jesus."

"I'm sorry." She really was, Carl could see that. She'd always hated causing pain more than anything else. "Christ, Wes, maybe you were better off thinking I was dead."

"I never thought you were dead." There was anger in his voice that seemed entirely out of place. Carl realized he'd let the scene slip away.

She reached out to Wes and took his hand.

Enough, Carl thought. He looked around for a way to take control again. There it was. Above them.

"Does this room look familiar, Jesse?" he asked.

She shook her head. "Of course not."

"But you remembered it. Look." Carl pointed up at the ceiling over the brass bed. There was a crack. Someone had painted an outline around it, conforming to the line of the crack and completing it as the shape of a rabbit.

Jesse stared at it and rubbed her forearms, as if feeling a chill.

Wes spoke up. "You used to look at that and say it reminded you of that line from *Madeleine*. So I filled it in one day."

" 'A crack in the ceiling had the habit of sometimes looking like a rabbit,' " she quoted.

He stood, excited. "You remember!"

She looked away. "Sort of." She moved over to the photograph Carl had examined before. Purple ink had been used to highlight the dark bruise on her rib cage, giving it an oddly erotic blush. "Why did you color that in?"

"It's beautiful. A bruise can be beautiful, don't you think?"

Jesse rubbed her side, thoughtfully. "I still feel it. How did I get it?"

Wes looked uncertain. "I don't know."

"Was it Martin?" she asked.

He leapt at that idea a little too eagerly. "Yes. I'm sorry. It was during one of your fights."

She studied it, looking very far away from them both. "I don't know . . . it doesn't scare me when I look at it. It's like . . . it's like it's a *good* bruise. Is that possible?"

She glanced back up at the crack in the ceiling. "It's funny . . . Was I ever here, during my seizure?"

Wes hesitated just a moment too long. "Of course not. Martin wouldn't have allowed it."

"Then why did I remember that?" She was talking to Carl now. "Amanda said I was just remembering things that happened during the seizure."

What Wes *should* have done was ask, "Who's Amanda?"

or "What do you mean you remembered things?" What he did say was: "You must remember it from before."

Jesse didn't answer, she was looking at the picture again, running her hands over it as if she were reading Braille. "Six o'clock."

Carl peered closely at the picture; the clock on the mantel read six.

"That's when I took it," Wes said, an edge of panic in his voice.

She was touching the picture again, touching the bruise. Then she pulled her hand away, as if hit by an electric shock. "I remember!" Her voice was trembling. "Something hitting my side. When I was being pulled out of the water. *Out* of the water. *After* I fell in." She turned to him. His eyes were wide and terrified. "That's when you took this picture. *After* the boat accident. That's why you never believed I was dead. You had me here all along."

22

"*S*omebody had to take care of you," he said, a help-less, vulnerable look on his face.

"How did you make everybody think I was dead?" she asked.

"It wasn't like that." Wes's face twisted in anger. "God, I should have told you right away, I know, but I'm telling you now. I'm doing the right thing."

After what happened on the boat, he said, he went home and stopped the clocks, looking at pictures of her and trying to build up the nerve to commit suicide. After a few hours, he drove to Ventura, rented a motorboat, and took it out to look for her. Not where the Coast Guard was looking, but miles away, where she'd really gone overboard, pretending he could find the right spot in all that ocean. Half planning to throw himself in there and drown.

But off on the horizon he could just make out one of the smaller Channel Islands—San Pasqual, it turned out to be. Much too far for Jessica to have reached it, assuming Wes had his boat anywhere near the right place. But it was something to do anyway, to put off admitting that he didn't have the courage to kill himself.

He anchored at the beach and took the dinghy ashore. At first he saw nothing but seagull bones and the ruins of old campfires. Spotting a trail, he followed it up a steep hill. He supposed there was something beautiful about the island in a barren, sun-blasted way. It amazed him that a place so empty and forgotten could be there, just a few miles from Ventura and L.A., that no one had found a way to build a shopping mall or an auto dealership there. It seemed otherworldly to him, almost like a dream.

He walked on up to the crest of the hill and found a little adobe cabin with a fenced-in yard, and he wondered who the hell could live out here . . . and then he saw Jessica.

She was sitting in the yard, stretched out in a lawn chair, sunning herself, for Christ's sake. Peacocks were strolling around her and he thought he'd gone mad, or that maybe he'd had the guts to kill himself after all, and she was here to welcome him into the afterlife.

"I walked up to you, but you didn't notice; I spoke to you, but you didn't answer; so I figured you were probably alive."

"How did I get there?" Jesse asked.

"There was a guy living on the island. Some kind of refugee from the sixties. I don't think it was entirely legal that he was there. I don't think anything about the guy was entirely legal. He'd been out on his boat the night before, during the storm, doing something he really didn't want to talk about. He saw you in the water and fished you out. But I guess the nature of his business was such that he couldn't call the police or the Coast Guard. Didn't want to chance them seeing his cargo, I suppose. So he was trying to figure out what to do with you."

"That's nice." Jesse didn't seem to like being referred to as a prop.

"It was so unreal. Some kind of miracle. I'd found you. Suddenly we were together again, and we didn't have to worry about Martin. I wasn't going to take you back to him . . . not after what he'd done. I paid the guy to keep his mouth shut. I'd take care of you myself. We'd live the life we wanted. Being together. Listening to music. Taking pictures."

"You wiping the drool from my face."

He gave her a cold look. "If need be. Yes, I took care of you. And I let you have a life. I knew that would cure you." He smiled now at the thought. "And I was right. Look at you. You're all well. Almost."

"How did I escape from here?"

He looked cross again. "It wasn't a matter of escaping. You were free to walk out of here at any time. One day, you did . . . Last Friday I went to the market and when I came back my BMW was gone. And you were gone. You must have just woke up, like I always knew you would someday, and just grabbed my keys and driven off. I guess his house was the first place you thought to go." Wes's glance at Carl was disapproving.

When he saw she had gone, he hadn't known whether to be happy or terrified, Wes told her. He had no idea where she was or what condition she was in. But he knew that she was moving on her own, he knew that her will had come back, so he was sure she'd return to him. He went a little crazy waiting. He'd drive the streets looking for her, then hurry home thinking she'd be there. He wanted to call for help, but he didn't know how. So he'd sit there by the phone, fretting, developing the pictures he'd taken of her. Coloring in the bruise, because it was a mark of her struggle to stay alive. A memento of her strength of will.

"Martin called me after you went to see him." Another glance at Carl. "He didn't know what it all meant, but I knew. Or I hoped. That she'd come to you. Then I heard the message on the machine in Oakland. And I hurried up, and there you were again. So, don't you see? That means something. It's no accident that I always find you."

The look of hope and kindness on his face seemed pure, spoiled only by a touch of pain, but Jesse still held back, bless her. Too many things didn't link up. "Why didn't you tell me this when you first saw me up in Oakland?"

"I was so shocked when you spoke. Then when I found out that you'd forgotten me, I just didn't know how to explain what I'd done. I didn't think you'd understand."

"I don't."

"But I've explained it to you. And you're better. And we've found each other. So . . . happy ending, right?" Hope was winning out over pain.

"I guess," she said. "One thing, though. When you were taking care of me here? . . ."

"Yes?"

"How many times did you fuck me?"

Wes folded over in two and dropped onto the bed, as if she'd slugged him in the stomach. "Never. Nothing like that happened. I swear to God, I lied about a lot of things. But I would never . . ." He looked up at her, looking so hurt that it seemed he was unable to comprehend why she couldn't understand. "I took such good care of you. I washed you and massaged you. I gave up my life for you."

"How noble." Her voice was cold now. Carl watched her—watched them both, ready to move quickly if he had to.

"It *is* noble," Wes said with a flash of anger. "I *was* noble. You're just too young and cynical to believe that. Jessica would understand. The only way I could reach you was through love. Giving you love, unconditionally, twenty-four hours of every day."

"And you never decided to slip me the real thing?" She was mocking him now; that dislike Martin had spoken of was naked on her face.

"No! God, how could you think that? We made love one time. One beautiful time." Jesus, that again. "I could never have spoiled that with . . . with necrophilia."

"Then why'd you keep me here like this?" She looked around at all the pictures. She had the bruise in most of them, Carl saw now. "Taking pictures of me like a bend-able, posable doll. Why didn't you just bring me home?"

"Because of Martin! I had to keep you safe from him."

"Martin never hurt her." They both turned in surprise as Carl spoke. "She wasn't afraid of her husband."

Wes turned to him with pure hate. "Who told you that? *He* did, I suppose."

"No." Carl looked over at Jesse. "She did."

He reached into his pocket and pulled out the folded sheets of paper he'd printed off Martin's computer. "I copied her journal from her PC in Oakland."

Wes stared at the pages in shock. "She didn't keep a journal," he said.

"Maybe she didn't tell you. Why should she? You weren't really friends anymore, were you? I just brought one entry with me. I think you should read it, Jesse. It's the last one you wrote. Dated the sixth of December, last year. The day before you went to see Wes. The day before you had your car accident and went into your seizure."

Jesse took the pages with an unsteady hand and began to read. Carl watched her, his throat tight with apprehension. To do this here, in front of Wes, might be the height of fool-ishness, but what choice did he have?

Jesse's jaw was clenched as she read. Her nervousness

didn't surprise Carl in the least. Reading these words was the closest she'd ever come to meeting the grown-up Jessica.

She looked up from the page. "This is strange, Wes."

Wes didn't move, didn't respond. Carl could almost feel him bracing himself.

"I'm writing about getting up the nerve to talk to you," she went on, glancing back to the page and reading aloud. " '*This thing has to end now or it's just going to get uglier.*' What am I talking about?"

"Your marriage," Wes said. Carl marveled at how the man didn't even hesitate. He just came right out with it. As if it were the truth.

But Jesse wasn't buying. "It sounds like I'm scared, Wes."

"You were," he said. "You were scared of him." Wes moved to the door. "We need to move. Martin might be here any—"

But her eyes were already back on the page.

Carl had gone over the same lines half a dozen times on the blue screen of the computer in Martin's study, before he'd snatched the pages from the laser printer and hurried here, praying he'd find her, praying she'd get a chance to see them for herself. He watched her and imagined he could tell from her body language each passage as she reached it.

Had she gotten to the part about the unpleasant scene with Wes last Thanksgiving? How he'd tried to kiss her when no one was looking? How he'd broken down and cried and stormed out of the family dinner?

Had she gotten to the part about the late night phone calls? About his sudden appearances at the house at ungodly hours? About the time she'd spotted his car following her on the Harbor Freeway? Had she reached the part where she said she was afraid of what Martin might do to Wes if he found out Wes was pestering her like that? Had she seen how she stopped using the word "pestering" and started using the word "stalking"?

Yes. He could read the words in her face. Her lips moved now, and he heard the words in his head as she mouthed them.

"Is this all my fault?" she'd written. *"I needed someone to talk to after Mom started to go. If Martin had been any use at all, I'd never have needed Wes's shoulder to cry on. So I complained to him about my lousy marriage and asked why couldn't I meet someone nice, someone who'd listen? Someone like Wes. God, why didn't someone shut me up?"*

Carl was startled to find that she was speaking aloud now, though he wasn't sure she was aware of it.

" 'I can't say I didn't guess he was attracted to me. I can't say I didn't like that a little. Is that a crime? How was I supposed to know he was a nut case?' "

Wes had seemed frozen in place. Now he moved forward, smiling, all reason and good humor. "That's taken out of context. We'd had a fight the night before."

Jesse didn't smile back. Her eyes didn't leave the page.

" 'When I realized things were getting out of hand, I tried to stop it right then. That's when the calls started coming. And the creepy poems. And the faxes. And the e-mails. And those disgusting pictures of himself.' "

"I can explain this," Wes was saying, still trying to laugh it off, to turn it into a lovers' spat.

Jesse didn't even stop for a breath. *" 'So it has to end. I'm packing all those stupid pictures he took of me into my car and driving to Pasadena. I have to say it flat out, so even a nut case will understand. I never want to see him again. Never want to talk to him. Thanksgiving, Christmas, who*

*gives a damn? No contact at all. It's better for him that way.
And if Martin asks why, I'll just tell him I can't stand the
guy. Which is the truth, isn't it?' "*

Wes jumped forward and snatched the pages from her
hand. Jesse backed up, and Carl moved in front of her.

Wes threw the pages down and raised his hands in
protest. "This isn't fair! I know it looks bad in black and
white, but you're only hearing one side of it."

"I know," Jesse said, in measured tones. "My side."

"No!" Wes was emphatic. "No."

Jesse moved to pick up the pages, but Carl stopped her.
"That's okay," he said, "you've read it all. She didn't get a
chance to write what happened next, did she, Wes?"

Carl's eyes locked with Wes's, and the aggressive hate he
saw in them made Carl's heart race.

Jesse spoke up before Carl's stare had a chance to
weaken. "What *did* happen when I went to see you?" she
asked Wes.

"I've told you what happened," Wes said. "Okay, you
wrote all that. But I told you, we were fighting our feelings.
So you came to see me and . . . that's when you realized I
was right. And we made love."

"Well, you must have quite a line, Wesley," Carl said,
" 'cause she doesn't exactly sound hot to trot here."

"She was in *denial!* We'd had a fight! She was trying to
justify rejecting me!"

"But you talked her out of it, right? And then you made
love one beautiful time?" Carl asked.

"Don't mock that!" Wes was screaming now.

"Why not? It's a joke!" Carl slammed his fist on the
bureau. "Martin didn't even know about all this. Jesse kept
protecting you, God knows why. But he read the journal
today. And he told me about your background. Your treat-

ment. Your medication. The restraining order your college business professor placed against you because you were stalking her."

Wes dismissed that, annoyed. "That was entirely different—"

"But it gave you good experience, didn't it? For breaking into my place? For following us? For setting fire to her house? I can just see you doing that. Did you take down all those pictures of her you'd hung back on her walls? Make a nice bonfire of them? Was that to punish her for sleeping with me?"

"I didn't do that! It was Martin!"

"Bullshit! Martin didn't follow us. Martin didn't throw her off the boat." Carl stood close to him now, eyes locked with his. "Who did that, Wes?"

Wes's mouth dropped open. "Did Martin see . . . ?"

Carl shook his head. "He didn't see anything. Because he was the one who was down on the deck. He was the one who was bleeding. And you were the one who picked her up, weren't you? You were the one who threw her into the water."

Wes didn't answer.

Jesse gasped and moved away. Wes turned to her. Pleading. "I'm sorry. I'm so sorry. I just got so *mad*. He had you. You were sick and I couldn't get you away from him! It was so unfair! And you didn't want to be with him, I could see that. Anything was better than that. So, I . . . I let you go. But I was so sorry afterward, so sorry. I wanted to die. And when I found you . . . God, it was like I could make it all better. And I could see it in your eyes that you'd forgiven me. That everything was all right."

She was staring at him now, dumbfounded. He reached out to touch her. Carl grabbed his hand to stop him.

A mistake. Wes wheeled around and punched Carl's jaw, knocking him against the wall. Photographs fell to the floor with a smashing of glass.

Wes kept hitting him. Carl wasn't able to count the blows or the passage of time. It seemed like forever, but it might have been seconds, expanded by the explosions of pain that came from his head and his joints where Wes was kicking him.

A momentary pause in the onslaught. Carl opened his swollen eyes and saw Jesse hanging on to Wes, clawing at him. Wes threw her off, furious. She crashed against the bureau.

That gave Carl time enough to scramble to his feet and brace himself for another attack.

But Wes didn't move toward him. He was staring at Jesse.

She was gripping the edge of the bureau, a bizarre, sickened expression on her face. Was it pain or horror? Before he could name it, it was replaced by another. Of surprise? Of sadness? Then another of anguish. Then more than he could name, one after the other, until her knees buckled under her and she fell to the floor.

Wes was bending over her, touching her face gently.

"Is she all right?" Carl asked, spitting blood from his split lip.

"I don't know!" Pure terror in Wes's voice. "It's like before! It's like she's gone again."

Carl fell forward against the wall to look down at her. Her eyes were rolled back in her head and there was a line of drool running down her cheek.

"Jesus," Carl lisped, "I'll call 911."

Carl couldn't quite walk, so he let himself fall toward the bed and reached for the phone.

A thunderclap exploded near his head and he fell to his

knees. A paperweight hit the ground with him and he realized that the thunderclap had sounded so loud because it
had been *inside* his head.

"She doesn't need doctors!" Wes was standing over him,
screaming.

Carl grabbed one of the photographs on the floor and
swung it up, using all that was left of his strength, catching
Wes in the jaw and raining shattered glass on the floor. Wes
dropped back. Carl stood up and slammed the frame on top
of Wes's head, once, twice, until it broke into splinters in
his hand.

Carl tossed away the loose picture, getting a glimpse of
purple as it fluttered to the floor. Wes lay still on the floor.
Carl fell onto the bed again and grabbed the phone. The
light must have been bad there; somehow he could barely
see to dial 911.

"A woman is sick here. She's not moving. We're at
18822 Arroyo Seco."

But there must have been something strange about his
voice because the next thing the operator asked was, "What
about you?"

"What?"

"What's the matter with you?"

He passed out before he had a chance to answer.

"Visiting hours start at nine in the morning. That's ten
hours from now."

"I need to see her."

"I'm afraid if you're not a member of the immediate
family, you'll have to wait for visiting hours like everybody
else."

"I'm her boyfriend."

The nurse sniffed once. "Her husband is in with her now.
How can she have a husband *and* a boyfriend?"

"You haven't lived much, have you, Nurse?"

"Visiting hours—"

"And I'm not a visitor! I'm a patient. See these stitches? I'm in room 395. Don't I get special privileges for being a member here?"

"If you're feeling well enough to wander around from floor to floor, maybe you should go home and free up a bed."

Carl gripped the edge of the receptionist's desk, partly to balance himself, partly to stop himself from gripping her throat. He released his hold and dropped onto the vinyl sofa.

After forty-five minutes or so, the nurse spoke again. "Are you just going to sit there all night?"

"Yep. I love this sofa. I'm buying one when I get home. I'm doing my whole house in orange vinyl."

"Are you trying to be funny?"

Carl thought that one over.

He must have thought himself to sleep, because the next thing he knew it was after 2 A.M. and Martin Ackerman was standing in front of him.

"You should go to your room and rest."

Carl shook his head and the immediate daggers of pain in his neck told him that had been a mistake. "No, I'm fine. How is she?"

"Asleep. She doesn't seem to want to wake up."

Carl felt a touch of dread. "Can she talk?"

"A little."

"So she's not . . . like she was before."

"No." Martin shifted from one foot to the other. "It's like she's just . . . shut down, or something." Martin started to move off toward the elevator.

Carl called after him, "She didn't . . ." He felt embarrassed to ask. Then he thought, The hell with it, he was never going to feel embarrassed again. "Did she have any message for me?"

Martin shrugged. "She . . . she wanted to ask you if you remember going to see the movie *Pretty Baby* with her."

"Pretty Baby?"

"She wanted me to tell you she liked it."

Carl frowned. He vaguely remembered taking her to see it, but he couldn't recall anything special about the occasion. "Is she delirious?"

"Maybe." He pressed the button and waited for the elevator. Carl limped over to him from the sofa.

"Where's your brother?"

Martin didn't answer at first. "That's where I'm going."

"I know you don't want to hear this, but he's dangerous. He tried to kill me on the road. He admitted he threw Jesse off the boat. You can't protect him."

Martin nodded. "No, I can't." Then he turned to Carl and spoke very simply. "He wasn't at the house when the paramedics got there. He took his car, drove to the Colorado Bridge, and jumped off. I have to go identify him."

The elevator doors opened and Martin walked in.

By four A.M. the nurse-receptionist had decided to feel sorry for him and brought him a blanket and a hard pillow. That woke him up just enough to realize what had been bothering him.

He hurried to the phone and called Kit.

"Carl! Jesus, God, it's good to hear from you. Are you all right?"

"What year was *Pretty Baby* made?"

"What?"

"Pretty Baby! Brooke Shields. Directed by Louis Malle. Written by Polly Platt. What year?"

"What the fuck, you call me at fucking four—"

"What year?"

A sigh. The sound of the phone being set down. Pages flipping in a book. "1979."

"I love you, Kit."

"I love you, Carl."

He hung up. He leaned against the phone, hanging onto the receiver to stop from sliding to the floor.

1979. '79, not '78. That was her way of telling him.

She was remembering.

23

*L*imping along the sidewalks of Glendale at two-thirty in the morning on a Friday night, Carl felt like the main character in a last-man-on-earth movie. Charlton Heston might be pursuing Rosalind Cash on the next block. Vincent Price might be hiding from vampires in the house on the corner. Harry Belafonte and Mel Ferrer might be fighting over Inger Stevens somewhere downtown, and who could blame them? The last man on earth was always busy.

Carl was bone-tired after another fifteen-hour day at the office, his aches and pains having resolved themselves into a constant throb of discomfort. He was ingesting painkillers at a habit-forming rate. If he became addicted and had to go into rehab, it would be a problem, since Kit had already used that as an excuse when he talked Dan and Mindy into giving Carl his job back. Drug addiction was so much easier to believe than the truth, Kit had told him.

So here he was, at the end of another work week. If he'd hoped his time with Jesse had changed him utterly, the gravitational pull of ordinary life kept telling him it wasn't so. He fought that dragging power, fought to cling to the previous days, to a self he'd thought he was becoming. For a week he had been what he always thought he could be; not a hack approaching middle age, but a hero, protecting the woman in danger, willing to sacrifice everything for the sake of love. Surely he couldn't just go back to being the same silly man he'd been before, could he?

During the weeks since he'd left the hospital, he'd tried a few superficial changes, hoping to cement his transformation. A new haircut. A new car; one of the new electric models, a hero's car, to prove how socially aware he was. The car was sitting two blocks down, having run out of whatever they ran out of. His Jeep, crushed but still operational, sat in his driveway. His insurance company still wanted to sell it for scrap metal, but Carl swore he would never let the dear thing go.

It's no use though, he thought, as he walked by the For Sale sign in front of his house. No matter what he did, what he thought, what he hung onto or what he let go, he was always Carl Rooney. He thought about that pernicious bit of show business jargon, "the character arc." Producer cant for development of the hero in a mainstream movie from a pleasant character in the beginning of a movie to an even more pleasant one by the end. Say if Robin Williams doesn't accept responsibility in the beginning, he'll be holding down that steady job by the end. Or if Tom Cruise is too "career-driven" at the beginning, he'll loosen up by the end.

The man who doesn't believe in love falls in love. The coward becomes a hero.

Just another way in which movies are lies. Because they're afraid to say the real truth, that the arc always completes itself in a circle and at the end you're still staring at the same face in the mirror.

By three in the morning he was sitting in his parents' bed, neck brace Velcroed around his throat, a cup of Fifth Sun cocoa steaming on the night table, combing flea eggs out of Roxanne's tangled pelt while her crusty eyes rolled back in ecstasy. There was his transformation. Now he could be a hero to his cat.

Snap. Rattle. His eyes flew open. He hadn't known he'd been sleeping. Dreaming again, he thought, cursing himself. Roxanne launched herself off his stomach and hit the floor with a wheeze.

Snap. Rattle. He sat up, eyes wide, knowing the sound but not believing it.

Snap. Rattle. He was on his feet, hurrying to the study. Just as he stepped through the doorway, the window crashed into pieces and a small rock fell at his feet among the broken glass. Stepping carefully through the shards, he made it to the window and peered down.

It was her.

"Sorry," she said. "I don't know my own strength." But she laughed, and he even laughed a little, as though a broken window in a house that was being shown to buyers tomorrow was of no concern. He sprinted downstairs, knowing he wasn't dreaming because of the sharp pain in his foot and the trail of blood he was leaving behind him. Another injury. He was starting to welcome them.

He paused before opening the French doors, wondering what was out there for him this time. He had never succeeded in talking to her at the hospital, and his attempts to call her at home had been singularly unrewarding. Martin or Mari the maid put him off enough times that he started to worry that there might be something wrong. Then Jesse finally came on the line. They'd had an odd, uncomfortable exchange on the phone, her voice rich with the kind of tension you get when you see some acquaintance the day after you revealed too much of yourself in drunken enthusiasm at an office party. Carl's worst nightmare seemed to have come true; in remembering her life, she must have remembered all the reasons they couldn't be together. In becoming again the adult Jessica, she had outgrown the affections of the young Jesse. The distance in her voice on the phone had sent him spiraling into a depression that had caused him to put his house on the market. So it was Brenda, his realtor, who was the real winner in this story.

He ran his fingers through his tangled hair. Tonight, in stark contrast to the last time she appeared here, his penis hung sleeping down his leg, seeming to share his hopelessness about this upcoming reunion. But as he opened the door and walked out into the warm night, it grew and nudged forward against his flannel pajamas. Hope is a thing with testicles. Trying to move in such a way as to conceal his misplaced enthusiasm, he approached her on the patio.

"Hey," she said.

"Hey," he said. "What's up?"

She laughed a little, but avoided making the cheap double entendres Jesse would have enjoyed about his condition. "You said you worked late Fridays, so I thought maybe you'd still be awake."

"I was," he said, knowing his bloodshot eyes made a liar of him. "You want to come in? Have some coffee?"

She hesitated. "I never did get to like that stuff."

"Cocoa?"

"God, no. How 'bout a Coke?"

So he led her into the den, limping from the glass in his foot and from the intricate lacing of pulled muscles that traversed his body. He watched her move and thought how different she seemed. Her gait was smooth and elegant, her clothes were tailored Anne Klein, her hair and makeup were done to nineties perfection. Even the way she sat was mature, legs crossed, elbows just so on the arm of the chair. Gone was the easy sprawling of last weekend. Carl felt a pang at its absence. Only when he gave her the soda did some of the teenager come back into the picture; she took a piece of gum out of her mouth and wrapped it in paper she pulled from her jacket pocket.

"Nicotine gum. I'm trying to quit smoking. Again. Thanks to you. Again."

Carl shrugged. "Just being a good host."

She shook her head, flustered. "This was stupid, coming here like this. I should have just called. But it seemed . . ." What it seemed she wouldn't say. She changed the subject by looking around the den. "God, I remember when I first saw this place the other night. It was like it was some kind of miracle. A room suddenly *appearing* where there wasn't one. Sometimes I miss that feeling. Everything seemed so shiny and new. So many possibilities. Hidden adventures around every corner. Now it's all just . . . you know, been there done that."

Carl stirred uncomfortably in his chair. It felt so disappointing to hear that late nineties cliché come out of her mouth; her speech had been refreshingly free of those before.

"Of course, Nicky says *I'm* the miracle. We finally got in touch with him in Peru. He said my recovery was a blessing from God. I told him I'd have preferred the blessing of skipping the whole damn thing. He didn't laugh. Never did get my jokes."

"So, you're back with Martin, then?"

She smiled and shook her head; even the way her hair fell seemed different. "No. I don't think that was going to last much longer anyway, and after all that's happened, well . . . it's over."

Carl poured himself a Scotch. "You're sure?"

She smiled, and it was that old mocking smile from the cafeteria a million years ago. "Curious, aren't we? Yes, I'm sure. I'm way too much trouble for him. I've been staying at a hotel for the past few days."

Carl felt a flare of hope and immediately squashed it, despising himself for his childish optimism. "How are you? You know, physically?"

"Oh, yes. The doctors say . . . Well, the doctors say so many things. Actually they say that I'm"—she gave him a long look, and went on—"perfectly healthy and they all want to write books about me and get rich and famous. How about you?"

"My whiplash will live longer than I will." He tried to smile, but it was a weak effort. "Look, there are some things I have to know. Some things . . ." But still he was afraid to ask the real questions. Embarrassment was back at home in his heart. "Did Martin ever tell you what really happened on the boat?"

Jesse said that she had finally gotten the story out of him. The two brothers had fought; Martin had bled profusely and fallen to the deck; Jesse had gone over; Martin hadn't seen how; Martin had taken the boat off as fast and as quick as he could. Later the boat struck a reef and sank. That much of Wes's story had been true. "He thinks I ought to hate him for it," Jesse said, "but I just can't."

Carl thought back to the moment when Martin had written him that check and wondered if he'd misunderstood. How much of that anger, how much of that impending violence had been directed at me, Carl wondered, and how much had been directed toward Martin himself? How much of that twenty thousand dollars had Martin intended as absolution? A guilty man's attempt to pay his conscience into forgiving him for running away?

So Carl couldn't hate him either. After all, what had been Martin's worst sin? That he'd been relieved to have Jesse out of his life. Hadn't that been Carl's own sin, back in '79? He quenched a pang of guilt by shooting down his Scotch.

She must have seen the pained look on his face and misunderstood it, because she said, "I'm sorry I didn't call. I should have, I know. But there was . . . there was just so much to assimilate. It took me days just laying there to sort through it all. I told Martin afterward, I felt like a computer rebooting"—she laughed at the thought—"just sitting there, whirring and whirring and doing nothing."

She told him she had already begun to remember in Wes's bedroom, when she was looking at the pictures. And that bruise. "But when Wes pushed me and I hit my ribs on the bureau, that's when it really started. It must have been like that guy with the tennis mistake Kit told us about. Something about the physical and the mental coming together like that. I just thought, I've felt this before.

"Then I remembered. Swimming in the water. Cold water. Wet hair streaming down my back. Being so cold. So afraid. Hitting my ribs on the side of his boat as that man pulled me out."

Carl asked if she remembered the entire rescue.

"Yes. And no. Or I mean, *more* than that. Because everything I remembered would lead to something else. So when I remembered swimming, I didn't just remember swimming that night. I remembered dozens of beaches and pools, places I'd never seen, never even heard of. And the cold made me remember ski trips and snowball fights that were all new to me. 'Wet hair,' and all these different hairstyles popped into my head, and all these faces and names of friends that went with them.

"I felt myself overloading, but things just kept coming faster. Friends would lead to houses and houses would lead to furniture and I'd get overpowered by silly details, like every telephone I ever owned just *displayed* itself in front of me like the different models of the starship *Enterprise* in Captain Picard's office on *Star Trek: The Next Generation*. And then I'd go off on thinking, Captain who? *Star Trek* the what? And all of a sudden I was off on remembering every movie and TV show I'd seen. And the commercials and the songs and the books and magazines. I could hardly breathe from it all.

"And there weren't any priorities; everything just came at me, the same volume, the same size. My first preppy roommate at Berkeley playing *Boston,* full volume, all hours of the day or night; me telling Mom I was getting married; seeing a cat run over and worrying that it was Patches and finding out that it wasn't. They just kept coming at me, like those spiders coming out of that egg sac in Big Sur. And all I could do was glimpse them before another one jumped out.

"I couldn't handle it all. God, I thought my brain was going to ooze out of my ears. Really, I didn't think my skull could hold it in. I didn't know where I was or how much time was passing. Then, slowly, I started to feel it all, I don't know, like, solidifying in my mind. You know, the way ice crystals form on a lake? Attaching themselves to each other, *connecting?*

"I was getting everything back. All the stuff I needed and all the stuff I didn't. My life."

She sat back, taking a deep breath. "I was at home, and it was days later before I could even sit up and talk or eat . . . And that wasn't the end of it, of course. Then there was the *dealing* with it. I mean, it all felt so new. It was like seventeen years worth of stuff had just happened to me, right then. How long does it take you to come to terms with that?"

"Forever?" Carl said quietly. "Like the rest of us?"

She laughed a little. "Funny thing is, when I didn't remember my life, when I just *heard* about it, it all seemed to make sense. Now, it's like I said, I'm lost in the details. No clear motives or themes; just me wandering around in a fog."

"Hey, that's all I do," Carl said.

She laughed. Just a little laugh at a little joke. But the connection was made, the smile in her eyes was there. Carl felt hope balloon inside him. If she could laugh at his stupid jokes, she was still the same person after all. Her character arc was circling back on itself too. This thing between them wasn't over yet. If Carl could think of the right thing to say, if he could build on this split second of communion between them, there'd be a chance for him still. So he was back in the cafeteria, trying to think of the right line to say. The right way to ask the one question that was on his mind: What were her feelings toward him? But his inspiration failed him, fear of failure fogged his mind, and all he could come up with was: "Did you remember what happened when you went to see Wes? Before the car accident?"

She looked off into the distance for a moment and swallowed, with a look on her face that told Carl he'd completely blown it. He'd asked a question that had pulled her far away from him, and their brief moment of connection was long gone.

"Well," she started, after a few moments, "like I said in my diary, I went there to lay it on the line to him. So, of course, I chickened out, at least at first. But then he started in with his creepy declarations and how much I meant to him and how much I loved him but I just wouldn't admit it.

It was too much. I let him have it. I told him he was wrong.
I told him I thought he needed help. I told him I didn't want
him and that he was crazy to be obsessing about me like
this."

She swallowed again and looked down at her manicured
nails. "I didn't know what I was dealing with. I thought I
was dumping some guy with a schoolboy crush. But
he . . . he went wild. He attacked me."

Carl felt sick.

Jesse shifted in her seat. "And that was his one beautiful
time."

"Oh, God."

"You don't have one of those cigarettes, do you? No?
That's probably good. I shouldn't be smoking. He broke
down and cried afterward. Kept blaming me for making
him do it . . . I started throwing things. I smashed that
damned clock. I ran out of that house. I wanted to fly out of
this fucking town and out of my miserable life . . . That's
when I plowed into the back of that car."

"Jesus."

Jesse looked at Carl's Scotch. "I wish I could have one of
those."

"I'll get it."

She shook her head. "No. Doctor's orders." She went
back to her story. "Wes was sick. I don't know. Maybe it's
because he's dead, but I can't hate him either. He had
enough hate for both of us. He hated his life. He hated what
he'd done to me. I think when he saw me in Oakland, when
he knew that I'd forgotten everything, he saw that as a second chance. He thought he could remake the past, improve
on it. Turn it into what he'd wanted it to be. Make it so that
I really had loved him. Like, if he could convince me it was
true, maybe I *would* love him. It's sad, really."

"I think you're letting him off pretty easy."

She shrugged. "Maybe. But he did take care of me when I was in his house, just like he said."

"You remember that?"

"Bits and pieces."

"You must have been terrified."

She shook her head. "I wasn't thinking that way. It was like I was watching myself from a long way off. I know he didn't molest me while he kept me there. I think he was telling the truth when he said he didn't want to spoil the memory of our one time."

"What do you think he'd have done though, after he took you away? After he found out you never could love him."

"God knows." Jesse shivered at the thought.

Carl reached out and took her hand. "I'm so sorry." It was a phrase that tried to encompass so much it ended up meaning nothing at all.

She looked down at his hand on hers. "Carl . . ."

He pulled his hand away; her voice had the tone of someone breaking bad news.

"I have to tell you something," she went on. She frowned, as if she was losing her nerve, then she went on. "Damn it, why is this so hard? I was *comfortable* with you before. The time we'd spent together in high school seemed so close, and you were still my best friend. Then all of a sudden that time just shot away from me, like I let go of a rubber band. There's this whole other lifetime between us now. I don't know if I'm comfortable with you anymore . . . I know that's not fair, but there it is."

"We're still the same people," he said quietly.

"Maybe . . . There's something else. I know you've been blaming yourself all these years for what you did back then . . . or didn't do. I'm *glad* you've been blaming yourself, it shows you're decent. But I don't blame you. I stopped blaming you a long time ago. We couldn't have gotten married and had a baby then, we were too young. Okay, I wish it had ended differently. We both could have behaved better. You *certainly* could have behaved better"— she laughed a little—"but that doesn't change what we were to each other. I know a lot of what you did for me was to make up for all that and . . . well, I want to thank you. You were there when I needed you." She gave an embarrassed laugh and said, with overdramatic sarcasm, "My hero."

"I didn't do it to make up for anything," he said stiffly. "I did it because I wanted to."

She looked a little hurt, gave a curt nod, and spoke more formally. "I'm sorry if I misunderstood your motives. Anyway, thanks."

Setting her glass down, half-empty, she stood and walked to the door. "I wish we hadn't kept getting interrupted. It would have been good to make love one more time. Would have given things a nice sense of closure."

So it was being closed, was it? Carl stood up a little too fast and let his drink slop out of his glass. "Is that what you're looking for?"

She looked surprised by the angry tone in his voice. "I don't know. I just think it's kind of funny, don't you? We make love one time with a busted rubber and I get knocked up. We make love one time in your greenhouse and . . ."

Carl felt his stomach flutter. "And what?"

"And nothing. We just obviously shouldn't get within ten feet of each other, we're too fucking fertile." She laughed as she spoke, but her voice broke and for a moment her face was very young.

"What d'you—what—what—what are you saying?" Carl sputtered.

"Nothing. I came here to tell you, but . . ." She shook her head, angry. "It isn't fair to you. I can take care of myself."

And she hurried out the door, letting him off the hook again.

Carl's body was frozen in shock for a second, then he dashed to the door after her, wincing in pain as the fragment of glass stabbed into the ball of his foot.

"Jesse!" She was already slamming a BMW's door and gunning the engine. Carl hop-sprinted after her, catching his foot on a sprinkler head and sprawling on the wet grass as she drove off.

Hobbling up the stairs, he slipped, cracking his knee twice on the hard tile steps, and fell over once while pulling clothes over his pajamas. He shoved his bruised and bleeding feet into a pair of loafers and searched wildly through the house for the Jeep keys. He found them behind those same books where he'd found the old pack of cigarettes, but by the time he'd stumbled to the car and pulled out into the night, his Jeep belching smoke and rattling like a kitchen falling down a flight of metal stairs, she was long gone, he had no idea where.

But he drove on through the night anyway, full of pain and ignorance, without a clue where he was going, except that he was going after her. Because that's what a hero did. And even if you could never be one, you could always pretend.